10.50

Praise for BLACK BIRD

"*Black Bird* rocks! An exuberant new Quebec voice that speaks for all of us who live in the spaces in between." Susan Swan, author of *The Wives of Bath*

"A work of terrific accomplishment. Basilières spent a long time writing *Black Bird* and it was worth it. The book has the unmistakable feel of an intelligent, gifted man who has found his voice." David Gilmour, author of *Lost Between Houses*

"*Black Bird* is a great, wonderful monster of a novel [and] ushers in a new, hilarious, wildly imaginative, powerful and heartfelt voice." Edward Carey, author of *Alva & Irva*

"Basilières' comic sensibility is as black and shining as a crow's wing. I believe Lovecraft must be sitting up in his grave and grinning." Gail Anderson-Dargatz, author of *A Recipe for Bees*

"Basilières' debut is a stronger, more original book than most novelists ever manage to write. Malicious, riotous, and moving, *Black Bird* is an anarchic *Two Solitudes* for the 21st century." Amazon.ca

"A giant mulligatawny of a novel . . . Wild and unpredictable, crammed with black humour, it reads like a very entertaining fairy tale gone wrong." *Books in Canada*

"An original novel with antic energy . . . Acutely observed . . . The powerful grappling of these characters with eternal human mysteries is what converts the magical fantasy from absurd to meaningful." *Literary Review of Canada*

"A funny, dark first novel." *Flare*

"[Basilières'] Montreal is indeed compelling. It's a gothic, violent, complicated, surreal Montreal. . . . At its core [*Black Bird*] feels more authentically Montreal than so many novels that strain to get it right." *Montreal Mirror*

"An outrageously Gothic novel . . . Basilières has created a Swiftian work of art, a novel that is both uproariously funny and devastatingly satirical." *The Sun Times* (Owen Sound)

"*Black Bird* is a macabre, funny and wonderfully malicious text that unhesitatingly moves between farce, black humour, satire and magic realism." *The Edmonton Journal*

BLACK BIRD

BLACK BIRD

a novel by

MICHEL BASILIÈRES

VINTAGE CANADA

VINTAGE CANADA EDITION, 2004

National Library of Canada Cataloguing in Publication

Basilières, Michel
Black bird: a novel / by Michel Basilières.
ISBN 0–676–97528–3

I. Title.
PS8553.A7858B58 2004   C813'.6   C2003–905690–2

www.randomhouse.ca

Text design: CS Richardson
Printed in Canada

2   4   6   8   9   7   5   3   1

AUTHOR'S NOTE

Readers with long memories or a command of
Canadian history will complain that the following
pages contradict known facts. Facts are one thing but
fiction is another, and this is fiction.

MONTREAL-LA-MORTE

Montreal, an island, placed a cemetery atop its mountain, capped that mountain with a giant illuminated cross and wove streets along its slopes like a skirt spreading down to the water. In this way, its ancestors hovered over the city just as the Church did, and death was always at the centre of everything.

Grandfather had one foot in the grave and the other on the shoulder of his spade. He pressed his weight on it; nothing. He stood on it, lifting himself completely from the earth—still nothing.

"No use," he said to Uncle. "The ground's already frozen. The season's over."

Grandfather eyed the lights of the city below glowing through the leafless trees ringing the cemetery. A single large flash winked at him like a bulb or a star going out; seconds later a sound like an enormous kettledrum drifted up through the cold air. The revolving beacon of a skyscraper swung overhead, and then came another flash, and another boom. There was silence after that, except for the wind in the trees. And then sirens. Grandfather watched the regular flashes of police cruisers and ambulances progressing along the lines of light that shone out of the darkness. Cops. They were never anything but trouble. At least tonight, he thought mistakenly, they were someone else's problem.

Cold and disappointed, the two men began the long walk home. Even if they could have paid for the bus that ran over the mountain, they couldn't board at the cemetery gate, in the middle of the night, with shovels and sacks. As Grandfather watched Uncle preceding him, he realized the snow was just as much an impediment to their work as the frozen ground: Uncle was leaving a trail of footprints, and Grandfather must have been too.

The season had definitely come to an end. What would they do now? This winter wouldn't be as easy as the last, when Grandmother's death turned out to be a boon to him in so many ways, large and small. Small, because it meant one less person to feed. Large, because it allowed him to indulge his hostilities, his grudges against the neighbours, and his fondness for drinking, all under the guise of his grief. But that lasted only through the summer, for as soon as Labour Day passed, the anniversary of her death, everyone began to remark that it was time to return to business as usual; the holiday was over, get a grip. In fact they might have allowed him a longer period of licence if he hadn't made it clear, after a certain amount of beer, that he'd not really been fond of her anyway, and what a relief it was turning out to be, being a widower.

This reaction surprised no one in the immediate family, but it was only after Grandmother's death that his true nature became obvious to the neighbourhood. She'd spent most of her life covering up for him and keeping him from them. After all, she was one of them, born and bred in the quarter, where her family was known and liked. He was the outsider, the stranger, the unknown quantity. Which caused a great deal of curiosity in the beginning, and a great deal of trouble for her.

He'd never shown any respect for her friends or relatives, for anyone on the street, for anyone who might give him a job, or even for his own children. She'd married him because he'd made an effort to impress her and convince her of his sincerity, and she'd never before been shown that sincerity was as easily discarded as an empty cigarette package. The rest of her life had been spent trying to make up to her children for so carelessly choosing their father, and overcoming her own disappointment, which he seemed to insist on reinforcing daily. He had the habit of reading aloud from the newspaper the story of some other family's tragedy and laughing at the details; of carelessly leaving pornographic magazines around the house where the children, her friends, and she could see them; of not replying to her questions.

She should have left him early on, but that would have meant returning to her parents' house, since she had no resources of her own. And return was impossible, because although they would have taken her in gladly and quickly, never asking why, they'd silently assume they'd been right, that she was returning in failure and despair. She could fight her husband's cruelty and indifference, a miserable struggle that would justify her life, but she couldn't fight her parents' certainty that she was incapable of a life without them. And in the end, the example of her strength in the face of his power was the legacy she would leave her children.

After Grandmother had received the last rites from Father Pheley, she summoned enough strength to look her husband in the face and, heedless of the presence of so many others, gave him her last words:

"Your heart is so cold it will lead you to hell. At least I don't have to fear meeting you again."

Grandfather couldn't bring himself to scowl or scoff, as he always had at any remark of his wife's. Not because of the presence of the others, or because she was dying, but because he still harboured his childhood fear of priests. The ensuing moment of silence, as her spirit left her with a smile on her face, gave him the chance to absorb one of the great lessons of his life: even in the presence of death and the entry into heaven, disagreeable people remain disagreeable.

Because he needed a cook and a housecleaner, Grandfather remarried quickly enough to cause eyebrows to raise, especially considering the difference in years between himself and his second wife. If his children had objections, in any case they kept silent. And the neighbours' speculations, typical in such cases, were off target. Grandfather had not been having an affair behind Grandmother's back—not that it

4

was beyond him, but he'd never bothered to hide his infidelities—nor had he lost his head, as foolish older men have been known to do. Neither had his new wife married him for his money, since he didn't have any. But it wasn't surprising that some might think so; although the family was never seen to spend lavishly, none of them were ever seen to have a job, either. And whenever the neighbours couldn't understand how someone could live in complete poverty, they assumed that person must be secretly rich after all. Under the mattress, in secret bank accounts, buried in the backyard: there was no limit to the hiding places, no matter how far-fetched, suggested by those unwilling to take the evidence at face value. Once the idea was planted, all common sense was discarded in the effort to bolster their belief, because nothing is harder to let go than the suspicion that someone else is guilty of hiding something.

Grandfather thought he remarried out of remorse. It occurred to him, in a rare moment of self-reflection, that he had devoted his life to his late wife's misery, and that wasn't enough. A man's life should count for more than one woman's. He would spend the rest of his days making up for this disappointment by ruining the life of another. He chose a woman from a neighbourhood where he was unknown, and won her by the simple process that worked on his first wife. He paid calls on her, smiled at her, told her amusing stories, looked her directly in the eye, gave her small presents, affected shyness and modesty. He lied and deceived with a practised hand, which a more sophisticated woman would have seen through. But a more sophisticated woman would have been a harder conquest and a tougher opponent. Grandfather chose his second wife precisely because she was unused to the attentions of men, unfamiliar with the real cruelty that exists outside of television, and unlikely to be self-assured enough to refuse his offer of marriage.

It's true that when invited to family dinners, she was puzzled how more than one of his own relatives, who seemed as well-meaning and kind as he was, took her aside to warn her he wasn't what he appeared, that he could only harm her. But she reasoned that they, like so many people, must be unable to understand the kind of friendship that she and Grandfather had found together despite the difference in their ages—a common prejudice that was hard to overcome. And if it were true that he was normally not as outgoing, friendly and generous as he seemed, mightn't that just be a sign that she'd brought him a kind of happiness? Couldn't he have fallen in love with her?

He couldn't. Despite his best efforts, his first wife resisted being driven to the grave long enough to die of natural causes; he saw this as a failure on his part, and for his second attempt he chose an easier mark. He considered this act as a kind of penance for the work to which he'd devoted his life: grave robbery. He felt that since death provided for his livelihood he might return at least one corpse. He was always attempting the least in everything. If he were a lumber-jack, he might plant a single sapling on the same principle: an eye for an eye. When he proposed to Aline, he thought he was making up for an earlier error, nothing more. And when she moved into the Desouche house to live the claustrophobic, uncertain and oppressive existence he laid upon her, with his small insults, sharp words, disappointed looks and everyday denials, he thought he was just being himself and could find no reason to put himself out on her behalf.

Now he worried how they would manage through the winter. Not that he was eager to work, especially since the digging got tougher every year; and then, the markets were drying up at the same time, what with so many people donating their bodies to science. Still, a living had to be made somehow.

The two men padded through the light snow to the unlit road. With the tall, empty trees overhanging the gravel path, they might have been in the country. Except for the continuous screaming of the sirens, the woods blocked the sounds of the city, and the sense of isolation was almost complete. Grandfather removed his gloves, brought cigarettes from his coat and silently offered them to Uncle. The lighted ends shone red. The men let smoke out through their nostrils, like dragons.

The road led them down to the lights and noises of the city, where it was warmer, but less comforting.

Once Aline Souris became Stepmother Desouche she quietly took over the kitchen. Although she was neither fond of nor good at cooking, it gave her an immediate and definite position in the house and kept her from feeling underfoot. Her natural shyness was brought out by her surprise at Grandfather's change in attitude towards her now that they were married, and reinforced by the Desouches' habit of speaking English, a phenomenon that made her feel as if she'd landed in a foreign country. In her previous life English had been as distant as England itself. It was the language of employers, bankers and politicians, not the language of friends or relatives.

The Desouche household was a fixture in its neighbourhood for several reasons, not the least being the sheer number of years they occupied the same building (much to the consternation of their landlord) in a city where families commonly packed up every July to move across the street or around the corner. Aside from legal responsibilities, because everyone eventually occupied everyone else's former premises, it was held sacred that the buildings not be abused or endangered by the tenants.

The Desouches were freed from this obligation by their immobility. They neither owned the property nor intended to leave, and practised a game of paying the rent just frequently enough to avoid a visit from the bailiff. All the landlord's efforts to have them legally removed were thwarted by the local laws protecting tenants, which the Desouches learned to manipulate to their benefit. The rental board was forced to rule in their favour even in cases where it was clearly reluctant. So the Desouches felt at liberty, over the years, to do to the house as they pleased, without the worry of any consequences.

Doors were moved, walls were struck down or created, windows bricked up, staircases added, balconies enlarged or destroyed. All this work the family undertook themselves because they couldn't conceive of paying the costs of unionized labour. So the neighbours became used to seeing deliveries of lumber, wallboard, sacks of plaster or other materials, and to hearing the sounds of power tools and hammering, not just during working hours, but at all times.

Of course, though each project began with a burst of enthusiasm, as soon as the inspiration had lost its novelty, work slowed to a crawl. Jobs that should have taken a few days stretched into weeks—even months. Simple tasks like putting up a new shelf consumed a week; repainting the kitchen was a month's toil; refinishing the living-room floor had been going on for a year. And there were even unfinished schemes older than Jean-Baptiste and Marie, who by this time were considered adults.

Aline found herself floundering in this ménage. The bared walls and rolled-up carpets had not been a surprise, but she'd assumed they were temporary and forgiven them accordingly. And now she realized, too, that her new relatives had been making a special effort to speak in French on her previous visits. As happens so often, special efforts were abandoned when the visitor became an in-law. She was hardly spoken to at all, and even then most often in English first. Only when she presented her pleading, puzzled face would they repeat themselves in French.

One exception was Marie, who hated speaking English even though her own mother was as Anglo as Aline herself was francophone. For this reason, Aline developed a certain fondness for her new granddaughter, who after all was not so very much younger than herself—a decade? More? Less? She excused in Marie habits and actions she wouldn't tolerate in the others. Although she would never express criticism of anyone, she took her revenge by leaving them out of her nightly prayers. But for Marie she'd make special allowances and requests to the Lord, minimizing her rudeness to the family—especially to her brother—her neglect of common decencies, and even her blasphemies. "She is young," Aline murmured into her fingertips, "and has endured unpleasantness. I am sure, just as for anyone else, enough success and encouragement would develop into happiness and then kindness. Do not forget her, Lord, and I will be grateful."

For the sake of the Lord, Aline prayed in formal French, not the joual in which she lived her daily life. It was sometimes hard to remember the elusive constructions that had been rapped into her head through her knuckles at school, but as her father always pointed out, only hard work earned results. She felt free to speak more colloquially with Marie, whose familiarity with vulgar phrases was astounding, and who expressed political opinions Aline had been used to hearing from her father. Both were summed up in the motto Marie cited most often: "maudits anglais"—damned English. However, Marie was less fond of Aline, whom she considered a yokel precisely because she was so astounded by common expressions, and because although she never disagreed with Marie on political issues, she seemed only to be avoiding discussing something she really knew nothing about.

Aline would have had more luck bonding with Marie's mother, who was now actually Aline's stepdaughter, though she was older by almost two decades. The two were alike, not only in temperament but also in situation, and Mother was the reason English had been adopted by the Desouches. Her case proved that the family didn't consider themselves above adapting to suit the needs of a new member of the clan, but also that they sometimes refused. Both of the women had married into the house, both were accepted only as necessary additions, neither was happy or comfortable. But the barrier of language kept them apart at home, just as it would have if they'd met on the street or in some shop. The two seemed to have an intimation that they were in some ways kindred spirits. They exchanged smiles and awkward hellos in each other's language, occasionally asked simple questions while pointing, helped one another carry things or fold sheets, even felt sympathy when the other was fighting with her husband. Aline and Grandfather, or Mother and Father, the scene was the same: the husband was angry and loud, the wife offered a moderate rebuke and then suffered an explosive retaliation that left her near tears and acquiescing in silence.

But neither could overcome the embarrassment of remaining ignorant of the other's way of speaking. Although each felt the possibility of a real friendship, comforting and fun, lying just beyond that linguistic horizon, neither could overcome the feeling that learning the other's tongue was a task too hard for her.

And then, relations with the rest of the household were equally confused. To begin with, as Grandfather's second wife, Aline was now stepmother to the older twins, Uncle and Father, as well as Mother, and grandmother to Jean-Baptiste and Marie. She couldn't tell Uncle and Father apart, and so never knew how to address them, until she saw that Uncle was missing a finger on his left hand. If it gave her some comfort to have a method of distinguishing her stepsons, it nevertheless made her uneasy to see that naked, tiny stump at the dinner table. But Uncle almost never said a word anyway, which relieved her of the obligation of making small talk with him. He spent much of his time following her husband in silence; the two worked together at the family business, an occupation no one had yet explained to her. On occasion Uncle sat with Father in the evenings, and over a table of empty beer bottles in the kitchen the two would trade stories back and forth, in English. It was practically the only time Uncle was talkative, as if he were releasing words that had been pent up in him until then.

At these times, Aline was uncomfortable even in the kitchen. She felt like an intruder in their private world, a world made up of anecdotes and tales that she suspected were crude, sensationalistic and unbelievable. She felt the brothers considered her immature because they were so much older than she was; and she felt their eyes on her body, which scandalized her. She was their stepmother, after all, a married woman and a relative. Because they displaced her, belittled her and looked at her as if she were a whore, she resented them even more than she was beginning to resent the new and unwelcome way Grandfather was treating her.

The only member of the family with whom she felt at ease was her new grandson, Jean-Baptiste. He had in common with his twin sister, Marie, the desire for a better life than that lived in the Desouche house. But while Marie was convinced of the necessity of political action, considering their problems the fault of the English, Jean-Baptiste felt the answer was internal and spiritual. They agreed, however, that the Catholic Church was an impediment to almost everything reasonable; and so he had turned to poetry, while his sister chose revolution.

Jean-Baptiste had taken the room on the top floor at the back end, the most remote and quiet in the house. Here, in what was almost an attic, he was insulated from the noise of the family and the street, free to read or compose his poems. His room was awash in books and magazines, papers and stationery. Since no one else would publish his works, he had decided to print them himself, and had installed a second-hand mimeograph machine in the attic, hemmed in by boxes of manuscript on one side and pamphlets on the other.

Jean-Baptiste was the only one aside from Marie who remembered that Aline didn't speak English. He understood perfectly well her feelings of isolation, since no one else in the family shared his interest in the arts. And since his mother tongue was English, he knew how hard it could be to learn another way of thinking. His French was not perfect, but he attempted to use it for her sake. However, he avoided spending time with Aline because he had no patience for those incapable of helping themselves, and it broke his heart to see her suffering. It's true he could have invested his own efforts in helping her, but he knew that she would never learn to walk for herself, without whatever crutch was at hand. Obviously, that's why she'd married Grandfather, who had behaved so much like a crutch during their courtship.

It was Jean-Baptiste who had warned her, in the first place, that she was making a mistake taking up with the Desouches, and now he felt the case was out of his hands: he'd done what he could and failed. But the more he avoided her, the more she followed him with her eyes, silently wishing she could win more real allies in the house, not knowing that this habit of hers gave him exactly the same feeling of being ogled that she got from Father and Uncle. It wasn't the arguing and yelling of the family, the small tricks and cruelties they played upon one another, the disrespect they showed for his work; it wasn't even the impossibly run-down physical condition of the house that made living there unbearable for him. More than anything else it was the quiet way in which Aline meekly tracked him from room to room, from dinner table to living-room couch to bathroom.

But Aline knew nothing of the others' feelings or reasons for behaving as they did; she only knew her own anxiety and unhappiness. She was baffled by their irritability, their relations to one another, their ideas, their jokes, their very being. Nothing turned out as she expected, and she was afraid of trying to change anything. Her only respite was in the kitchen, where, if she had no natural talents, at least she had cookbooks. So she timidly advanced from frying eggs and bacon, soaking peas for soup, boiling beef and potatoes, to stuffing chickens, making simple spaghetti sauces and packaged cake mixes. She had no kitchen timer and relied on the clock, but was always forgetting to consult it because she was listening to the radio, so that her dishes were always either over- or undercooked. But if she treated food as if it were someone else's children, she at least became familiar enough with that one room to feel at ease when she was alone in it. The worn table, the overpainted cupboards, the ancient, round-edged refrigerator under which linoleum had never settled: these were the physical things, along with Grandfather's body, which by their own age had drained her of enthusiasm, ambition and self-confidence. Hers was the domain of the defeated, the unrealized and the barely adequate; and only there was she comfortable.

While Aline slept, while Grandfather and Uncle were returning from the cemetery, while Jean-Baptiste wore out his eyes with a novel, while no one could say where Marie was or what she was doing, Father and Mother were exercising their conjugal rights. After years of unhappy marriage during which each secretly resented in the other what they forgave in themselves, making love was the only time they forgot each other's ugliness.

Mother couldn't help her disappointment at Father's shiny scalp, which emerged where once had been a thick, dark web of hair. Or when his hard, smooth belly had softened, distended and almost maliciously grown the hair he lacked elsewhere. Or especially at the way, even after a bath, a shave and a liberal application of cologne, he still smelled like his own cigarette case. For his part, Father dreaded the scars motherhood had left on his wife and was nostalgic for her former firmness, smartness of dress and coquettish manner.

Both were reluctant to get into bed at night for fear that the other might be overcome with desire. But even so, when they did make love—once their initial reluctance and embarrassment was behind them, once they had resigned themselves to the effort—they found themselves contemplating the selves of their youth. Neither heeded the wrinkles, the greyed eyebrows or the extra pounds. Both remembered and re-experienced the wordless pleasure of each other's warmth, the languid expression in the other's eyes, and the disappearance of the musty room, the unpaid bills on the coffee table downstairs, the whole rest of the world around them. But this brief, infrequent transcendence could neither be lengthened nor multiplied and was for them not the precious gift of a sanctified marriage, but the cruel temptation of a mischievous creator, or the restrictive proscription of an oppressive society. It made them both realize that it wasn't the deed itself they were reluctant to enact but the partner they were stuck with who drove their eagerness away.

They were incited and saddened by the sight or company of others to whom they felt physical attraction. They knew they no longer had the youthful vigour that attracts partners and had once attracted them to each other. Nevertheless, they both still had the desire for youth and beauty just as they had the desire for the material things they saw advertised all around them, on billboards and buses, on television and in magazines. Cars, clothes, vacations; blondes, brunettes, redheads. Because there was so little in their own lives, they wanted so much. And they believed that somewhere people enjoyed possessions without responsibilities; people who were younger, thinner, more handsome than themselves; people they imagined they were with when they were together.

The banging door and stomping of Grandfather and Uncle up the steps broke their spell; they opened their eyes on each other. Numb, neither could be bothered finishing and so they lay panting. It was just before dawn. Together they resented the returning men who hadn't the decency to tread quietly. They were tired and drifting off, but jarred awake more than once by flushing toilets, heavy steps and the cawing and flapping of Grandfather's pet crow. The scratching and whining of Uncle's dog abated with a few yelps.

One of Father's few saving graces was his refusal to take part in Grandfather's crimes. Mother thought of this and moved closer to him in the bed. In the dark, in their cramped room, he put his arm around her, thankful too that he was here with her and not with them; and also thankful that Mother had never complained of his lack of a steady job, that he'd tried and failed at so many things. For both of them, even indigence was preferable to the family business.

It wasn't necessary for Marie to stand by and watch her bombs go off. Timers were accurate, and she knew her business. But she was a perfectionist and insisted on being available in case anything went wrong. Sometimes she wondered exactly what she would or could do if there were no detonation. Would she dare try retrieving the package? If she did, what could she do with it? It was more dangerous to take a bomb apart than to put one together. But she couldn't bring herself simply to set it and walk away. That was too impersonal, as if she were an anonymous quirk of fate rather than an active, intentional being. That would be like one of those unsigned statements her comrades in the Front de libération du Québec—the FLQ—were always sending to the newspapers. Like the diaphanous, ambient noise of the city itself or like messages from unknown spirits transmitted by Ouija boards. Her work was hers alone, and her insistence on watching it to completion was her way of signing her statements—for they were political statements—just as an artist would sign a canvas, or her brother sign his poems.

Tonight's operation was a masterpiece. She dropped the package into the mailbox outside the restaurant just as she'd planned with her cell. The place was full of drunks, stuffing themselves sick with smoked meat after boozing it up all night in the bars. Anglos mostly, of course. The bomb went off like a charm at three-twenty.

Torn metal, shattered plate glass windows, people screaming and bleeding their way across the floor, across the sidewalk. The fire, the noise, the ambulances, and lastly the reporters with no sense of the humanity of it. It was a symphony of lights. First the explosion itself, a great orange fireball; then the blinking flashers of police cars and ambulances; finally the flashbulbs and floodlights of photographers and video cameras.

She stood within a crowd of onlookers, herded back by patrolmen, watching the countless cops, firemen, paramedics, victims. When the detectives finally came around to ask for witnesses, she slipped away.

Her report was for her cell. And it wouldn't do to be identified at the scene.

She walked slowly along the still busy rue Ste-Catherine, mulling over the events in her mind. She ignored the drunken advances of a handful of boors being turfed out long past last call. She walked as if by rote to the meeting place, gave the correct knock at the door, entered. Several faces gazed at her inquiringly. She began to speak. As she related her triumph to her unit of the FLQ, she heard her voice as if from a distance, the words indistinct in her own ears, like the prayers of others in church. But the images in her mind were vivid, the lights blinding, the heat of the flames blistering like an open oven, and adrenalin flowed through her just as it had through those whose world had been suddenly shattered by her actions.

When she was done, the others began chattering excitedly, smiling grimly, gesturing importantly. Now it was time for the press release. Marie's job was done, and theirs began.

She would let the others contact the media. She wasn't interested in words, unlike her brother. Words were so anemic compared with actions; words were the weapon of her enemies, the English politicians. What had she heard but empty words all her life? No, they could stay up the rest of the night arguing over their text. Marie was going home to a well-deserved rest; next afternoon she could read in the paper just what an impact her actions had had, and what the press and the public thought of her companions' words.

She left the basement room by the rear, into the lane. A receiving dock blocked one end. The vapour rising from a sewer screened the other, which opened onto the street. No one would see where she had come from. She would appear out of the mist like a ghost or a banshee. In the dim light just before dawn, if anyone saw her at all in this district, she would likely be taken for a streetwalker.

Her route took her back past the scene of the bombing. Already the windows were being boarded up and the shattered glass and debris had been swept off the street corner. A single patrol car remained.

Early morning buses were already running, empty, through the downtown streets. She passed through the campus of McGill University, crossed in front of the building that had been her high school, turned onto her street. At the top of the block the mountain rose, grey from the leafless trees, the fields around it white with snow. Halfway up the block, directly in front of the Desouche house, a police car was parking.

Uncle's dog woke before his key turned in the lock, and whined ceaselessly while waiting for him in his bedroom. It leapt and circled him until, receiving a smack for its trouble, it settled back to sleep when Uncle slid into bed and began to snore. When the doorbell rang, the dog's head snapped erect. Uncle rose and went to the window and looked out, leaning the balls of his hands on the sill. When he saw the police cruiser his chest began to punish him. He ran to Grandfather's room.

Grandfather had been trying to silence the crow, which had begun its morning screeching as soon as he opened the door. Aline turned her face to the wall, burying herself in the pillow. She couldn't understand why he wouldn't keep the crow elsewhere. Unless he got some satisfaction out of displeasing her. She was surprised to see it when she moved in. He never mentioned it before their marriage. The sight of the enormous, ragged black scavenger sealed the lid on the idea of any time alone together, hidden away from all the rest of the world, even if no real honeymoon was possible. The presence of the crow transformed their marriage bed into a bier.

Uncle pounded on the door, yelling "Police! Police!" and set the crow off again. Even Grandfather gave out a little screech. He tore the door open. Uncle, in his underwear, grabbed him by the shoulders and shouted again, "Police! Police!"

Aline sat upright, confused and terrified by the sight of Uncle nearly naked in her bedroom. "What's going on?"

"Shut up," said Grandfather. It wasn't clear whether he was addressing her or Uncle. He disappeared into the hallway and Uncle followed him. Aline sighed and lay down.

Grandfather stomped down the hall and banged on Father and Mother's door. When Father answered he said curtly, "Tell them we're not here. We're not here, you don't know where we are. Understand?" Father nodded. Grandfather grabbed Uncle by the arm and ran him down the stairs, careful to stay out of sight of the windows. The two men hid in the basement.

But when Father finally answered the bell after the third ring, the police asked for Mother.

Jean-Baptiste was only a few pages from the end of *The Unbearable Lightness of Being*. He was dazed, still caught in the dreamlike state of reading. He had just read the line, "Our lives may be separate, but they run in the same direction, like parallel lines," when Marie knocked at his window. He left the warm bed, his body startled by the change in temperature, opened the window and retreated before the blast of winter air. Marie climbed in without a word, carefully closing the window behind her.

She whispered: "Tell them I've been with you all night. All night, understand?"

Just at that moment the doorbell sounded downstairs.

Jean-Baptiste looked towards the door. "No, I don't understand. Okay, you want me to cover for you, but what will they think if we say we were here together?"

Marie got into his bed and pulled the covers under her chin. "For God's sake, they'll arrest me."

"Coat, boots and all," said Jean-Baptiste. "Would you do it for me if our positions were reversed?"

They were silent a moment.

He asked, "What did you do?"

"Nothing. Does it matter? I did what was right."

"I just want to know what kind of criminal I'm harbouring. That's a crime too, you know. I want to
know how serious this is."

Now there were people walking about the house,
making noise.

"Don't be so self-righteous. Will you turn me in?
Would you turn in Grandfather and Uncle?" She was
struggling to take off her clothes under the blankets.
There was a knock at the door.

Jean-Baptiste got back into bed. His sister was cold
beside him.

Father burst into the room. "Jean-Baptiste, wake
up. Angus is dead."

Angus was his other grandfather, Mother's father. She
sat on the divan sobbing; Father spoke with the police.
Marie quietly went to her own room; Jean-Baptiste
looked suspiciously after her, but said nothing and
instead made tea. Aline began to fry potatoes and
bacon. Grandfather and Uncle sat silently in the dark
basement, looking up through the narrow window to
the street until they saw the wheels of the patrol car
driving away. Then they went back to bed.

Angus had lived on the slope of the mountain,
on a street that would someday be named after a
man Grandfather counted among his customers,
a man famous for opening up people's skulls and
prodding them with electrodes while they were still
awake. A man who was the Desouches' family doctor
because he could be paid in trade instead of cash. It

was a prestigious street, where many foreign countries had their embassies in large rambling houses older than their countries and more solid than their governments, and where behind closed doors, worse things were done to people still awake.

Angus had been proud to live there. He'd seemed to think his street somehow more worthy of respect than others. Perhaps because it was higher up the hill, or because so many of his neighbours were mysterious men in dark glasses. Or because so many of the houses were surrounded by fences and cameras. At any rate, he had a way of suggesting that Mother's street was beneath him in more than just the literal sense.

It was never any use pointing out to him that he could only afford to live there because he lived alone in a small apartment and spent no money on vices of any kind, or even simple necessities like clothing, preferring to wear what he still insisted were the perfectly useful shirts and pants he'd been issued in the army. Or that, really, it was past time to cancel his dead wife's pension.

None of this or any other opinion contrary to his made any impression on him, for Angus was one of the world's freelance wise men. They're not rare, these savants, but those to whom they offer advice curiously ignore them. And they're often intentionally thwarted by their inferiors just to keep them from influence and power or even simple respect. They've always paid less than you have, and for better goods. They invariably shake their heads as they say they told you so. They always have another suggestion for getting your life in order. They have a great respect for their own experience, but scoff at anyone's education. To them the words "expert" and "intellectual" are insults, and metaphors are clouds of smoke and halls of mirrors.

Angus had been proud of serving in the army, although he'd been drafted and then discharged as soon as the war was over—as soon as they were done with him. He was fond of such abstract concepts as Duty and Honour. To him the abstract was that to which he couldn't explain his sentimental attraction. But it left him with lifelong respiratory problems: he'd been gassed in those trenches. Which taught him something you can't learn in school. Which left him teary-eyed still, whenever he heard "God Save the Queen."

Mother kept thinking to herself, "I'm an orphan now . . . I'm an orphan now . . ." She remembered those things about him that he'd never shown to the others. His sudden changes of heart when he switched from chastising her to forgiving her: "Ah well. You're still my girl, aren't you? I guess you'll just have to take me as I am." His habit of paying their debt at the corner grocery without telling them. The way there was always more food in the house after he'd been invited to dinner than before. How he used to take the children down to the harbour to see the boats.

Now there would be the problem of dealing with his things. His apartment. His funeral. Now there would be a dreamlike week, during which everything would be centred on the absence of him. And why had he suddenly been taken in the middle of the night with the desire for a smoked meat sandwich, anyway?

Mother couldn't stifle a burst of abuse against "those bastard felquiste swine," meaning the FLQ; meaning, if the family'd only known, Marie. And then she dissolved again in her own tears. Marie, pale, accepted it silently. She was overwhelmed; her world had changed unexpectedly. It would take her weeks of sullen silence to digest it. It had never occurred to her that anyone she knew personally would be affected by her terrorist acts. Everything had always been aimed against an ill-defined "them" and not an all-too-familiar "us."

When they went up to Angus's apartment they were surprised to find everything already packed. Only the most essential items were unboxed: a single towel, a couple of mugs, his toothbrush and comb. It was precisely as they'd left it when helping him move in years ago after his wife died. The hall was lined with boxes and bags, furniture was stacked upside down and the dresser was empty of its drawers.

He'd been fond of saying, "Properly used, a single spoon can last a man a lifetime." Now Mother realized what he'd meant. He left no insurance. He'd always waved his bankbook and said, "Here's my insurance. Why give money to those crooks?" But Mother wasn't allowed to draw from his account. Until the estate was settled, the Desouches were forced to pay the outstanding bills and the burial expenses. That was bad news for their already frustrated creditors.

The services were arranged with the undertakers who occupied the adjoining building on the south side of the Desouches' own house. They were given a special rate because for one thing they were neighbours, and for another, since he'd been so close to the blast, there just wasn't much left of Angus to embalm.

For years, they'd watched others dressed in black filing in and out of the parlour next door. They played a game of counting the limousines and hearses they'd see in a week, or run to keep Uncle's dog from wandering in to join the bereaved. In summer, Uncle sat on the porch in his undershirt, beer in hand, as mourners slouched on the sidewalk, hot in their suits and dresses, self-conscious beneath his unfriendly stare.

Now the Desouches all donned their formal clothes. Stiff and not much used, they were long out of fashion and obviously unsuited to their lives.

When they entered the funeral home for the first time, Grandfather cased the joint like a professional housebreaker. How much easier would it be to collect his merchandise here than to have to tear it from the ground like a miner? Alas, he noticed the building was fitted with an alarm system beyond his abilities to circumvent: tiny cameras in the ceiling corners and motion sensors on every window and door. And as Uncle pointed out, here the corpses would be missed immediately. But Grandfather couldn't get over the feeling of being let into a bank vault. He fled the parlour "for a smoke," which he sucked on like an infant at a bottle.

Passersby saw him tremble and jerk the cigarette in and out of his mouth, saw his discomfort in the suit, saw him standing before the funeral home, and murmured their condolences on their way. Grandfather wondered what they were on about.

Until Grandmother's recent demise, Jean-Baptiste had never actually known a dead person. Now, with Angus, it was still a novel enough experience to inspire a glut of new poems which—because they were about the death of his grandfather and because he was so young— were atrocious. But he loved them enough to want to print them himself and hand them around to anyone who would take them. Eventually he had enough to fill a small pamphlet, and began to think of how and where he could find the paper and ink he needed.

In the meantime, he decided it couldn't hurt to submit some of these new works to local magazines— even if there were no chance of acceptance. The problem, he knew, was that he just wasn't sociable enough to become part of the right circles. Which was obviously the only way anybody got published, especially locally. Everybody knew everyone else and they all published one another in their reviews and magazines, and went to each other's readings and launches, and wrote about each other in the local newspaper, which made them all seem very worldly and important. And no one bothered over whether their work was really any good or whether it was enjoyed by anyone but themselves.

Jean-Baptiste knew the real problem was that they didn't recognize good work when it bit them, because they never read anything but each other's work, and because they watched too much television. The anglophone literary community of Montreal was very small. Although they had heard of people like Calvino and Goethe and Bulgakov, they thought these people were foreign dictators or film stars. Therefore Jean-Baptiste was quite surprised to receive a reply from an editor who, while rejecting the poems he had sent, offered encouragement, asked to see more work and invited him round for a chat.

"I feel a little like Artaud," Jean-Baptiste said as he sat opposite the editor.

"Who?" the editor asked.

"Never mind," said Jean-Baptiste.

The men borrowed a truck and moved Angus's things to the basement. Mother wanted to sort through them, knowing she'd discover much of it difficult to discard. She spent days below ground looking at brown photos by the light of an unshaded bulb, trying to bring herself to throw out old shirts, opening letters he'd kept from people she'd never heard of. And then closing them again as if afraid of being caught.

When Father suggested it was really getting time to begin disposing of some things, she protested.

"No, not yet. It's so comforting having them near. Later, in the spring." For once, Father didn't press her.

But Angus's boxes in the basement were no comfort to Marie. They were a secret torment she dared not share with anyone. It mattered little to her that others had died or been injured. She'd expected that—she had wanted that. It didn't even matter so much that someone she knew personally, her own grandfather, had died. Truth to tell, she hadn't liked him very much. He was too much of an Anglo. Too much of a slave to his masters, who preyed on his simple ideas of how the world worked. And used him, as he thanked them for it. If he'd been smarter or more clear-sighted, she could at least have respected him personally, even if he was English. No, she lost no love over Angus. The hard part was watching her mother's grief. And knowing she had caused it.

Never before had her mother's feelings mattered. She'd always felt Mother's feelings were the result of erroneous ideas, that if she could only see the truth she'd be ashamed of her heritage. The same way Marie was ashamed of her anglo blood. When she was small, even before she began to form her political ideas, Marie had looked at her mother and decided she would not be like her. She wouldn't be subject to someone else's will, the way Mother was to Father's. And when she became a teenager, she began to see the French and the English as being in the same relationship.

Nevertheless, even if Mother made her angry and represented something she hated, even if Mother had no place in Marie's world, she was still Marie's mother. And to see her staring vacantly, to hear her spontaneous sobbing, to watch her face drawn with expressions of madness, was agonizing. Marie knew that as long as those boxes of Angus's were in the house, she couldn't bear to be.

She didn't even tell them she was leaving. She took nothing with her. She simply stayed away.

The rift between Aline and Grandfather had been growing since the day the police came. Though Aline was not brave, and was now frankly afraid of Grandfather, she was even more afraid of the police. She'd always believed that anyone who hid from them had reason to. The thought that she'd married a gangster mortified her.

"This business you're in with Uncle," she asked, "it isn't criminal, is it?"

Lifting his eyes but not his head from the newspaper, Grandfather mocked her voice. "*Criminal*. That's not an absolute, is it?"

"Mon dieu," said Aline. Her heart sank. It was the final degradation. The intimacies they'd shared sprang into her mind and repulsed her. She left her pan at the stove, sat at the table and cried.

"Someone has to pay the bills," said Grandfather. "Look, we're months behind on everything. We have to eat."

Through her hands, Aline said, "Then it's true crime doesn't pay, isn't it? Good Lord, help me."

"Fuck the Lord," said Grandfather. "He never bought me a meal."

She couldn't get any more than that out of him. He wouldn't deny the illegality of his activities but he wouldn't describe them either.

Now she was glad that Grandfather had a nocturnal schedule. It relieved her of the burden of sharing the bed with him. While he slept during the day, she worked in the kitchen and did the shopping. She tried to encourage Mother to join her at the shops. It had been Mother's task until Angus had died, and though Aline welcomed the excuse it gave her to leave the house, she thought it would be better if Mother came out of the basement and her depression. For the rest of the time, when Grandfather was not in his room, she slept.

Eventually she grew used to the crow flapping in its cage and unless it screeched it no longer woke her. Its squalling became her alarm, signalling the entry of Grandfather into their bedroom and prompting her to rise for the day. While she dressed it would continue screeching. It was a great annoyance to Grandfather. Wanting to sleep, he'd bury himself in the bedclothes.

At last a curious thing happened: Aline began to like the crow. She took its squawking as her own complaining, complaining that she was much too timid to undertake herself. Every time Grandfather flinched at a piercing cry, she felt as if she herself had screwed up the courage to yell at him. As soon as this occurred to her, she ceased resenting the crow's waking her. She ceased to fear it or be surprised by its sudden outbursts. She began to feel relief; the more it cawed, the calmer she felt. There were times when its screeching scaled ear-piercing heights, spurred on by Grandfather's desperation, his covering his ears or slapping at the bird. Times when she realized she was actually smiling as if at the laughter of children.

Naturally, the more Aline came to like it, the more Grandfather hated the crow. Although he'd never been fond of it, now it irritated him more and more, until he couldn't remember why he'd taken it in at all.

It had been a whim at first. One he expected to give up after the inevitable fight with Grandmother—this had been while his first wife was still alive. But for a reason Grandfather couldn't understand, she never said a word. His unstated surprise at her silence had quickly turned into a challenge. If she wouldn't object to it being in the house, she certainly must object to his moving it into their bedroom.

Of course Grandmother was not such a fool as her husband, and after so many years of his persecutions, she knew instantly that the filthy bird's only purpose was to annoy her. Long practice had taught her that her only weapon against Grandfather's taunts was an iron skin. She ignored the bird.

Grandfather, on the unimaginative principle that he was more stubborn than his wife was patient, swallowed his anger at this trick turned against him. He too ignored the crow. So successfully, in fact, did they both overlook it that it became just another unpleasant part of being in the bedroom. Like the dull peeling wallpaper or the draft from the hall, or each other's proximity.

Now when it seemed that his second wife was actually going to enjoy the presence of this creature, Grandfather was furious. For the first time in years he moved it out of his bedroom and into another part of the house. He placed it on the enclosed back porch. Aline used the excuse that the unheated space was too cold for the bird and brought it back inside the kitchen. She fed it scraps after their meals and bits and extras while cooking. She cleaned its cage, watered it and even let it fly about the room and stretch its wings. It perched on the countertop or the kitchen table, watching her go about her business as if genuinely curious. It followed the movements of her hands with a cocked head and hopped around for a better view.

Aline's disposition improved. Yet she dreaded returning to Grandfather's bedroom every night, even if he wasn't there. He never made the bed, so his presence was always impressed upon it like a weight on her soul. But it was impossible for her to think of leaving her husband. Her own sense of shame and the proscriptions of her faith saw to that. But the duty of sharing his bed was an albatross round her neck. Then one day as she closed the windows before giving the crow the freedom of the kitchen, she suddenly realized that if it could leave its cage, so could she.

She moved her things into Marie's room.

"Where do you think you're going?" demanded Grandfather.

"If thine eye offend thee," said Aline, "pluck it out."

TWO

RESURRECTION MAN

They had run through the letters and past-due notices, they had weathered the storm of phone calls, they had swallowed the abuse of bill collectors; they had even pretended not to be home when the gas man came calling. But eventually he showed up with a bailiff, and Uncle grudgingly answered the door.

"We would pay it if we could," he said truthfully. The men nodded, and politely removed their galoshes so as not to track snow into the house, and Uncle led them to the basement door. "Find it yourself," he said, and left them.

They discovered Mother among Angus's worldly remains, like a child with dolls, and they exchanged hellos. When they explained who they were, she showed them the furnace. Under the eyes of the bailiff, the gas man sealed the meter, and the furnace went out.

When they left, Uncle took a pair of pliers from the pantry, wordlessly passed by Mother and her things, and broke the seal on the meter. He lit the pilot light, waited a moment to make sure the settings were correct, and went upstairs for a smoke.

37

Later the landlord, who was equally unsuccessful in collecting his rent from the Desouches, called the gas company to inform on them out of spite.

The phone calls began again. Father tried patiently explaining that winter was a bad time for them financially, and also no time to do without heating. But like all public utilities, the gas company was heartless; its employees were the kind of uncaring functionaries who do so well in totalitarian regimes, precisely because they're able to bury their humanity under their position so completely. They merely follow the rules, as if such abstract guidelines affect only other management decisions and not people. When the woman berating Father for being a deadbeat made this perfectly clear, he hung up the phone, collected a hammer and nailed shut the door to the basement. The gas man showed up not just with a bailiff but with the police, and Uncle himself handed them a crowbar to wrench open the door. When they flicked on the light, they discovered Mother still down there.

Grandfather, Uncle and Father held a conference around the now permanently sealed meter. Though they had some elementary knowledge of how to jimmy various kinds of meters, plumbing and fuse boxes, they couldn't simply snap a wire this time. It was already getting colder in the house; but at least that got Mother up out of the damp, unfinished basement.

Next day Father walked over to the main branch of the public library across from Lafontaine Park, and found a book on natural gas with colour illustrations and complete details on the workings of the system. It never occurred to him that the library would issue him a card, so he simply stole the book, secreting it in his armpit beneath his winter greatcoat. The three men pored over the book all day, getting colder and colder, putting on sweater after sweater, drinking too many cups of hot tea.

At last they decided they had only two choices: to pay the bill, which was impossible, or to direct gas from their neighbour's line into their furnace, which was dangerous.

The house on the north side of them was occupied by an old woman and her retarded son, which would have made it ideal, but it was heated by electricity and anyway they were already siphoning that. This fact was never noticed by either the old woman or the electric company because Father had discovered that by removing the meter from its housing and simply replacing it upside down, it ran backward. Every morning one of the men would go out before dawn behind the house and turn it right side up again; and so the meter reader never realized it had been tampered with, and in fact the old woman's bills decreased. But the Desouches didn't have any electric heaters, and thought it best not to press their luck anyway. So their only choice was the funeral parlour on the south side.

That evening, behind the protective wall of dead Angus's boxed possessions, with their work-heavy exhalations rising like steam from the ground, they began digging into the black, hard-packed earth.

Despite the cold, their heavy jackets, scarves and gloves left them sweating.

Upstairs, huddled around the kitchen table, with the oven door open and its element glowing red like lava, the rest of the family were freezing. They too wore coats and toques and gloves, but they weren't sweating. By this time Aline had said, "Que c'est froid, tellement froid!" often enough that Jean-Baptiste no longer had to translate it as "It's too fucking cold" for Mother. Nor had he to translate Mother's "It's like a grave in here" for Aline.

Through Jean-Baptiste, Aline had been trying to convince Mother to take up her old chore of shopping again, at least by accompanying Aline if not going alone, and if only to get into a building with some heat. Aline herself was finding any excuse to run to the corner store or the grocery, scrounging up what little cash was in the house on the pretext of needing more oregano for the spaghetti or another jar of jam for the toast. But Mother wouldn't go with her. Though she shivered and suffered with the rest of them, she seemed so comfortable in her mourning that nothing would move her.

"One step at a time," said Jean-Baptiste. "At least she's out of the basement." Aline nodded.

Jean-Baptiste had become the link between the two women, translating freely for each what the other had said. But because he resented this position immediately, this extra burden imposed on him by their ignorance of each other's language, he took to translating quite freely indeed. Usually he would deliver intact the general idea of their statements, but often in a way which he knew would incense them unexpectedly.

When Aline said: "Mother, if you come outside the house with me, you'll feel much better. You'll begin to come outside of yourself," he translated this as:

"She says you should get out more, you're just feeling sorry for yourself."

And Mother's response, "Like anyone else, I treat my own suffering as well as I can. And I can't help thinking about my father," was heard by Aline as:

"What do you know about suffering?"

But on the other hand, Mother absently accepted a cup of Earl Grey from Aline and only later thought that Aline must have discovered it was her favourite from one of the others and bought it on her own initiative; and when Mother couldn't finish her morning toast, she had saved it specifically "for Aline's bird."

The two women came to regard each other as capricious and unpredictable, and in the end, although they thought of him as their bridge, Jean-Baptiste became just another obstacle between them.

And an irritable one at that. Jean-Baptiste was increasingly unsatisfied living in the family home. He'd never really liked living there, and he was coming to that age when the idea of living away from his parents was transformed from a nightmare into a dream. And ever since Marie had demonstrated that it was possible by disappearing, he had been trying to imagine how he too might leave. He was held back only by the unfortunate curse shared by all the males of the Desouche line: he didn't want to work. That is, he couldn't bear the thought of a regular job, of rising early to ride a crowded bus, of having a boss.

And recent developments had only nurtured his desire for freedom: Mother's turning away from life, Aline's growing dependence on him, and now the freezing cold. The only one in the house who seemed unaffected by the drop in temperature was the crow; and as they huddled around the table, it nonchalantly stared at them all from atop the refrigerator, its head held first at one sharp angle and then another, as if trying to figure them out. In the chilly kitchen, its cawing was like derisive laughter.

"That damned crow," said Jean-Baptiste.

"That's what Grandfather calls it. Please don't call it that," said Aline.

"Well, it needs a name, then. What am I supposed to call it?" asked Jean-Baptiste.

At that moment Father burst into the kitchen from the basement stairs, flinging open the door with a crash. The crow screamed and flew about the ceiling, colliding with the light fixture and sending it swaying to and fro like a pendulum.

Mother jumped up with her hand on her heart and exclaimed, "Gracious!"

The silence seemed sudden afterwards. Shadows rose and fell on the walls; the crow settled on the washing machine's wringer.

Jean-Baptiste said, "How about Grace for short?"

The family had silently assumed that Marie disappeared out of shame at being found in her brother's bed. Only Jean-Baptiste knew that if shame was the reason, it was another kind of shame that had driven her from the house. But even he had no idea where exactly she'd gone. Uncle was of the opinion that "A young woman can always find a bed. There's no reason to worry." But Father remained concerned, perhaps more than he might have been if Mother had been up to carrying some of the anxiety. It seemed to him that no one else was paying proper attention to her absence; of course, he didn't blame Mother. And Jean-Baptiste had had an earful from him about not going anywhere near his sister. And what could Aline be expected to think? But the sheer disregard, even scorn, that came from Uncle and Grandfather was a growing irritation that did nothing to soothe his misgivings.

Hour after hour, Father shovelled and sweated in the dark, cold, damp basement, while his two companions silently smoked with a shovel in hand, or grunted to each other as if over the years they had developed their own system of communicating without bothering to speak full sentences. Father found it wearisome. And Grandfather had told him pointedly, "Look, son, you can either talk or shovel. But it's too hard to do both. Take my word for it."

"Hell, I'm worried about my daughter—your granddaughter," he'd said angrily.

"I never worry about women," said Uncle, and he smacked a rat with the flat end of his shovel.

"Christ," said Father. "I can't dig any more, I'm not used to it like you two. What with everything, it feels too much like we're digging our own graves. I'm so tired I could just fall in beside that rat."

The others took over. Watching their rounded backs rolling, he stood there for a moment under the burden of their contempt. But he shook it off, and went upstairs to his wife.

Where had Marie gone? Like anyone else who needs a place in a hurry, Marie had gone to her friends'. The Desouches, of course, hadn't the slightest idea who her friends might be. For them, she had simply disappeared. Naturally she had chosen to associate with people her family would never have had anything to do with—idealists.

Marie's friends considered the English to be an occupying power, as they were in Ireland and as they had been in India and so many other places. *Anglophone* and *English* were synonymous to them; they couldn't accept anglophones as Canadians, even though they saw themselves as Québécois, distinct from the French of France. And if you had suggested to them that in the eyes of the natives forced onto reserves, they were just as much occupying foreigners as their perceived enemies, they would certainly have angrily explained the difference to you.

Despite so much historical evidence to prove that their own politicians and businessmen had much more in common with their anglo counterparts than with them, that their own journalists and pop stars were just as much lackeys of the local money lords as were those of the Anglos, and that any of them would renounce their linguistic and nationalistic patriotism as so much fascist obfuscation the instant they were offered any personal material benefit, those at the bottom of the social ladder—Marie's cell—clung foolishly to the belief that the French were a nation loyal to their kindred. Marx had been wrong: it was not the power of money that grouped or divided people. It was language, pure and simple.

Meanwhile, lawyers, politicians and businessmen, anglophone and francophone alike, learned one another's language, made deals together, enacted labour laws benefiting the moneyed, carved up monopolies between them and charged their champagne expense accounts to the working taxpayers in two official languages. In Canada and Quebec money had always been and would always remain bilingual. And as always, for those who had it, it provided not only their continuing comfort and success, but also the despair and failure of those who did not. It bought, through the offices of the media, the illusion that if only it were printed in a different language, it would multiply and disperse more evenly and equitably.

But money was a thing that worried Marie's FLQ unit only in a practical sense and not as a political force. It worried them only when the bills from those monopolies had to be paid: the telephone company, the electric company, the cable TV. Communications, heating, the flow of information: they were billed in

French, and so they paid happily. Or if they didn't, or couldn't, they were hounded by French bill collectors; and eventually, their services were cut off by French workers.

Fortunately, the political struggle cost them far less than their rents. They stole guns, explosives, cars—anything in the way of tools needed to mount their operations. And when it was unavoidable, when they could do nothing without hard currency—to pay off their French lawyers, police friends or drug suppliers—they stole that too, with the same guns and getaway cars. They were careful to observe their linguistic barriers here too; they did not rob the local Caisse Populaire, but instead targeted those great, oppressive anglophone institutions, the Royal Bank and the Toronto-Dominion. Their very names were arrogant affronts to francophones everywhere: Royal, meaning the Queen, and Dominion—need that be explained at all?

As for moral quibbles, they were more than just easily brushed aside; they were never raised in their minds at all. it was a simple matter of necessity: in order to carry on the great struggle, their basic material needs had to be met.

Some funds came from sympathizers of all sorts—the unemployed, the working poor, artists, members of the Church; even some Québécois businessmen, who realized that local customers were silent sympathizers and a little word-of-mouth was good advertising. But since their federal unemployment insurance cheques were pitifully small, the bulk of their living expenses had to be charged up to the cause and paid for out of its treasury. Which meant that a good deal of their time was spent planning and executing what they described as their "capital campaign."

And so they turned Montreal into the bank robbery capital of North America.

Marie was in her element. True, she was sleeping on couches, on floors, on camp cots in basements. But here she felt alive, she felt purposeful, she felt vindicated. She missed nothing from her family home. Except, perhaps, the regular meals. But youth and idealism know no hunger save lust, which always seems appropriate to grand ideas. Though they often missed meals or ate badly, and though she and the few other women in those circles were expected to prepare what meals there were—along with performing all the other usually female duties—Marie was pervaded with a sense of self-importance that verged on the sacred.

Their leader passed an infectious inner strength to her through the group's debates, through tirades against their enemies, by their sexual union, and by his very gaze. It mattered not that living conditions were primitive, that personal hygiene was neglected, that the bourgeois affectations of social conventions were ignored (i.e., that the women were sometimes beaten, often insulted or shouted down). What mattered was that in the end, once victory had been ensured and the people of Quebec were commanding their own destiny, they would be able to build a society that would no longer have need of these crisis conditions. An independent and more confident

Quebec would be able to consider such currently unspeakable ideas as anglophone rights, and then to turn to such secondary matters as personhood for women, linguistic tolerance, a healthy economy.

But in the meantime, there were mailboxes to be blown up, store windows in anglo neighbourhoods to be broken and perhaps even visiting ambassadors to be kidnapped.

Uncle and Grandfather were in a quandary. The digging was done; they had access to the gas feed into the funeral parlour's basement. It was now a simple matter of shutting the valve from the rear of the property and joining a line to their own furnace. But once they did that, there would be no reason to dig any further; and the thought of tunnelling right into the mortuary itself so tantalized them, the same way that the thought of a bank vault would have tantalized Marie's friends, that they stood silently staring into their own hole, unable to go upstairs and complete the work. Neither said a word—they only infrequently glanced at each other—but both were thinking that Father would not permit the mad scheme they were dreaming of: to operate out of the family home was to invite disaster upon them all. Their work was tolerated by the others, even those who found it distasteful to varying degrees, but to make accomplices of the whole household would be going too far. And altogether it was just too risky; these were bodies not yet relegated to the machinations of the earth and its creatures, not yet ceremonially put out of mind. Once their absence was discovered, their route would quickly follow, bringing scandal and police in their wake.

Weighing their desire against practicality, the two men sat on boxes and smoked. They shuffled their feet; they flung their cigarette butts carelessly into the pit; they shivered. Finally, hungry and bitterly cold, they rose and mounted the stairs.

It wasn't long before they had completed the dangerous task of welding a supply line to their own furnace. The one detail they couldn't properly manage was a regulator on the line. It opened full throttle or not at all, but since they would never see the bill, it mattered little to them. Within an hour the family thankfully began to peel off their layers of clothing and go about the house comfortably; by bedtime, they were finding the air a little stuffy.

Tossing in their sleep, they threw off their bed-clothes and lay naked on their mattresses; when they woke in the daylight, they were sodden with sweat, and threw open the windows to let in the cold air.

Afraid that Grace would fly out the kitchen window and fail to return, Aline devised a collar and a line for the crow's leg from the elastics she'd saved off lettuce heads. "Why don't you just let the damned thing go?" growled Grandfather. Grace leapt at him from her perch on the fridge, screaming and pecking at his face and batting him painfully with her wings. Aline still had hold of the line she'd been affixing to the bird, and she pulled on it with all her strength. Grace resisted and the elastic merely stretched. The noise drew the others to the kitchen, where they saw a black storm of feathers where Grandfather's head should have been, and Aline shouting out to the Lord while she tugged and drew on the line as if she were flying a kite.

Father and Uncle managed to subdue Grace, and Grandfather escaped with only some bloody scratches on his bald head and his dignity battered. But when order had been restored, everyone suddenly noticed they were soaked with sweat, even though the winter wind had the freedom of the house.

Grandfather had never been gentle with the crow, but neither had it ever been aggressive in return. Now Grace pecked and flew at him whenever the chance arose, almost as if the mere fact of possessing a name had endowed her with the right to hate and persecute just as people do. Whenever the two came together, one would scream and yell, the other caw and squawk, with wings flapping and arms waving, as vicious as the tomcats in the lane.

As the house grew warmer day by day the crow seemed livelier and happier, but Grandfather grew more and more afraid of entering the kitchen and so began to take his meals elsewhere—leaving dirty dishes all over the house despite everyone's annoyance and Aline's pleadings that he clean up after himself. "That's your job, not mine. Anyway, it's your buzzard keeping me from my own kitchen."

And they all took to wearing as little as decency allowed inside the house. Less, in Uncle's case, Aline felt, though even she discarded long-sleeved blouses and dared a cotton skirt that rose above her knees, for the heat was now terrible, especially when she was vacuuming. And the effort of keeping the house at least clean, if not orderly, was a constant and increasingly necessary one: for the first time in years, neighbours began calling at their door.

It was the heat, of course. In a neighbourhood as poor as theirs, everyone kept their homes as cool as they could bear, preferring to wear sweaters and huddle under blankets in their living rooms rather than burden themselves with larger utility bills. Over the past few days, the neighbours had begun to notice first the open windows, then the snow melting from the Desouches' roof, and finally even the drifts in the small front yard begin to shrink, turn black and soak into the ground, as if spring had descended upon their house alone.

It was a thing of wonder, but nevertheless to be taken advantage of. Under the pretext of "seeing how Mother was getting along with her grief," her friends, the women who gathered at the local dépanneur, who'd earlier cautioned each other against disturbing the frail, shattered woman's peace, came looking for a cup of tea and half an hour in their shirt-sleeves.

Aline was burdened with hosting them, of course, for which she was angry but at the same time grateful, for they did have a positive effect on Mother, who slowly seemed to benefit from their selfish solicitude. Mrs. Pangloss was loudest as usual, even when trying to be considerate of Mother's precarious condition. She shrieked at the others to speak quietly, slowly, and to refrain from laughter. This last was directed mostly at old Mrs. Harrison, who was the very image of a witch and who never lost the opportunity to claim she was related to a Beatle.

"Ah, you're full of shit!" was the inevitable response from Mrs. Pangloss, a woman who admitted that everything in life was false and base; but since she hadn't the imagination to make any difference in her own life, she accepted as an article of faith that God was doing his best even at this very moment, no matter what disaster was in progress.

They treated Aline as if she were the maid. She brought them little sandwiches and cookies, and they thanked her too loudly, as if she were deaf, and then turned immediately to plying Mother with stupid remarks:

"At least he didn't suffer; it was quick." Who could tell what sufferings had been involved? thought Aline.

"Everything's for the best, dear, you'll see." Aline was offended by that one.

"Was there a will, dear? Did you do all right? He must have had some pile stashed away. He was always so tight with his money." As if Mother would somehow have been consoled by money, and as if a trait they had reprimanded Angus for in life could be counted as a virtue in death.

Yet Mother seemed to believe that their concern was genuine and their prattling more than just thinly disguised malice. She smiled whenever one or more of them came by; Aline would have preferred to toss them on their ears, but for Mother's sake she swallowed her feelings.

If Mother had no use for any possible inheritance, the same was not true of Father. He perked up at the mention of a will. Who would have suspected any relative of his would have a will? What of any possible value would anyone have to leave? But now he realized this woman could be right, for he remembered Angus railing against insurance companies while fluttering his bank book. He'd forgotten about the unsettled estate, what with Mother's fragile condition, Marie's disappearance and the cold.

But now the returning heat had brought back thoughts of money. He tried to speak of it to Mother, but she pointedly told him she didn't care about the money. He wanted to know how much there would be, and how soon it would come. He dreamt it would be enough to make an actual difference, enough to invest or to seed a business with. Not merely enough for a good drunk or new clothes or to pay the outstanding bills, but a large enough roll to gather some momentum and change things permanently for them.

It wasn't the first time Father had schemed a way to financial security. He'd tried a few things in his time, turning his hand to all sorts of trades and occupations. It wasn't really out of desperation that he'd done so but at least partly out of a feeling that a man of his talents could mould them to almost any task. Therefore he'd tried making badges and ribbons, he'd tried driving a taxi, he'd tried clerking in a bank, he'd tried being a barber—he still insisted on inflicting haircuts on his relatives—he had tried everything a reasonable man might do, and failed at them all. It wasn't that his practice proved inadequate to his theory, but that the real market never met his expectations.

Except that one time he'd been a clerk. The problem there had been getting caught. The episode was occasionally referred to by Grandfather or Uncle as "the Bank Job," but never to Father's face.

Father discovered that getting Angus's money was just a matter of pushing the forms through, and so he spent the following weeks pushing. While he awaited the arrival of the cheque, he looked round at the overcrowded hallways and rooms, at the broken, scarred and second-hand furniture. Couches were draped with faded bedspreads to hide their torn fabrics; chair legs were held in place with glue and baling wire; lamps were turned so their cracks and chips would face the wall. He'd always longed to be able to afford genuine antiques instead of junk furniture.

Suddenly he had the brainstorm he felt would shape the rest of his life: he would open a shop and sell and repair antiques. Further, he would open it right next door. That old woman and her son didn't need the huge old house all to themselves, and he would get it from her. If he had to, he'd bully her into an arrangement; they could live on the top floor, and Father would even give the boy a job, something he'd never had. He'd pay them a woefully small amount of money to rent the entire ground floor as a showroom, and the basement as a workshop for repairs. At first he worried he'd be unable to find real work simple enough for the boy to do. Bah! he decided, he'd merely set him to driving nails into a plank for no reason at all, and give him five dollars at the end of each day. Father imagined himself driving around town to visit decorators and other antique dealers and architects and designers, and standing them all drinks and dinners to drum up business. He'd buy himself a fine grey suit with a bowler hat in which to look his best for his "clients."

Mother's grief became his happiness. Her father's death was as great a blow as a father's death always is, no matter how loud he yells or how disappointed he is or how angry, intolerant, even destructive; still she cried for her father because she'd never have another. But for him, his father-in-law's death was a boon: no more awkward Sunday dinners, no more meddle-some, disapproving advice, no more struggling for the acquiescence of his own wife. For her it was the end of a kind of life, but for Father it was the prom-ise of a new beginning.

In Grandfather's life there had been little joy or hap-piness, and he had worked at keeping that little bit hidden. In a world of poverty and numbing physical labour, happiness was a weakness, a kind of lever to be used against its unwary possessor. A happy person was an unsuspecting person, and an unsuspecting person was, well . . . victimized.

The Desouche family history begins in mystery because Grandfather was an orphan. In the aftermath of the last great cholera epidemic in Montreal, before the Great War, he became one of dozens of children who were merely deposited at Catholic schools without references. Thousands of parents had died, but most of them were known or at least known of. Grandfather had no memory of his parents and never knew if they'd died friendless and unremarked, or had simply taken advantage of the general tragedy to relieve themselves of the burden of an infant. It wouldn't have been unheard of in the days of Victorian poverty, when it was hard enough to find a bed space for one, let alone two or three.

Grandfather was given a dormitory bed and meagre meals, and classes taught by local priests. And when he was old enough—eleven—he was told to find himself a job. The orphanage's method of encouraging job hunting was to turn all boys over ten years of age out of doors after morning porridge. Thus Grandfather found himself wandering within the watching crowd one bright spring day, as the ice was cracking on the St. Lawrence River. It heaved house-sized blocks atop one another and over the banks, creating massive white dams, which diverted not only the bored and sensation-hungry residents of higher ground—who had nothing to fear—but the river itself. The first of the joyous rites of spring: the annual flooding had begun.

With a stolen clothesline and a spade—his first, but
not his last—he walked down to the shore and saw the

tenements of Griffintown sinking like the ghetto of
Venice into canals where streets had been. Furniture
and wooden boxes bobbed and drifted with the
waves and the current; blocks of ice as big as trucks
snapped signposts and broke whole door frames as
they slammed past; dogs swam, happy or confused.
Families were leaning out of upper-storey windows,
calling for help or waiting it out. Neighbours from
the ground floor and even higher were doubled up
with relatives and friends still higher, if they were
lucky. Some not so lucky were gathered blocks away, in
the street above the high-water mark, with whatever
they'd saved thrown into a pile; some were trying to
start a fire to dry out. Here and there a boat went
along the street, bringing bread and dry blankets to
the stranded, throwing them in through windows.

Out of this misery, Grandfather created his first
job.

He hunted along the shore until he found them:
two lengths of wooden sidewalk not washed into the
St. Lawrence, but dumped well up out of the swell
into a cramped back lane. It was a large job for a
young boy by himself to drag them into the street. He
arranged them side by side and tied them together
with his clothesline. Dragging and pushing, he finally
got the damned things afloat, though he'd been
soaked with frigid water up to his chest.

Hauling himself aboard with a grunt, he cast the
spade over his head and the momentum lifted him to
his raft, which pitched violently. The spade made a
poor oar, and the raft tended to spin. He found

instead a pole floating by and, taking it up, became a gondolier, ferrying the stranded to solid ground.

The job had its dangers. His ankles were always awash in filthy, freezing water; some customers insisted on overloading the raft and tumbling everyone and everything into the drink—for which Grandfather was not paid—or simply ignored his calls for payment. Grandfather quickly learned to get his cash up front, and was not one to bargain. Late in the day he'd come back to the orphanage exhausted, starving and shuddering, but with money in his hand.

Flooding was a short season, only a matter of days, so Grandfather worked as long and hard as he could. As the waters and the ice began to recede, the shoreline became a gauntlet of slime and mud, with half-buried objects or drowned cats or rats, and a hellish stench rising in the spring sun. It was a relief to get to the water and rinse his feet, even though it chilled them to the bone. Now, too, was when the unlucky ones were found: those caught by surprise, or too old or sick to flee when the warning came. The drowned.

Because his raft was large enough, Grandfather got the job of taking empty coffins around to the houses of the dead and bringing them full back to shore. Only one at a time would do, for a drowned corpse is waterlogged and heavy, and even one by itself was probably not safe, with the slats of the raft barely lifting above the brackish water.

It was a crowded district, this slum below the tracks, and though they'd been dealt a severe blow, the inhabitants, like anyone else, couldn't stay forever grim.

With the waters now receding, the work of taking stock and rebuilding however they could was under- way. Even though they were still wading or swimming or canoeing to their doors, because they weren't idle, they were as noisy and cheerful as people at work can be. For once, their work seemed to have a clear purpose, and that was a relief from the grinding meaninglessness of their factory jobs.

And then Grandfather came poling up the street from the river, a small boy beside a large pine box mak- ing for the shore, where waited a Catholic priest in a black cassock, a bereaved family and a barking dog.

Hour by hour the poling got harder, for the water began flowing back into the river. Grandfather was weary and hungry. Despite the sight of the bloated corpses being loaded into his coffins, his stomach growled. Now it was after five, the shadows lengthen- ing, and here was his last passenger of the day: a fat woman. As she was lowered from the second-floor window—one man holding her under the arms, the other in a rowboat beside the raft, taking her legs— Grandfather worried. She was too big. No telling how large she'd been in life, but now, with probably a good fifty or sixty extra pounds of river bilge in her lungs, her stomach and the Devil only knows where else, Grandfather was afraid she'd sink him.

When they finally laid her in the coffin they couldn't nail it shut, for every hammer blow threatened to capsize the raft. At last it was simply tied shut with cord, and Grandfather hesitantly began poling the four blocks to the shore.

But her weight, the cumulative exhaustion of the last several days' hard work and the ebbing water were too much for the eleven-year-old's frail arms. Just as he was coming to landfall, with the waiting party of grieving relatives looking on in horror, he slipped to his knees on the slimy planks and, breathless, couldn't get up again. The raft began to float back to the river. As he lay watching the group ashore recede, they jumped and shouted and wailed like stricken animals. The raft, now totally at the mercy of the current, turned a corner out of their sight and Grandfather turned onto his back, watching the lights go on in windows above and around him, residents pointing and shouting to one another. Just as the street disappeared from his view and the St. Lawrence began to roar in his ears, someone jumped from an apartment window into the water and rescued him. As a strong arm clasped round his tiny chest, and his eyes closed with fatigue, he could just make out the coffin floating downstream to the Gulf.

When Grandfather woke, it was slowly and reluctantly, for he had a fever in his aching joints and had not slept off his labours. But the cold, bony hands of the priest cared not. Grandfather was spared less pleasant fondlings and extremities only by the priest's discovery of the purse hidden in his underwear. Where else would he have put it, a child without a room to himself or hope of a bank account, or even pockets to his trousers? The priest's hands hesitated; retrieved the knotted cloth; and then troubled Grandfather no more. Four days of playing Charon, rafting and struggling in filthy, cold water, all to buy nothing but the time to sleep it off.

Was this the value of honest labour?

Even so, considering the alternative, Grandfather was not bitter.

Yet.

Grandfather was an unkind man, but not a stupid one, and so he took life's lessons to heart. To be happy was a mistake; to be kind was a waste of effort; and to plan for the future was to miss today's opportunities. Accordingly, he never considered that all the small cruelties he inflicted on Grace, his wife's crow, were like a savings plan: tiny daily deposits that accrued so slowly their day of redemption seemed infinitely removed. However, Grace had a way of descending on him so unexpectedly that if he'd ever bothered to think along these lines, he would have concluded that all of life's mysteries are equally impenetrable, and who could say whether *any* hopes or fears would pay off, ever, in any sort of way? So he continued throwing pencils and forks at the bird, or striking out at it with his hand, but almost always missing, since Grace was as wary of Grandfather as were his wife and family.

But unlike the others, Grace was confined to the kitchen and her cage, and couldn't escape Grandfather's presence merely by leaving the house or retiring to another room. So the crow took to perching on the lintel of the kitchen door whenever she was let loose. There she could see Grandfather before he could see her; and she often took what advantage of this she could. If he entered the kitchen without his old man's hat, she would defecate on his bald head. If he wore the hat, she would swoop down and snatch it away, and Grandfather would be reduced to chasing her about the kitchen with the broom, swearing and knocking things off shelves and the tabletop. Once, the bird dropped the fedora into the soup, which so distressed her mistress, Aline, that from then on all soups were simmered with the lid on.

One evening, as dusk was settling, Grandfather woke and groggily bethought himself of breakfast. He found the kitchen empty except for Grace, whose cage was set at the open window. Running his hand over his tired, bald and now always scarred head, Grandfather suddenly thought how easy it would be, with no one watching, to open the cage door. At least one of the problems in his life could be easily solved. If Aline wanted to know who had let the crow loose, he could be just as puzzled as she or anyone else in the house. Of course she would *think* it was him, but that didn't deter him. He had been on decreasingly civil terms with his wife since she had moved out of his bedroom, until now he frankly cared nothing for what she felt or thought, just as he would never stop to consider the feelings of his victims—who of course could have none—or their families.

He tied the sash of his dressing gown and cautiously approached the cage. Grace watched him with her usual indecipherable stare, head atilt. The crow shuffled to get farther away from him, but when it was clear he was coming for the cage, she broke into screeching and flapping as if he were already poking at her.

Grandfather retreated, listening for any reaction from the rest of the house. None. Good. But how to open the cage without sounding the alarm again? He settled on a yardstick, and held it out at arm's length, trying to force the small sliding door upwards. Grace watched as if curious, her head swinging from left to right, occasionally pecking at the stick, once grasping it in her beak until Grandfather cursed and yanked it back. Eventually the deed was done, and Grandfather almost smiled as Grace realized she was free to leave.

She hopped onto the threshold and tilted her head in the direction of the open window, and then, as if suspicious, towards Grandfather. "Go on, go on," he murmured. She seemed to consider first his words, and then the darkening sky, before finally she hopped to the sill, spread her wings and leapt into the air.

Grandfather leaned out the window to see her go, but she was already lost against the deep blue night sky. Could it be true? Was he free of Grace at last? He thought he heard the rustle of her wings; he leaned further out and turned his head to look up the wall above. Suddenly a rush of air hit him in the face as he heard Grace screeching. He swung his head back quickly but couldn't make it inside the window before she was on him, pecking, cawing and batting him with her wings. Her feathers were razor-sharp, and he felt his cheeks and neck wetting with his own blood under her attack.

Halfway out the kitchen window, with all his weight bearing down on his chest and unable to get a proper footing in his panic, he grabbed at the bird and tried to tear her from his face. That was a mistake. Now Grace panicked. For a second she was still; inside, Grandfather's feet slid on the kitchen linoleum as he struggled to brace himself, instinctively squeezing the crow's breast between his hands—not to disable her, but as if it would somehow steady him. Breathless, Grace let out a mournful rasp, reached over to Grandfather's red, strained face and plucked out his left eye.

The bird nested on the roof and hung over the house like an ominous cloud. She swirled joyfully in the air through the uproar: Grandfather's pitiful screams, the resultant howling and barking of Uncle's dog, the shocked exclamations of the family as they came rushing to the kitchen, even the whine of the ambulance pulling up to the door. She followed to the hospital on the mountain, circling the ambulance all the way, cawing in rhythm with the rise and fall of the siren. She circled and pecked at all the windows until she found him lying in a public ward. And she sat herself down on the nearest window ledge, waiting.

She caused a little stir on the ward, the nurses and other patients wondering at this marvel. Grandfather explained, "That bird has my eye."

"Oh yes," said a nurse, smirking. "I see the resemblance."

64

Before the Quiet Revolution—when Quebec woke from the Great Darkness imposed by the Catholic Church, big business and the Duplessis government— the Royal Victoria Hospital was known as a good medical clinic. Afterwards, it was known as one of Montreal's Great Anglophone Institutions, and climbed up the slopes of the mountain slowly. From the original red stone structure it spread into newer wings and outbuildings, aligning itself with another Great Anglophone Institution, McGill University, for which it became a teaching hospital. Now it served the larger downtown community of immigrants, Anglos and francophones without discrimination. But like so many other aspects of what was in spirit a late-colonial society, it failed to recognize the current place it held in the milieu.

Up the hill to the corner of University and Pine avenues was the first and lowest of the buildings composing the complex—the oncology clinic; just above it was the original main building, now given over to general practice and administration; higher still, the women's pavilion; and finally, hidden back and up behind a few stands of trees and sloping lawns, the Allen Memorial—the psychiatric unit.

From bottom to top, almost as if on purpose, almost as if reflecting a moral hierarchy, the hospital mapped out a spiritual ladder. First and lowest: cancer, darkest and most frightening of diseases and swiftly becoming one of the most common. Then, only slightly more elevated, only slightly less horrific, came the bureaucracy no institution can survive without—literally the backbone without which it would all collapse into a shapeless, purposeless mass. Above this, the maternity unit, that place where all mysterious ventures either up or down start, where the shocking fact of Being begins in pain and fear, despite all the medical establishment's desperate attempts to contain, control and neutralize the essential and primal nature of our births. Weighing down upon this, as if in warning, the Allen. The psychiatric unit. The mental hospital. Madness. Above birth, above the regulated normalcy of life, above the lurking of cancer; more frightening than all of these, hidden by its height and least understood, hardest to deal with of all human conditions because it denies all others validity.

On the mountain only two things lay above the house of madness. First, the cemeteries, and then, above everything, the cross.

Through the frosted glass the dark silhouette of the crow shuffled back and forth on the outer sill, protecting her perch from pigeons, and every now and then scraping away the frozen condensation with her beak—now to Grandfather's mind so like a scythe—and pressing a single eye to the glass, reassuring herself that Grandfather still lay inside. During the night the scratching and shuffling could be heard throughout the ward, and occasionally a low, quick cawing, like laughter.

✤

Overnight began one of those snowstorms that visit Montreal several times each winter, and that people elsewhere find hard to credit. The clouds had rolled in without warning, against all predictions, but brought no lessening of the cold. The wind toppled trees, radio towers and headstones on Mount Royal and then swept down along Park Avenue, its natural conduit, and passed the Desouche house so quickly that it blew the hallway and bedroom doors closed. By morning it was clear the city was already paralyzed; the radio was announcing that all schools were closed, advising people to stay home, and pulling out weather data and statistics designed to amaze and awe their listeners: *not since; surpassing even; in contrast to.*

By noon the wind was gone but the falling snow had not diminished. The Desouches happily opened the windows again to let in some cool air. It was impossible to see anything but an ever-changing, ever mobile, ever white expanse of snow drifting down to the street. Cars, mailboxes, even the other houses across the way were only vague outlines against the blank landscape. Vehicles large and small lay abandoned at odd angles in the street; trails where brave or desperate people had waded, waist-deep, were smoothing over and filling in; the iron finials of the Desouches' fence, poking blackly out of the drift, seemed to slowly sink and disappear.

Aline opened the kitchen window. She watched loose flakes of snow tumble inside and drift in the breeze, melting quickly on the sill. She closed the birdcage door, wondering where Grace had gone. She listened to an unearthly silence; the snow insulated any noise, and anyway there was no traffic or sound of neighbours, who were all locked in their houses. There was not much sound inside her own house either. Jean-Baptiste was back in his room as usual; Uncle was probably, and thankfully, in his with his dog; Mother was dazedly staring out the living-room window, perhaps thinking of Angus, perhaps waiting for another visit from her friends; Father was in the basement, but he wasn't digging. Aline had never known real silence here; almost suddenly, she realized how empty the house felt: Marie, Grandfather and Grace were all gone.

She was upset by what had happened to Grandfather not so much because she still cared for him—although it had proven to her surprise that she did—but because she was unused to any kind of violence happening in her world. Now here was the second act which had impinged on her personal life, after Angus's sad end. And she was shocked that Grace could have been capable of it, even in desperation. Naturally, she assumed Grace had acted in self-defence. She was neither surprised nor disappointed that Grandfather had attacked the crow; it was hard for her now to be disappointed with a man who had proven so low after appearing so elevated. But at the same time it was hard for her not to worry over his injuries, which were after all considerable. They had left him in the hospital with his whole head wrapped up in bandages to hold the wound closed, and red gashes on his face and neck where claws and wing tips had done their less severe but still evident damage.

Grandfather had quite rudely suggested that her vocal prayers were not only useless but annoying to himself, the patient. But she had prayed anyway, that some good might come of such a dark event; though she had done so only later, at home and in silence.

Now, in silence, she took out a cookbook and absently leafed through its pages, looking for a recipe to match the few ingredients she had on hand.

In one respect Grandfather had been lucky: he'd arrived at the hospital before the blizzard. By the evening the police were asking for the public's help and commandeering snowmobiles for emergencies and sleds to be towed behind them. It was clear that even once the snow stopped, it would be days before the city regained its normal life. Although the streets and sidewalks would eventually be plowed, some of this snow would last until the spring thaw, turning to black ice, invisible and treacherous to drivers and pedestrians alike.

And when the snow did stop, the clouds dissipating and the sun bouncing off everything in a dazzling and painful display, the cold set in with a vengeance. With the silence still largely unbroken by normal traffic, the Desouches were near enough to the slopes of the mountain to hear the trees snapping as if they'd been struck by lightning, with a crack not of thunder but of the ice in their trunks, and a horrible quick ripping sound just beneath the sharp report.

It was at this time that Marie chose to return.

Marie didn't stay long enough to find the cause of the two things that surprised her: that Grandfather was missing, and that Aline was installed in her room. She didn't stay long enough to be plied with questions about her absence. She barely stayed long enough to observe that the other women's meek expressions revealed their clear memories of which bed Marie had been found in. All those trivial things would have to wait for some other lifetime, one less consumed with the enormity and urgency of the work to be done. And at the moment, that work consisted of enlisting her brother's aid.

She knew he'd refuse; she'd told her friends so from the start. "He'll never help you. He's too much an Anglo for one thing, and too arrogant for another. He's a poet, and thinks he's above all worldly troubles. He'll never consent to writing your articles for you."

Marie had always been troubled by the propagandistic strain in some of her friends. She was uncomfortable with manifestos, letters and proclamations of any sort, partly because she'd always had a tendency to turn away from her brother and his interests—so reading and writing impressed her as something only someone as goofy as he was could make use of—but also, truth to tell, because she had been raised bilingual, and that made reading difficult for her to learn. She had initially been unable to distinguish between the languages, because although her parents spoke to her in either one or the other, she and her brother had spoken them both interchangeably.

Jean-Baptiste was already reading his mother's English magazines before he was five, before he'd been sent to school. When Marie got to school, she discovered that much of the language she knew was not just unknown and unused, but actually discouraged. She was reprimanded for using French, and handed poor report cards and extra work. After only the first year she insisted to her parents that she wouldn't return to school if she was going to be punished merely for speaking. She was sent to a French school. There, she did better, hated it less, but the unpleasant associations—words and letters, Jean-Baptiste and the English—remained, and she was never able to overcome them.

Nevertheless the others convinced her that his help was needed, and she was sent to ask for it. And she couldn't deny to herself that a brief respite from underground living would be a relief. Or so she hoped. The long walk through the snow and wind from the East End cold-water flat in which she was hiding with her friends (convinced they were known and hunted) actually cheered her. Even without proper winter clothes and boots— which she had left at home and now anticipated reclaiming as a benefit of the trip—there was a refreshing, cleansing spirit in the overwhelming quantity and purity of the snow. She took a lesson from the weather: that it was possible to remake the world, to purge it of its worn, decayed and corrupt face, and invest it with a uniform and absolute innocence, a zero-point from which to begin again, and avoid past errors. But this was only possible by an action that would catch the old, complacent order by surprise, leaving it inundated and defenceless. Something sudden, total and overpowering. Like a blizzard.

How could it have been anything but awkward?

"Where have you been?" asked Mother, not in anger but in sorrow.

"With friends. And I'm going back. Where's Jean-Baptiste?"

"In his room, of course." And as Marie mounted the stairs, "For God's sake, Marie, don't."

"Mother, it's not what you think."

"It never is, is it?"

And then, with her brother: "I've come to ask you to help us."

He snorted. "I don't know who you mean."

"Of course you do. And you know what kind of help we need, too. They want you to write the statements."

He put down his book. "You mean they want me to think I'm needed so they can use my press. Go away. The next time I see you will be in jail."

Marie wasn't surprised by her brother's negativity, but she was surprised that she hadn't discerned her comrades' motives herself. As soon as he'd said it, she knew it was true. They would never think themselves incapable of the task; they had been carrying along writing their own pieces for years, and only now had they thought of outside help. What angered her was that they lied to her; they hadn't the confidence in her to reveal their true motives. Which only showed how badly they'd read her, how poorly they troubled to know her. She would never have been reluctant to use her brother; she had only resisted being in debt to him. She slammed his door behind her and marched to her own room—Aline's room.

She was turning out the closet in a fury, searching for her boots and winter coat. Aline, hearing the slamming doors and marching steps, knew immediately where Marie was. She left her boiling stewpot and hurried up the stairs.

"Marie, forgive me. Now that you're back, I'll find another place."

"Forget it."

"No, no. I can move my things, it's your room." And she began to gather up her clothes from the bed.

Marie emerged from the closet with her things, flung them onto the bed and pulled off her shoes. "Forget it. I'm leaving."

Aline was silent as Marie pulled on her boots.

Mother had followed Aline up the stairs and stood in the doorway watching. "Stay for dinner," she said, "at least."

Woken by the noise, Uncle had come out of his room and sleepily made his way to the water closet, pausing long enough to say, "I guess it's not dinner she wants. Unless her brother's on the menu."

Marie looked up, aghast. "Jean-Baptiste, Jean-Baptiste," she yelled. "That's all you can think of, so you think it's the same with me. I'm not the sick one. It's not me. You have those thoughts, not me."

Her yelling had set off Uncle's dog, who barked behind his door. Now Jean-Baptiste appeared. "I'm trying to read."

Marie pushed her way through her family and ran down the stairs. "Fuck you all," she yelled.

They stared over the banister as she ran out the front door, slamming it in her wake. Father entered from the kitchen, where he'd come up from the basement. He stood in the hall, looking from the door up to the landing where the rest of them gazed down. "Was that Marie? I missed her."

Outside, the snow began to fall again.

At the library, Jean-Baptiste returned some American novels that had only depressed him, and exchanged them for novels from France. He had bad luck with the Americans, who despite the lavish accolades printed on their back covers, seemed somehow false, precious; so strained in their attempt to be literary that only other Americans could fail to see that the emperor had no clothes.

He sat at his leisure in the library's greenhouse, daylight filtering through the snow-covered glass roofs and the extravagant, enormous leaves of the tropical palms down onto the pages before him. As soon as he began to read—Flaubert, Camus, Voltaire—he was comforted, soothed and cheered by the ease and the grace that poured out of these French writers and lay still and tranquil on the page, as if warm in their beds, while the storm raged, impotent, outside.

When it pleased him, he was so relaxed in the act of reading that he lost track of the words themselves. He didn't see the printed pages but saw right into the action of the text, not as if looking at images or as if dreaming, but as if the pages were fields of space in which another kind of existence held sway; an existence that engulfed him as completely and convincingly as reality, and one subject only to the powers of the words themselves. Adjectives tumbled into one another, displacing sedentary nouns; modifiers soothed and slackened the sharp verbs; metaphors invisibly bridged the gap between pages; phrases and tropes ran circles around subjects.

Briefly, a pang of guilt crossed Jean-Baptiste's mind as he remembered he was reading English translations. Time and again he'd regretted not being master of his paternal tongue. Time and again he'd wondered if, as much as he identified with these interpreted French words, wouldn't he be so much more consumed by them in the original? Ironic, then, that he was so close to and so comfortable with the English language that when reading its writers, he could spot in an instant, in only a phrase, in merely a few words of a sentence, all of the author's conceits, all of the author's frustrated hours poured into an attempt to look at ease and in command of the broad, swaggering, American tongue, but tripping over his own idiom by bending his tools to insignificant subjects and overworked commonplaces.

No wonder it was so hard for his own works to find their way into American, Canadian or even local journals. For not only had he no desire to write in the acceptable North American manner, but he realized he had no desire to read those works either. That no matter how much attention these works received, no matter how highly they were praised, by no matter what authorities, they still seemed to him sterile, empty, somehow not genuine. It was as if all those involved in the enterprise—the publishers, the writers, the reviewers and even the readers—were somehow fooling themselves. As if they were all engaged in a mutual hallucination of meaning.

What a funny, awkward place to stand, between two languages, as if he had one foot on each rail of a train's track. He admitted: he disliked novels written in English, but he couldn't read those written in French.

Mother tongue English, father tongue French. Both solitudes. English was feminine, welcoming, mothering—but also guttural, Germanic, a precise and at the same time crude language full of words and phrases stolen from others to shore up its own metaphorical poverty. French was the father: always disappointed, always driving, always stern, always ambiguous, always fighting to beat down the Oedipus in the son—but at the same time, French was so fluid, so romantic, so Latin and Mediterranean, so sunshine and Eros.

In the greenhouse, lost in *The Temptation of Saint Anthony*, among the towering palms and lush undergrowth, with the rich, sweet smell of the earth and the

moist, warm air enveloping him, he was sheltered
from the Arctic winds battering the city, from the
droning growl of the heavy plows, and from the cloy-
ing and musty smells of Aline's heavy cooking.

THREE

Since it was now an established fact that Mother's friends would visit several times a week, Father made the effort to put the front parlour into a condition to receive guests. The furniture was removed, the floor swept and washed, the imitation oriental rug unrolled after so many months, and the nesting spiders relocated into oblivion. Finally, the furniture made its return, in a new arrangement supervised by Aline, who swooped down upon this chance to make a mark of her own on the house and revealed a startling capacity for self-assertion. She even suggested a new renovation project, that a door should be knocked out of the rear wall to provide direct access to the kitchen through the pantry and eliminate the need to carry trays up and down the long hallway. There was an idea for Father to ponder.

Mrs. Harrison arrived amidst a cloud of tobacco smoke, frail and bent as driftwood, mumbling her hellos and putting out an arm to steady herself in the hall. She was so small she needed Aline's help to hang her cloth coat up on the hook. Mrs. Pangloss, who had never been shy of showing her hostility to Grandfather, and who had already had the news of his misfortune, reacted by storming in as if she were home, quoting the Bible. Just as Aline was bringing in the tea, she bellowed, "An eye for an eye, my dears. The Lord gives us what we deserve," and nodded her head vigorously in agreement with herself. Aline, who only half understood what had been said, was frightened by the remark because it stung her with the memory of her own words to Grandfather.

When Mrs. Harrison ventured that her remark "wasn't very nice," Mrs. Pangloss replied that the Lord was not obliged to be nice, on account of his mysterious ways. Mrs. Pangloss never hesitated to identify her own will with that of the Lord because there were always plenty of people—Father Pheley, for instance, or any number of doctors, or many of her fellow callers to phone-in radio shows—who readily agreed with her quick grasp of that clearly defined line between right and wrong. Though truth to tell, it's possible some of them had simply learned the futility of argument. And speaking of doctors, had Mother yet been to see her own regarding her over-long mourning?

Mother's eyes rose to meet Mrs. Pangloss's gaze. Had it been that long? Just how long had it been?

A cigarette quivering in her outstretched hand, Mrs. Harrison said, "Leave her be," as best she could while trying to retain her ill-fitting dentures. Clacking them into place, she continued, "Everybody's different. She needs her time."

"Maybe you should talk to Father Pheley," insisted Mrs. Pangloss, who, although she knew her friend to be Presbyterian, felt everyone ought to be Catholic and refused to believe those disgraceful rumours about the Church and its servants. "He'll put you right."

As if there were something wrong with me, thought Mother. She remembered the rumours all too well—Angus had been fond of referring to them—and the incident in Marie's childhood.

"He's Catholic," objected Mrs. Harrison, puffing.

"You old fool, of course he's Catholic. He's a priest." Mrs. Pangloss's temper rose with her exasperation. How anyone could tolerate that brainless harridan was beyond her.

"She should burn sandalwood." By now, the two were speaking as if Mother were absent.

Mrs. Pangloss pulled herself erect with a hand on her hip, tilting her head. "What in God's name are you talking about?"

"It'd make her feel better. The smell. It smells good."

"Fer crying out loud." Pangloss paused. "You think smelling up the house will make anyone feel good? That's for witches. That'll give her a headache."

"I saw it on TV."

"Oh, it must have been a horror show."

"No, it was Mass. From Rome. The Pope. The Pope."

For once Mrs. Pangloss was silent.

"*He's* a priest," said Mrs. Harrison.

✤

Mrs. Pangloss continued to encourage Mother to see a doctor, because although she still believed that whatever took place was the will of God, she was not a Mormon, and thought that doctors were also the will of God because many of them had told her so. While no one else thought this line of reasoning made any sense, everyone agreed a visit to the doctor—any trip out of the house—would probably do her some good. Mother finally cracked under the pressure and went to her family physician.

Dr. Hyde hadn't seen her since he'd delivered her of twins, and so happily went about a battery of tests when Mother couldn't be more specific than to say she felt "under the weather." He made her undress and weighed and measured her; he took her blood pressure and her temperature. He had her pee into a cup; he examined her urine as closely as he could. He examined her breasts for lumps. He wasn't sure, so it took a long time. He made her put her feet into the stirrups and bent into her with cold, dry implements. He was thorough. He put on rubber gloves, which he lubricated, and was more thorough. Finally, as she lay with her legs still spread into the air, he simply stood and stared at her for such a long time that she slowly turned completely red; and then, just as slowly, she resumed her natural colour; and then she began to worry. At last he announced he could find nothing wrong with her.

Why then did she feel so out of sorts? Gently, the doctor tried to suggest she was just having trouble accepting her grief, and therefore was, well, mentally unbalanced. Perhaps she simply needed some rest.

In any case, he would do for her what he did for everyone when he had no idea what was wrong with them: prescribe tranquillizers.

The small square of paper he handed her at least made Mother feel she hadn't endured the whole ordeal for nothing. But *unbalanced*? She was puzzled and tried to decide how that could be. It was a fact that since she was a small girl, she had developed the habit of sleeping on a different side each night. Because Angus had tried to raise her with a sense of regularity, she took to sleeping on her right side on even-numbered nights, and her left on odd-numbered nights. But suddenly she realized that the calendar is mostly made up of odd-numbered days. Whenever the thirty-first came along, she would sleep on her left side. But the next day, the first, was also an odd day. So in fact she had been sleeping more often on one side than the other. She realized that all these years of asymmetrical sleeping must have made her brain slide around in her head, until now it wasn't sitting straight in her skull. The doctor was right: she was mentally unbalanced.

What to do about it? Well, he'd said rest, and given her tranquillizers. Obviously she needed to correct the imbalance. She would go straight home and start sleeping on her right side, regardless of whether it was an odd or an even day. And she would sleep until she had regained her mental equilibrium.

It took quite some time.

❧

Uncle was introduced to his first dog when he was only a child. Fittingly it was just a puppy itself, and he hated it instantly because it refused to be paper trained. But taking it for a walk was something of a pleasure, if only to get away from a house which even then abutted on the funeral parlour on one side, and a crazy woman's on the other.

Grandfather's preferred method of instructing his children was to beat them when they acted contrary to his wishes. So there had been a loud row with Grandmother as Uncle cowered upstairs, listening without his supper. For once, Grandmother had won: instead of being punished for killing the neighbour child's hamster, Uncle was to be shown the value of life and the responsibility of owning a pet. (In truth, Grandfather was not upset at the slaying itself, but that a child of his took no care to hide the crime. An attitude like that was the privilege only of those beyond the law by reason of birth or wealth or sheer force of personality—a Bronfman, a Van Horne, a Duplessis—but certainly not a Desouche. Regardless, this quibble had no bearing on the argument over an appropriate punishment.)

Next day, Grandmother took him on the streetcar to the SPCA and kept him there until he had chosen a puppy. Understanding that the lesson he was being taught was not one he could acknowledge and then forsake immediately, he whined and protested. The thought of a lifetime of daily caring for and nurturing his sin was as repellent to the child as it would be to any adult. Grandmother, who considered this method of educating him a gift and would never have understood his reluctance even if Uncle had been able to explain his reasoning, was as startled by this reaction as were the clerks at the animal shelter.

"Never seen a young boy didn't want a puppy," they exclaimed and remarked, and called in every one of their co-workers to see the petulant and contrary child.

At last Uncle broke down, not under Grandmother's patience but under their collective gaze of wonderment, and grudgingly chose a listless young animal that seemed to him older—and closer to death—than the others. In fact, it was merely sick and undernourished. Under ordinary circumstances Grandmother wouldn't have allowed an unhealthy dog into her house, but she was compelled to consider she'd won some sort of victory, and perhaps nursing it back to health would produce exactly the effect on her young son for which she was hoping.

It didn't. Uncle clearly wanted nothing to do with the creature and there was something about it so indefinably unsavoury that no one else could take any pleasure in its presence. Nevertheless, Grandmother spent more energy ensuring that Uncle looked after it than she would have doing the job herself. Reluctantly he fed and watered and walked it twice a day, even though when he did, the other children in the neighbourhood took care to be absent. It remained a sickly thing, head drooping, eyes watery, rarely a wag of the tail; it remained untrained, and Grandfather bellowed and cursed whenever he set foot in its droppings in his own house. But it remained only as long as it had to, for one day, long, weary dog-years later, it disappeared.

No one knew whether it had got loose and been struck by a car, or struck out on its own for its own mysterious reasons, or even whether Uncle had finally done something about it. But as Uncle grew into adolescence he left it behind with the rest of his infancy, and it simply was no longer a part of his life, like so many childhood sins, until on a summer's dog day, it seemed to have simply evaporated in the heat.

The black dog followed Uncle home the first year he began working with Grandfather, in fact on his very first job. It was one of only two times they were discovered at work.

Who this witness was they never knew. Whether some groundskeeper or some darkly romantic soul taken with wandering through graveyards in the middle of the night, or simply some homeless unfortunate. It mattered little. But discovery was unacceptable. Discovery was death to them—arrest, shame, unemployment—and so it meant death to their discoverer. While Grandfather kept the man's attention, Uncle moved behind him and swung the shovel like a baseball bat. Almost, the anonymous head flew out of the park; the blow, at least, was strong enough. But the spine and neck would not let go, and it merely leapt forward first, before the rest of the body came crashing behind it.

"Criss," said Grandfather.

A discussion ensued. Could they take this one to the doctor's back door too? That was a tempting plum: two bodies to sell, for the work of just one.

But no, Grandfather reasoned, a medical man could easily spot the difference between a disinterred corpse and a murder victim. And though it might not make any difference to him, it might. It just might. Or then, it could be a fact taken careful note of and stored away for maturation, like a wine or a cheese, only to be resurrected at some future opportunity, to be enjoyed in the fullness of its strength.

Either way, it was simply too great a risk. When Uncle, a greedy neophyte, protested too much caution, Grandfather reminded him of the legendary status attained in their profession by Burke and Hare, and how in that case only the doctor had got off scot-free.

Reluctantly, then, Uncle pushed the fresher of the corpses into the grave, at the foot of which sat the dead man's dog. It neither howled nor barked, not raising any kind of a protest or even sniffing its master or his new resting place. It merely yawned and watched. And when the two men took up their burden of shovels, lanterns and sacks, it trod along behind them as if it had done so all its life.

It would not be got rid of, and Uncle discovered he felt quite at home with his anger towards it, and the practice of kicking and slapping it. And so he settled into a life with it.

❦

The second time they were caught, they were just lowering a coffin back into the ground. A figure ran screaming out of the night, right into the grave, and lay startled and injured in silence.

Uncle looked in. "It's a woman," he said.

Grandfather turned on his flashlight. It was a man in a dress.

Two more figures came running over the hill. Grandfather snapped off his light and began to move away. The fellow in the grave pleaded. "Don't leave me with them."

They were cops, from the neighbourhood. They had no pants.

On opposite sides of the open grave, the four men recognized each other. Slowly Uncle turned and gathered up their things. He and Grandfather took up their large, full sack.

"Tabernac," said the younger cop. He was panting.

The older one said, "Ferme ta gueule."

"And keep your pants on," said Grandfather. He and Uncle turned their backs and walked away. They weren't stopped, and if they heard any noises behind them, they made no comment.

Ville-Marie de l'Incarnation Desouche and her brother Jean-Baptiste were born only an instant apart in those brief seconds between 11:59 P.M. and 12 A.M. either on June 24th, if one wanted it to be St-Jean-Baptiste Day—as Marie wanted, and why couldn't she have been named for the Fête

Nationale?—or on June 25th, if one liked the idea of being the antipode to Christmas—which Jean-Baptiste did, for poetic reasons that he himself couldn't clearly define (or at least, that's how he thought of it; but it could simply have been an inherited grasping for symmetry and balance, passed down through Mother from Angus); and perhaps because of that they retained something ineffable about them, as should the day. Or its cognate.

Further, the event took place not at the Royal Victoria but at the Reddy Memorial, a lesser anglo hospital that stood on Atwater Street. The same Atwater that divided (English) Westmount from (French) Montreal, the same Atwater that was so treacherous with black ice on dark winter nights. Born at midnight, on that border, a boy and a girl, of an English mother and a French father.

Could they be anything but doomed?

One chose words and the other actions, but they both believed in exploding complacent notions of the status quo; one revered Artaud, the other Che Guevara, both of whom upheld, at heart, the idea of honesty.

Thus, Marie was furious with Hubert.

No matter how long and hard Hubert tried to explain to Marie that he felt it necessary to act as he had, to deceive her in the greater interest of their cause, it made no difference: she slapped him and spat at him when he tried to take her around the waist, to fondle her bosom, to calm her in their bed. He realized now, of course, that his precautions had been too stringent, that she could be trusted totally.

Yet couldn't he be forgiven for treading lightly on family connections, especially in a mixed family?

Well, that deserved another blow; after which, "I am Desouche," cried Marie. "I have proven myself in direct action, with dynamite. Have you? You're a scribbler, like Jean-Baptiste. You do nothing. And you doubt me?"

Her words stung. True, he was their ideologue: he was their only university-educated cell member. True, he'd had the same difficulties with his former professors as he was now having with Marie, that they refused to see he was right, that they stubbornly clung to their bourgeois faith in political, not revolutionary, action. True, further, that his passionate tirades against their complacency, which was tantamount to collaboration with les têtes carrées, netted him only expulsion from the Université du Québec.

But he was no coward. Hadn't he authorized all the bombings? Hadn't he planned the bank robberies? Hadn't he stood in public distributing pamphlets and haranguing Anglos? Wasn't he always the one urging action, casting the deciding vote in favour of change, not caution?

Hubert had never flinched in a crisis, never hesitated to give orders, to decide. As leader of the cell it had been his role. Some others were smarter, including Marie, and some were better connected; and he was always silent in debates, letting others argue and discuss. But whenever there was a deadlock or doubt, all turned to him to break it. And having listened to all voices, when it was clear the issue wasn't clear at all, he decided. Always on the side of instant action and today's goals, always for the good of the cause. Always what he imagined he would someday be rewarded for, when Quebec was its own sovereign nation, by its own head of state. By the very man presently both premier and leader of the Péquistes— the Parti Québécois.

Hubert considered the Péquiste premier to be the future of Quebec: "He is our destiny." And he considered all his fellow felquistes as the natural, military extension of the Péquiste political party. He knew that someday, when separation had finally been achieved, all felquistes would be lionized and welcomed to places of honour in the new nation.

In fact, Hubert dreamt of receiving a medal from the premier himself, on a platform before a cheering crowd. And that was just the beginning. On occasions when he allowed his fantasy to flow out to its end, he became not just a decorated hero of the revolution, but afterwards a revered public speaker and journalist, and finally a respected and tenured professor of political science at that same large French Montreal university that had turfed him out in his youth. He would be appointed to chair committees on social and cultural issues, his classes would be crowded with silently awed young faces receiving the wisdom not only of his thoughts but of his active experience, and the hallways would be cloudy with the cigarette smoke of the Revolution.

In other words, Hubert's idea of revolution was not to change at all the way in which Quebec society treated itself, but merely to change who was cracking the whip.

In this respect Hubert's nationalism was traditional, one might say even orthodox. The French in Canada had not, on the whole, ever been treated very well, even before the British Conquest; but at least in the early days the poor illiterate farmers were spat and shat upon by their own landlords, the Seigneurs, and shat and spat upon by their own curés and confessors. Unlike France, where the Ancien Régime was deposed with a fury that negated the ideals of Liberté, Égalité, Fraternité, Quebec didn't mind so much an enormous gulf in wealth and privilege—as long as it retained a French face and a French voice.

But it would be a mistake to think Hubert and Marie and all the rest didn't have legitimate complaints. For too long had the French been excluded, in practice if not in law, from too much in Quebec: from government service, from higher education, from business. While it's true that the poorer English were too, at least they could read the application forms; at least they could be understood in banks and stores.

And although bigotry abounded among the English, just as it did among the French, it was true (and still is) that anyone, English or French, could succeed at whatever he or she wished, given the right quantities and proportion of three essential qualities (no, not talent, ambition and charm): hypocrisy, money and friends. This was proven by the fact that as many political and business leaders in Canada have been French lawyers as have been English, more or less, but that none of these leaders has ever been a farmer or a labourer.

Nevertheless, Hubert had made the mistake of confusing Quebec with a totalitarian country, of confusing Canada, a Western capitalist state in which he was free to organize whatever political or labour unions he wished, to speak and vote freely, to work as hard as he felt necessary to effect political change, with countries where people were tortured and murdered for these things. In his confusion he adopted the methods and rhetoric of revolutionaries from such countries, because all over the West it was becoming the thing to do. Germany had its Baader-Meinhof, Italy its Red Brigades, Peru its Tupameros. He explained to Marie that "louder votes count for more. Votes that explode are supreme."

Hubert, Marie and the other felquistes rejected much that was common in Quebec. They rejected foremost the idea of a nation that spread from sea to sea; they rejected the idea that a social conscience and responsibility could cross linguistic lines; they rejected the thought of common goals providing common solutions. They rejected even the feeble Canadian notion of patriotism. But they held dear conceits that every people regards with a sentimental nostalgia: that by birth they were entitled to their land, that blood will out (one way or another), that outsiders were depriving them of their natural rights. They would not allow Ottawa to administer social programs and they would not allow English to sully the French face of Quebec. But because nationalism glorifies blood relations and the extended family of a common religion, they would sell their souls to the Devil to be home at Christmas.

And they couldn't see the irony in that.

Instead, they celebrated the fact in myth, made it a cultural sacrament taught in their schools and literature, and elevated it to the status of a founding paradigm. Fur traders stranded far from home at Christmas were carried by the devil to their families in a flying canoe. It became a sentimental Christmas display on a downtown Montreal street, a giant inflatable parade float for the Fête Nationale and the illustration on a beer label: Les Maudits. The Damned.

Jean-Baptiste was visiting the shrunken heads at McGill University.

McGill still maintained a small Victorian museum housing the various trophies, plunder and knick-knacks retrieved by the pompous during years of empire building. A great domed central area housed the skeletons of several dinosaurs, surrounded by second- and third-floor galleries displaying insects and geological specimens. Other wings contained stuffed mammals, large and small, set against painted dioramas of the settings they'd been shot in. A sequence of enormous glass cases held a parade of simians from tiny spider monkeys through chimps and apes, each slighter taller and more upright than the last, culminating in a human skeleton displaying a sign that read: Darwin's Proof.

Jean-Baptiste had been visiting the Redpath Museum since childhood, when Mother and Angus had brought the children to the campus for picnics. When he was old enough, he came by himself. In truth it was a small and unimportant museum scientifically, but it did have its treasures, which lured him back time and again. It was here he'd first seen skeletons of any sort, and here they were in abundance. Tiny rodents, bats, larger predators; serpents, from garden snakes to giant constrictors out of darkest Africa, sabre-toothed tigers, the aforementioned dinosaurs and, yes, even humans. Here was a display of marvels more chilling than any Hollywood movie, because these were real.

They held an eerie fascination for him, these relics, because on the one hand he knew them to be the real remains of once-living creatures, but on the other, the manner in which they were displayed was itself a relic of a once-living era. The mammals, for instance, were stuffed and posed and set against a backdrop painted to look like the wilds of nature—yet so obviously artificial—and had been in place since before the vogue for zoos (that is, for actual living creatures) had supplanted such exhibitions as these. And truth be told, there was something about the cases themselves, with their mahogany trimmings and plate glass, and the sheer age of the mounted and mummified corpses, that bespoke age and dust and decay.

Of course, the Redpath had its own real mummy, a glorious and mysterious object contained in its own room. The brightly decorated coffin stood open for inspection with the rag-and-bone princess summarily exposed for any eye to behold, in total disregard for her noble origins and surely her own and her long-gone family's desires for her dignity. Still, since immortality had been the goal of her funerary preparations, she could be said to have achieved it, even in this debased and insignificant form. Her hair escaped the crumbling wrappings but still clung to her skull. It was thin, bleached grey not by the expanse of time since her death but by the comparatively brief exposure to the blazing overhead lamp. Her hands had been clasped on her breast while they were still clothed with flesh but now had fallen—both of them, her fingers still entwined—to her right side. The remains of her face had shifted to stare at her hands as if she were mourning the loss of their use. If she were not so obviously dead, she might be sleeping.

All these items radiated an exoticism only magnified by the accompanying explanatory cards and crumbling black-and-white photographs illustrating the remote, dark corners of the world where the brave safari-suited scientist-explorers had risked all to procure them.

For Jean-Baptiste, the most alluring of the oddities in this phantasmagoria were two simple items almost hidden from view in a little-used stairwell, which he'd only discovered while hunting for the washroom. In a modest case, surrounded by poisoned arrowheads, bone needles and a leather pouch spilling powerful magic, were two shrunken human heads.

Balls of chocolate-brown leather misshapen from (some kind of: what?) misuse, topped with tufts of silky black hair like tassels hanging from the handlebars of a child's bicycle, they were mounted at the ends of sticks smooth and free of bark, whose bottom ends were wrapped in leather (leather?) grips.

As a child these curios had been enough to distract him from the washroom he'd been seeking. He'd stare eye to eye with the tiny people, their eyes sewn shut in an almost sleepy expression, their mouths sewn shut with lips (and here's how he would ever after understand this phrase) *pursed,* and wonder: What had they seen? What had they said?

As he'd grown he'd been forced to crouch lower and lower, in order to look them in the face, until finally he now resorted to sitting back on his knees as the only proper way to get a look. It had always seemed wrong to do other than face them, since they were still, after all, human beings. He couldn't bring himself to weave his head about and around the glass case in order to glance behind or above or beneath them, the way others did, or the way he could with statues or mineral specimens. Even the mummy princess was mostly hidden by her centuries-old roll of cloth so that one knew she was a corpse, although her desiccated ashes and dust retained only the vaguest of human forms.

But these heads weren't objects; these heads had real, recognizable faces. These were people.

Which always led Jean-Baptiste to wonder at the status and fate of people who lost their lives, or pieces of them. Where were their bodies now, what had become of them? Were those bodies also people? Had they ceased to be human when they lost their heads? And whatever had happened to Uncle's missing finger? Was it still in some way human, was it still in some way Uncle, or had it instantly, on the point of separation from the rest of him, become something else? A mere thing?

This he'd wondered time and again over the years as a child; today, he also wondered: and what about Grandfather's eye?

Aline was praying for both Grace and Grandfather at the chapel where she had once been in the habit of going every Sunday with her own father. St. Joseph's Oratory stood on the slope of the mountain opposite the Royal Vic, which put both the Catholic and Jewish cemeteries between the two and gave it the highest elevation of any church in Montreal. Aline would never have had enough pretension to travel out of her local parish for the sake of worshipping at this grandest of cathedrals, except for the fact of her being present at a particular Christmas Eve's midnight Mass, when the relic of Frère André's heart had bled in public.

This rare miracle had marked her and her father in a bond with St. Joseph's, and they never afterwards resisted the temptation to worship where God had chosen to bridge the gap between heaven and earth. It seemed an unquestionable sign, a direct invitation to these meekest of the flock to remember that after all, since they would eventually inherit the earth, they might want once in a while to gaze at the riches they would then enjoy.

The Lord of the Poor was never one to stint on His own house, and this one, named after His own earthly father, was no exception. It was purposely erected at the top of a hill so steep it required a stairway like those in Hollywood fantasies of the Ascent to heaven itself. And a funicular for those who could pay the penny. The doors were so large it seemed a giant's castle. The vaulted ceilings were so high the light-bulbs must have been changed by God Himself, and He probably didn't have to stoop. Where it wasn't covered in jewelled relics, embroidered tapestries, enormous stained glass windows or painted biblical scenes, it was merely gilded. The enormous volume of space within its walls produced the requisite booming, medieval echo as the numberless white- and gold-robed priests chanted their way across the altar. The pipes of the organ, pointing straight up to God, loomed so large over the congregation they might have been taken for factory chimneys. The nave seated thousands, so that communion became the endless parade of Judgment Day and the beginning of eternity.

In short, it made Aline feel small, poor, nervous and insignificant.

Just as it, and she, were intended to.

But despite this—or maybe, as they say, because—it made her feel closer to God than any local chapel ever could. Especially during that particular midnight Mass.

Frère André—a doorman—had been revered in Montreal and even beyond as a living saint: a tireless worker for his flock, a gentle and generous soul, the very Platonic ideal of a Christian shepherd. He lived a long and selfless life, was much loved and never maligned, and at the last he welcomed the summons of the Lord with a humble contentment.

As a reward for this exemplary life, the faithful tore his heart from his corpse and hung it up in public. What, if any, compensation was granted him by the Lord is not on record; but for what it's worth, he was beatified by the Pope a decade after he died.

The heart was treated for preservation and mounted on a golden silk pillow, in a case handcrafted of purest silver; it was viewed not through mere glass but through a lead crystal window. It was placed in its own permanent niche in the church, and proved itself a worthy attraction. The devout remained so, the wandering returned to the fold and the curious began to pay a token into the poor box for their visits. Prayers, which had previously been divided fairly evenly between the Lord and St. Joseph, were now just as often addressed to Frère André.

Eventually the heart itself showed the weakness of the flesh, and as it dried and hardened, it darkened in colour until its purple was black. But because it was mounted high enough above the heads of even those who didn't kneel to gaze at it, no one minded. Or perhaps no one noticed; at least, no one ever remarked on it. In time it became another fixture of the chapel, like the altar, the organ or the cross. It was noticed only as it served a particular purpose.

Even Aline approached it as she did the other artifacts of worship, as if it were not a person or a divine spirit but only signified the proper place to perform the rituals of her religion, simply the object that served to remind her of her devotion.

Until.

Midnight Mass is as much a spectacle in the Catholic Church as it is a religious observance, and as much a social occasion for French-Canadian society as a spectacle. On Christmas Eve, after the enormous traditional dinner and the clamouring for presents that follows, the children are dressed in their finest, no matter how loudly they complain. For once, they want to go to bed. They're tired, after all, from the excitement of the day and the abundance of material goods afforded by the holiest of Christian observances. But no, the parents all insist, Mass must be observed. They've paid to reserve space in the pews; it's an obligation not only to the Church but to their neighbours, to see and be seen; and to be seen to be devout. So devout as to be able to afford a pew up front.

The Church spares nothing. There is music; there are carols; there are innumerable candles of all sizes everywhere; smoking censers are swung in one hand while the priest reads, chanting, from a psalter. St. Joseph's is jammed. Every seat is taken and the corridors are full. The multitude patiently wait their turn at the door, stamping their feet in the cold, their breath billowing. The crowds pass in and out of the church for hours. Confession is taken, with penitents lined up waiting their turn like the poor at a soup kitchen; absolution is given in solemn tones; communion is taken with necks bent, silently. The priest mumbles continuously and drops the Host onto outstretched tongues like a machine stamping out parts.

Aline, out of breath from the climb to the Oratory, and her father, yawning despite the frigid, clear air, waited patiently for the line ahead of them to shuffle its way inside. Once they were through the doors, the interior space was bigger than expected, as if the confines themselves increased the volume they enclosed. The temperature was rising with every exhalation of the flock and with each new candle lit for a remembered loved one. It did no good for Aline to open her cloth coat and loosen her knitted scarf. Her father too complained of the heat.

The monotonous droning of the chanting priests and praying crowds . . . the languid swelling and swirling mass of people . . . the air thick with incense and the smell of paraffin . . . the hypnotic twinkling of the candles . . . the late hour, the heat . . . by the time they'd shuffled their way up front near the altar, Aline was afraid she'd pass out.

Instead, as they passed in front of the niche displaying Frère André's heart, she prayed for strength. She crossed herself and stared into her hands, chapped from the cold. She closed her eyes but immediately felt vertiginous. She gave up praying and reached for the rail. Her father steadied her. When she opened her eyes and looked up to the relic, it was bleeding.

Aline silently contemplated the vision before her and tried to determine if it was real or merely induced by the atmosphere. Could she be witness to a miracle? Had no one else seen it? Her father too was staring, but silent, and might just have been in prayer. Surely the Lord would not choose her from among all the faithful to witness His presence? Surely others were more deserving? Her father returned her gaze and she realized he too was seeing the vessel fill with blood. He'd been thinking similar thoughts; and they both now knew their vision was true, and miraculous.

It was left to someone else to cry out in the crowd:

"It's bleeding. The heart, Frère André's heart! It's bleeding!"

A clamouring began. Communion, confession, prayer were all forgotten. At first there were cries of "Silence!" from the priests, in anger that Mass should be violated, and "Ta gueule!" from some outraged but less refined of the faithful.

Aline and her father were no longer looking at Frère André's heart, but into each other's joyous eyes; and as the crowd began to press and howl, they retired together from the church, straining against the flow of bodies. They had seen, and had no need to gawk like children; and they had seen *first*. Aline was bursting with the warmth of a communion she'd never before experienced, and so must her father have been, for the two remained silent even when their eyes met.

The mindless fervour of the crowd could also see nothing but the bleeding heart, and so ignored the overturned votive candles. When the flames took hold and some close to them began to shout the danger, they went unheard in the cacophony of prayer, amazement and denunciation:

"Fraud!"

"A miracle, for Jesus' birthday!"

"Fire!"

"Praise God Almighty!"

"Don't push!"

By the time the draperies were aflame, Aline and her father had left the church by a side door and, despite the cold, were slowly making their way down the cathedral steps. So taken were they with the miracle that they never remembered precisely how they'd gotten home; whether they rode the bus as they had come, or hailed a taxi, or even walked the entire way.

There was no newspaper on Christmas, but the following day—Boxing Day—as Aline was pouring her father's morning coffee, he looked up from the paper and said, "I don't remember a fire at the Oratory. Do you?"

"Oh, no. No, I don't."

"No one seriously hurt." He read further down the column. "A miracle, they say."

"Yes, with the crowds."

And so, from that day on, whenever there seemed

some especial reason to speak to God, something out of the usual line of *Bless Papa and bless Mama and bless the neighbours too*, Aline made the trip to St. Joseph's and knelt before the relic of Frère André.

For the sake of an eye, for the sake of a bird, she prayed to a shrivelled black heart. "Forgive and heal my husband in your mercy, Lord, and bring Grace back to me."

⚜

On the afternoon Mother went to sleep she'd been thinking about Angus because his death was the cause of her grief and his insistence on regularity was the cause of her malady. And so his was the face that first took shape in her dreams.

Angus had never been in a dream before. He'd had them like anyone else, but this feeling was something different. It was still amorphous, still entirely unpredictable and absurd, still faded at its edges into an insensible void, still finite but unbounded. But it was also definitely not like any dream he could remember because he was inside it, instead of the other way around. Things happened, time passed back and forth, immense objects appeared in his path yet failed to obstruct it. Primal fears took hold instantly without warning or reason, but without incongruity: he was naked before an immense crowd; he'd been climbing a staircase forever; he fell from an immeasurable height; he flew; the car's brakes failed; he made love to Isabel; he slept; his daughter dreamt he was approaching her.

He asked her, "What the hell happened to me?"

"You died in the war," she said. "Don't do it again."

The peasants were storming the castle and the dance of pitchforks and torches overwhelmed their conversation like surf on the beach. Both tried to speak and failed.

It did no good to turn her as Dr. Hyde had suggested, to prevent bedsores. She simply returned to her side as if she were a boat righting herself. She slept so much they thought she must be sick. Yet she had no fever, never moaned or cried out in delirium, didn't even toss and turn during her dreams; she always seemed simply and happily asleep. The medication was slowly disappearing, which was a mystery since Mother was never awake to take it.

The more and better she slept, the more fitfully did Father; which eventually brought the solution to the case of the disappearing pills. He tossed and turned, aware of the unnaturally inert form of his wife. He'd gotten used to her immobility, so that when she did move, it woke him instantly. And this time he saw her sit up, open the vial, shake out two pills and swallow them with water before settling back in bed. And he realized she'd done so entirely in her sleep.

After days of sleeping beside her, he could stand no more. It was just too creepy; he couldn't share the bed with her any longer. Since there were no available empty rooms except the front parlour, that's where they moved her—and her friends continued to visit her, as if she were in a hospital bed.

She lay semi-fetally as if in prayer, with her hands clasped together and her head nodding towards them, her thin grey hair clinging from neglect.

At first Aline was shocked by what seemed to her Father's disposal of his wife: how could he not have wanted her in his bed? But as she began to assist in the minimal care Mother seemed to need (an airing of the sheets, an occasional sponge bath, feeding like a baby) she came to understand how uneasy her condition had made him. It was certainly unnatural, and yet nothing seemed the matter with her. In fact, if it were possible to judge by her face and the lack of tension in her body, she seemed now to be content, practically happy. It was almost as if she were simply awaiting something and had stopped bothering to suffer through life in the meantime.

When Mrs. Pangloss arrived the day after they'd installed Mother on a folding cot in the parlour, she began a panicked keening: a screeching wail pitched as high as she could manage without cracking her voice. It was her instinctual and habitual way of entering a wake, beginning high and loud with shock and disbelief, and it usually gave way first to a moaning despair and finally to a quiet sobbing in a corner, with only an occasional outburst designed to refocus the other mourners' attention on herself. Funerals are, after all, for the living.

Aline didn't know much about Mrs. Pangloss's habits but she could tell instantly that she thought

107

Mother was dead. Mrs. Pangloss managed to choke out the usual baffled questions—"What happened? Was it an accident? I didn't know she was sick! Oh, the poor woman. Was it quick? Did she suffer?"—and as usual didn't bother to wait for the answers.

Aline attempted to calm her by mustering what little broken English she could, but under the rush of Mrs. Pangloss's exclamatory grief she was reduced to tugging on the woman's sleeve and muttering, "Non, madame, non."

And then, unexpectedly, Mrs. Pangloss did something Aline would otherwise have judged as impossible as anything absurdly imaginable, like walking on the Sun or meeting Elvis; something which shattered totally her view of the woman and cast into doubt her opinions of all Anglos.

Mrs. Pangloss spoke in French.

Aline stepped back under the blow.

Haltingly, as if the words had made no sense to her, she framed her simple reply almost as a question: "Elle dort." She's sleeping.

Mrs. Pangloss moaned hugely and all the tension lapsed from her face; she slumped into an overstuffed armchair and buried herself in the cheap cloth coat she was still wearing. She breathed ferociously, holding her heart as if to keep it in place. Aline couldn't tell if she was relieved or disappointed.

Aline stood nervously, not daring to approach the woman, not knowing what to say or do. Should she take her coat? Should she try to explain Mother's condition, when it had commenced, why they had moved her to the front parlour? Should she speak in French or English?

At that moment, Dr. Hyde arrived and relieved her of any responsibility. Aline was torn between her resentment of his presumption of authority in what was really *her* house and not his after all, and her relief at not having to choose a course of action. She hung both their coats and retired to the kitchen to prepare tea.

"Bodies," said Dr. Hyde, "are fascinating and disgusting."

He took Mother's pulse. "They are always with us; they are perhaps the sum of our existence. Yet we always feel as if they were adjunct to ourselves. They are filthy and they produce filth. We may lose parts of them, appendages or even internal organs, and go on living feeling that we are still ourselves. So we speak of them as if they were separate from our existential selves."

He listened to her heartbeat. "We have mapped them, inside and out; we have charted their histories and divined their workings so that we know what parts belong in which place and how they are supposed to function. We have experimented with them and subjected them to torture, chemicals, extremes of climate, so that we know more or less the conditions necessary to their well-being. We have deduced a Platonic ideal against which we measure ourselves and our patients: this is the practice of medicine."

He placed the stethoscope on her back and listened to her breathing. "Yet we are forever stumbling across exceptions, aberrations and inexplicable circumstances. Miraculous cures, astonishing survivals, even unaccountable deaths. And this, Madame Desouche's curious repose."

Mrs. Pangloss nibbled a crustless devilled ham sandwich and nodded. She firmly believed that when one found oneself in the presence of a professional, educated man, one should take advantage of listening to him in order to better oneself. Especially if he was a doctor. It had always puzzled her that her friends the Desouches should have Dr. Cameron Hyde as their family physician, and it stunned her now to see that not only had they been telling the truth about it, but he would deign to descend from his famous institute on the slopes of Mount Royal and actually pay a house call.

He was, after all, a famous man who had done unbelievable things. An indisputable genius since the days when *Time*—an American magazine, mind you— had put him on its cover, he was invested with all the unquestioning confidence of the hospital and the university to which he'd brought fame and money by his brilliant experiments into brains, bodies, psyches and souls. So overwhelming was his authority in Montreal that not even those whose heads he'd cut open (whether in an effort to shrink them, or merely to introduce needle-thin electric prods), or those to whom he'd sequestered in sensory deprivation tanks and secretly administered the new, mysterious lysergic acid, or those whom he'd restrained, doused, disoriented or otherwise tortured—not even those poor people (and they were usually poor) had once imagined that their "treatments" were anything but proper. No one had ever thought that Dr. Hyde's actions might be unorthodox, unethical, illegal . . . monstrous. Not for years would anyone suspect that they might be actionable, although frequently they were acknowledged, sometimes by Hyde himself, as "experimental." But then only grudgingly.

And besides, he (or they) would say, just look at the results. More donations to the hospital, more government and private funding of research at both McGill and the Royal Vic, more acclaim within the medical community for both Hyde and hospital.

But damned few cures or recoveries. Never mind; if none of the ex-patients were complaining, there must be good reason. Many of them were dead or vegetative or otherwise, but that only proved the need for further research.

Mother's case was quite interesting; she simply lay down to sleep and refused to wake up. It certainly wasn't anything he had told or asked her to do, or thought might do her any good, or even thought of at all. True, he had a ward full of comatose and vegetative cases up the mountain, but they were mostly in reaction to "developmental treatments" or "radical therapies."

"Why's she asleep, Doctor?" asked Mrs. Pangloss.

He opened Mother's left eye and shone a penlight into it as if he were looking for something that had rolled under the bed. "I don't know. I've done nothing to her."

"Didn't you give her some pills?"

"Yes, but she's taken them all and I won't give her more. Besides, they wouldn't account for this."

"What is it, then?"

"She's simply asleep. It's a mystery."

Mrs. Pangloss gulped some tea. "The Lord, then, eh? Mysterious Ways. That's what Father Pheley says."

Dr. Hyde put away his tools. "Yes. Well, it would help if His ways were not so mysterious to physicians."

Mrs. Pangloss was devastated. It was too much. On the one hand, here was the city's most celebrated man of medicine attending her friend in her very own home, in Mrs. Pangloss's own presence. On the other, he not only could do nothing for her, he admitted he was baffled. Further, she suspected his remarks bordered on blasphemy. Not only Mysterious Ways, but a clear-cut example of Giveth and Taketh in the same instance.

When Father and Jean-Baptiste entered to hear the diagnosis, the doctor prattled on in the most extravagant of Latin phrases about what exactly he had done and in the least common medical jargon about what exactly he had found. Jean-Baptiste was looking at him quite suspiciously. Father finally pressed the point.

"But what is it?"

Dr. Hyde donned his greatcoat and heaved a sigh. "Brain fever," he said.

"Brain fever? My God. What can we do, Doctor?"

He put on his hat, took his gloves from his pockets. "Keep the windows open. It's too hot in here. And wait."

Father was clearly burdened with this news. Why wasn't there something to be done? A prescription, a treatment, even an operation? Why couldn't it simply be over with, and let them all get back to their lives?

When Dr. Hyde had left and Aline was clearing away his untouched plate and cup, Mrs. Pangloss remarked, "He's not so smart. Great Man. In a pig's eye."

"What the hell is brain fever?" asked Father.

"A usually mortal affliction in Victorian novels," said Jean-Baptiste.

Father's voice broke. "What!"

"Nothing," said Jean-Baptiste. "It's nothing at all."

Mrs. Pangloss asked, "You mean it's like *psychosomatic*? Is that the word?"

"Yes," said Jean-Baptiste. "Except it's the doctor imagining the illness, not the patient."

So Mother slept and life was easier for her; but Grandfather couldn't. There was, first of all, the pain. Although now it had dulled considerably, it was still constant and likely to stay that way for some time, according to Dr. Hyde. And whenever he closed the other eye, he still tried to close the absent one and received a stabbing reminder that he couldn't. And then there was the intermittent presence of Grace at the window. She was like Captain Hook's crocodile, hanging around as if she wasn't finished with him.

There was also the proposal Dr. Hyde had put to him to consider: transplant or artificial? Though it was now almost too late for a transplant—too much healing would preclude the idea. And there was the problem of a suitable donor. Besides which, the thought of someone else's eye in his head was not a pleasing one. Would it even fit properly? What would he see with it? Would it match the other? No, better to go without. A simple patch might be best—wait, now we're back to Captain Hook and that damned bird.

That was it, then. A glass eye.

Just as Grandfather made this decision, he received a visit from Mrs. Pangloss, who came to the hospital despite her dislike of him simply because he presented her with an opportunity to visit someone else's misery.

He groaned when he saw her, which she chose to accept as a greeting.

"I had to visit Billy Berri anyway," she said. "He's just had a prostrate operation. Insisted on showing me his catheter." And she made a noise something like a giggle, but altogether too much like a cackle. She sat beside Grandfather's bed, trying to look around and under his bandages to see the wound. When she couldn't, she surveyed the ward in the same manner.

"You don't look so good. Coming along? Well. Christ, you want to get out as quick as you can. House of horrors in here. Creepy old place. Not that you're not used to that sort of thing, that house of yours, next to the funeral parlour. Nurse! Nurse! Open a window. We need some air in here, it's not a morgue. He he hee."

There was one thing the two could agree on: the hospital was no place for a sick person. Both were old enough to remember the days when few people ever returned from hospitals, and the association was still strong in them: hospitals were houses of death. What

114

do you expect when you put so many diseased souls together in one place? Whatever germs, microbes, viral infections, diseases and bacteria you were relatively free of before going in would surely be coming out with you—if you survived. If they didn't kill you, they at least made you a carrier, a host.

Aside from that, there were the surgeons to fear. Mrs. Pangloss suspected the very idea of tampering with God's work: if He'd put something in there, who were we to take it out? But she was forced to admit their successes and grudgingly bowed to an intelligence greater than hers; which after all was also a gift from above.

Grandfather, however, was on familiar terms with at least one surgeon, his own family doctor, Cameron Hyde. And this certainly did not put him at ease. It wasn't a question of religion with Grandfather. He'd never been convinced that human life, or any life, was in any way connected to anything supernatural at all. If asked, he'd deny entirely the very existence of the supernatural. No, his doubts were quite firmly based in the physical. He knew a thing or two about bodies and how they fitted together. Surgeons, however, always seemed more interested in getting them apart.

In a word, butchers.

So the idea that he'd been under the knife himself was one he was having trouble accepting, one he was in fact trying to suppress, and the thought that he might have to undergo yet another operation unnerved him.

Bandage; eye patch; glass eye; perhaps even a human eye. But never again his own.

Grace scratched at the frost-covered window, startling Mrs. Pangloss. "Crikey, is that your wife's buzzard? No wonder you won't open the window. What's she doin' here, trying to get another taste? Hee he hee. Oh, that's a filthy bird. You must be glad she's out of the house."

Strangely, thought Grandfather, another point of agreement between them. Or at least it would be, under ordinary circumstances. But at the moment, since he was not in the house, he would prefer that Grace were. Or at least that she were somewhere away from him. He sat up a little and turned his own single, baleful eye upon her.

With a screech, she flew away.

FOUR

Somehow, they were all home for Christmas. As usual, there was no money for extravagances or even decent presents, and not enough real cheer among them to warrant giving one another anything frivolous. Mother slept through it, of course, but Father slipped her present, a new pillow, tenderly under her head. Aline had taken up a collection and they'd all scraped up enough money to make a down payment on Grandfather's new glass eye. Aline herself received a set of aprons and oven mitts; Father and Uncle got cigarettes. Jean-Baptiste had been put in charge of his sister's gift and agonized over it. What would she want? How little he knew her, how little they had in common, he realized. He fell back on buying her a book, of all things, terrified she'd throw it back in his face. But what else did he know? At least he'd tried to find one on a subject that might interest her, and presented her with Marighella's *Manual of the Urban Guerrilla.*

The rest of them, especially Father, might have been happy to consider Marie's mere presence gift enough from her. Yet she had insisted on doing her duty to the family and ungrudgingly moved herself to choose Jean-Baptiste's present. And since she couldn't

help herself in the face of the overwhelming sentiment of Christmas, which, even if it has no spiritual
meaning, retains for most Québécois the enormous
force of the most important of family rituals, she
tried her hardest to choose something that would
genuinely please him.

Everyone expected it would be a book. There was
little point in buying him anything else. That had
been learned by them all through years of experience.
He might scorn any kind of practical or well-meant
trifle—a sweater he'd never wear, chocolates he
wouldn't eat because they were milk, not dark—but no
matter what book anyone ever gave him, it always
elicited a genuinely grateful response. Even if it was
one he'd no interest in reading.

And indeed, the package was obviously a book. But
when he opened it, it so surprised him he found
himself without words.

"Let's see," said Father. "What? It's blank!"

Uncle scoffed. "What good's that?"

The blank book had given Marie a lot of trouble.
She'd struggled with a desire to fulfil a familial duty
that opposed her own sense of the uselessness of literature. She felt almost as if she'd been asked to buy
booze for an alcoholic, or smack for a junkie: it wasn't
going to help anyone.

She was gratified, at least, by the sight of the sign
above the shop, which read: *Livres.* It was a lovely soft
word, a French word. Not like that harsh, alien,

English word *Books*. It was soothing and familiar, yet it reminded her that political change was possible, that the power of the francophones was growing. For it was posted above an English bookstore, which like every other business in Quebec was required by law to post all their signs, inside and out, in French. Despite stocking nothing but English books, the proprietors were forced to replace the sign over each section inside their store. In here, you couldn't buy a mystery novel; you had to settle for a Roman Policier. There was no science fiction, but there were Anticipations; no health, but Santé; no fiction, but Romans; no travel, but Voyages; and no humour at all. This method made it so much easier for the French to buy English books.

It made entering the store so much easier for Marie, where she found herself surrounded by words. Despite her initial fears she found that the thousands of volumes, shelved against the walls, arranged in pyramids on the floors and piled in stacks at the ends of aisles, didn't threaten her. They weren't her enemies, for there was nothing in them or about them that could do her violence, simply because she refused to engage with them, and that rendered them powerless.

Neither were they a temptation, a seduction away from reality or practical work, because they were in themselves a kind of work: she was a poor reader who expended effort in any kind of reading; and surrender has to be effortless.

As she browsed she noted the other customers' seemingly unconscious slavery. They ran their hands

119

over spines, read front matter and dust jackets, opened volumes and lost themselves in the pages. They rarely spoke to one another and looked only at the books. When they did converse, it was only to recommend the relative merits of particular books, like born-again proselytizers or hosts for parasitical alien invaders. They were like opium smokers: calm, contented, alone with their thoughts and heedless of time or space.

It gave her the creeps.

And finally she realized the worst of the problem: Jean-Baptiste couldn't read French. She might have given him *Prochain épisode* or *Nègres blancs* or even *Bonheur d'occasion*, but he couldn't read them. What was she to do, give him *Two Solitudes*, or *Duddy Kravitz*? No, that was too much to be asked, to spend her own money on the Anglos and their Toronto publishers. She simply could not give him an English book.

So if both French and English were out, there was not much left. But there was a display of diaries, calendars, notepads and—blank books.

Instantly she grabbed one up, with a simple blue cover. Blue was Jean-Baptiste's favourite colour. She stood in line to pay and thumbed through it. No dust jacket, no title page, no gaudy coloured painting (English books were so tasteless in presentation; at least the French were restrained). And best of all, no *maudit anglais* type.

And, she reflected, here was a perfect symbol: a book that was not a book. Empty. Meaningless. No matter how hard he worked at its contents, he could derive no pleasure from this one, he couldn't make it mean a single thing. It was a nothing, just as all books were nothing, just as his life was shaping up to be nothing. And it wasn't in English. Although here he couldn't possibly read between the lines, her message would strike from the pages of this blank book the instant he opened it. It was more than just bilingual, it would transcend all language in its direct, violent attack on his wasted, counterproductive obsession: bang, you're dead.

When Jean-Baptiste opened the book, words deserted him.

What is a blank book? he thought. It's a book waiting to be written. It's not simply blank paper, on which one can scrawl anything: lists, phone numbers, meaningless doodles. It's cut to size and bound in boards because it's a complete object whose leaves follow one another from beginning to end, continuously, like a journey or a lifetime. A blank book is not nothing, it's simply an untaken journey, an unlived life. It's a concrete potentiality and, as such, an invitation and an affirmation. It's an acknowledgment that a book should be written upon it, that it can become anything. It can mean anything. And because its meaning must be physically manifest upon its blank pages, it can mean precisely what its owner—its writer, its reader—wants. The giving of a blank book is the giving of a voice.

"Thank you," he said. "Thank you, Marie. It's perfect."

There was something so white, so pure, so sacrosanct about a blank book. Dare he spoil that with words?

Oh, hell, yes. That's what it was for, after all. Marie's intent had been clear, at least to him. She'd swallowed all her own hatred of his obsession and given him permission to indulge himself. Now, after that, could he refuse? It would be an insult to refuse.

He moped about for days. He took up his pen, flung open the stiff cover and hastily inscribed: "Chapter One."

He scratched it out. He'd suddenly realized what a huge commitment it was to have written those two little words. If he began a chapter one, he'd be pledging himself to a chapter two at least, bare minimum, even if not to chapters three, four and so on. No, that was too much.

Don't scare yourself. Don't make any promises. See what happens, ease into it. No one gets married on the first date. He jotted down some notes. A day later, a scrap of dialogue came to him, and then a response. He put names next to the voices.

Within a week, he was writing a play.

Given the peace offering she'd made, Jean-Baptiste couldn't refuse to let Marie bunk down among his papers and pamphlets and ink and stencils in the attic. Though he'd come to consider it his own space, it was still technically a common part of the house;

and Marie was in fact being generous, since she had given up what was after all her own room to Aline, who still refused to return to Grandfather's room— even though she was often in and out of it, ministering to his wants and pretended sufferings.

And it was making Father happy again to have Marie back amongst them, and a little joy here and there couldn't be a bad thing at the holidays. Especially now that the house was turning into some kind of sanatorium, with Mother in the public ward downstairs and Grandfather in his private room upstairs. Father was full of his plans for the new business and hoping to conclude his bargain with the neighbour woman any day now, and hoping also that Grandfather would be about again as soon as possible so that he and Uncle could help with the renovations of the basement while they had no work of their own to do.

As far as Grandfather was concerned, his principal work for the foreseeable future was to get used to his new eye. He was no longer vain enough to care that it didn't match his own in colour; or at least, his poverty had thus far overcome his vanity, although it couldn't be vanquished totally and leave him satisfied with a plain patch. In respect of his lingering if dwindling pride, Father conspired with the family to withhold from Grandfather the knowledge that in fact the eye in question was not new.

Father had purchased it at a reduced price from their neighbours, the morticians. No more need be said about its origins or the character of the funeral directors, or indeed of Father, except that this wasn't the first time Father had bought or sold something to or from them, and therefore they understood one another well enough to introduce such delicate topics as the sale or purchase of items, implements and ephemera.

Grandfather began by inserting the eye for only a few moments at a time because he discovered it irritated more than his first pair of dentures had. Dr. Hyde had warned him there would be a period of adjustment, but this seemed beyond expectations. He could only keep it in a few moments, had trouble stopping it from rolling over in his head even though it wasn't symmetrical, and shuddered every time it bumped up against the socket in his skull when he tried closing his lid over it.

Aline was frightened of the eye. It was gruesome. Even though Grandfather's socket had more or less healed, this business of taking it out and putting it in again often resulted in a kind of rheumy pus being emitted. She brought him iodine and an eye cup to rinse with, and a bowl of hot water and alcohol so he could clean the eye. She herself refused to touch it.

"Why don't you clean it for me?" he would whine.

"You're old enough to clean yourself. It's disgusting. I won't touch it."

"But it causes infections!"

"Mais voyons, is that my fault? Take care of yourself."

"Some wife."

And that remark stung her. But then, what kind of a husband was he? If only she'd the strength to say that and not just think it. He was worse now that he'd returned from the hospital, more easily angered and demanding. She couldn't do enough for him. She brought him meals and drinks, the newspapers, his prescriptions, disinfectants . . . she even gave him sponge baths like a nurse. And everyone knew there was simply nothing wrong with his legs, there was no reason for him to be bedridden, except that he seemed to like it.

Aline found herself actually missing that brief period of his absence from the house. The only thing that comforted her was that for some reason, when Grandfather had returned, so had Grace.

The very same day that she'd carried his things up to his room and turned down the bed for him, Grace came fluttering in through the kitchen window and into her open cage. When Aline came down to make tea for Grandfather, there she was. She was cheered to see the bird, and cooed at her and offered her bread crumbs. Grace tilted her head, hopped about and cawed in response. Aline was convinced there was a communication between them.

Marie wasn't the only felquiste who'd gone home for the holidays. The long months of underground living had taken their toll on the whole cell. Some had neither seen nor talked to their relatives at all since the summer. For most there had been no other human contact, and their only experience of the outside world was the cold wind blowing through the newspapers.

Their tight-knit, tight-lipped world of politics and paranoia was long on sleepless nights and short on long baths, big meals and the unselfconscious camaraderie of beer and hockey games on the family TV set.

They struggled with the idea that now was the perfect time to stage an event, what with everyone preoccupied not by the language laws but by the holiday. Security would be lax.

On the other hand, so much of normal life was closed down and discarded by the season that there might be smaller chance of disrupting it. In the end, they gave in to their own sentimentality and risked blowing their covers by leaving their basement apartments. Of course, they left by night and flew home as fast as they could to avoid detection; of course, they'd be back in only a few days, after the New Year, before anyone in Quebec woke up again.

They were ever conscious of being in danger in the public eye. In broad daylight they might be recognized by the police or journalists or ordinary citizens—yes, even by their own families. They were being hunted, according to the papers, and they believed it, for in the eyes of bourgeois society they were already convicted criminals: murderers and bank robbers, anarchists, terrorists. They were the damned.

In some ways it would be a hard holiday. They would have to lie about where they'd been and what they'd been doing. There were things you just couldn't tell people, no matter how close you were to them. But the lure of réveillon was too strong: the thought of Christmas dinner and their mothers happy to see

them, of sharing a drink with their brothers, of trying to show they really did love their families (and if
they didn't, what was their work for, after all? One of
the hardships of the lot they'd chosen was physical
separation from those they loved; but how much
choice was there? Who was going to do the hard work
of nation-building if everyone stayed home before
the fire?), that lure was strong enough to overcome
their fears.

But it wasn't easy for Hubert to forget his politics,
his life work, even or especially in his parents'
Outremont home. It was warm, it was comfortable,
but it was paid for by his parents' years of slow
progress and advancement, by their acceptance of the
status quo and by a slow-witted provincial bourgeois
mentality that infuriated him.

Although his father was no fool. If he didn't dare
think that his son was a murderer, a terrorist, certainly
he was afraid that he was at least a fellow-traveller, a
misguided, hot-headed youth who never realized
when he had things good.

And so eventually the spirit of the season was forgotten. The father and son's conflicting ideas of
what was important and the amount of Christmas
cheer they'd poured down their throats combined to
topple the tree, to revive the old, unsettled arguments. Whether Hubert had left in disgust or whether
his father had thrown the bum out, neither could
really say, but somehow Hubert found himself out-
doors in the cold, with pine needles and strands of
silver tinsel in his hair. On New Year's Eve.

Hubert had been thrown out of his parents' house before, but at least this time he had a place to go. It would be lonely, what with the others still at their family homes. He was thinking mostly of Marie, though even if she'd been waiting in their unmade bed, he was now too drunk to enjoy her presence. And it was late, calice. He waited far too long at an unsheltered bus stop, hanging off the post, before a lonely police car came by and the cops chased him home. So there was nothing for it but to walk over the mountain and down to St-Henri. At least it was warming up. He was feeling nauseous, and his head felt so small it hurt.

The Desouches kept Christmas for the family, but on New Year's they invited what friends they had. Principally this meant Mother's friends Mrs. Pangloss and Mrs. Harrison. Since poor Mother was still asleep, they invited themselves on her behalf. Father had invited Mrs. McCairn, the elderly woman from next door, and her simple son, Moonie. Not that they'd ever been particularly welcome before, but given his plans for the new business, he thought it wise to treat them as he would anyone else he wanted something from.

Mrs. McCairn, after years of trying to bring her son's intellect up to her own level—and failing miserably, her head simply being too weak—decided that rather than bear the shame of a retarded son, she would bring her own mind down to his reach. She began by trying to make them both happier, and celebrated their birthdays whenever the spirit took her. She was already an older woman, but because she'd found this way of increasing the number of her birthdays, she rapidly became the oldest person in the neighbourhood. Even her son was soon older than people who'd visited the maternity ward when he was born. Because she spent the evenings talking about her own childhood, her own parents and things that had taken place in the neighbourhood, and because the sound of her voice lulled him into a trance that was so like his own dreams and memories, he began to remember things he'd never witnessed. His name was Martin, but for years the neighbourhood had known him as Moonie; her name was Diana, but she was only ever known as Mrs. McCairn. No one had ever seen Mr. McCairn, who had died in the Great War, and by the time anyone saw his photo, clean-shaven, smiling in his uniform, sepia brown, Moonie was showing it off as a picture of himself.

"Captain Moonie," said the local wits behind his back.

"Ach, it's a fine uniform," Angus had said. "I'd one like it myself but not quite so grand. Be proud of it, boy. It's more than most around here have got."

The three women (Mrs. Harrison bent almost far enough over her own knees to fall out of her chair, Mrs. Pangloss with "Go on, just a little punch—Stop! For Christ's sake, d'you think I'm a drunkard? Hee hee hee," and Mrs. McCairn suspiciously looking down from side to side at the chair she was in, as if afraid it wouldn't hold her) settled together at Mother's bedside. Soon they were all enveloped in the cloud of Mrs. Harrison's cigarette smoke; occasionally her cackling or Mrs. Pangloss's mirthful shrieking or even Mrs. McCairn's polite giggling could be heard from within.

Father had also invited the mortician from the other side, who showed up only because he had just concluded two transactions with the family: one re Angus and the other re a certain lump of glass. Of course he wore the same suit he was always seen in, as if he hadn't another. And why should he? Formal wear was never inappropriate, was it? And black is never out of style. Father himself was forced to speak to him, since no one else seemed to want to, and the mortician, trained by years of funerals, was very much used to standing discreetly by and not disturbing the mourners. And there *was* that woman over by the window. Was this, after all, some kind of a wake? Or perhaps a death watch? In which case, it would be the first time the mortician had shown up in advance of Death's knocking on the door. Though he was never far behind.

Marie and Jean-Baptiste argued over who would help Aline in the kitchen and who would entertain Moonie. Jean-Baptiste lost.

"I got a baseball bat for Christmas," said Moonie.

"I got a book," said Jean-Baptiste.

"You want to play ball?"

"Uhm, some other time."

"I'll get the bat, and you bring a ball and we'll have a game in the lane."

"The lane's full of snow."

"So?"

"Listen," said Jean-Baptiste. "I heard you were studying to repair radios."

"Yeah, by mail."

"How did you do?"

"I got a certificate. It's hanging over the TV."

"Well, look. I've got an old radio you could fix for me."

Moonie looked alarmed. "It's not transistors, is it? 'Cause I didn't learn transistors."

"No, no. It's tubes. I told you, it's an old one, short-wave. Angus used to listen to the BBC with it."

Moonie looked relieved. "Oh. No, you can't repair tube radios."

"What? Why not?"

"They blow up."

When Jean-Baptiste started to argue with "What do you mean?" Moonie's face betrayed his fear. "Oh," said Jean-Baptiste. "I get it. Okay, forget the radio."

"Who's Angus?" asked Moonie.

"No one, any more."

"You want to play baseball? I got the bat new for Christmas."

⚜

Angus was dreaming again. It was winter, but he was sweating in the heat. Perhaps he was in hell; at least it seemed certain he was at a funeral, and he thought he

131

heard people talking about him. Over in the corner, in a cloud of fog, he saw a woman in a coffin. Three other old women attended her, while off to the side stood a man who looked like Death, or a monk. As he approached the woman, without walking over to her, he saw that it was Mother.

It became much hotter. Steam was rising from her. He felt compelled to wake her up. He reached out to shake her, but either his arms didn't respond or he no longer had any. He began to shout, trying to direct his voice into her ear. It seemed to do no good.

Aline was a little nervous working with Marie on the food. She was worried about the food, too, but Marie had never seemed to like her. Yet she had made the gesture of giving up her room, as if she understood just how intolerable Aline's marriage had become. And here she was volunteering with the refreshments and chatting without once sneering at God or the Anglos. Together they had prepared Mother for the reception, washing her hair, changing her robe, even giving her a sponge bath. Aline was becoming an expert at it now, like a real nurse. But Marie had held and moved and caressed her mother almost as if she were her own infant, and Marie herself the mother.

Of course, Aline couldn't know that those were the particular moments in which Marie was feeling her guilt. She saw now that Mother had found life unbearable without Angus, taken as he was so unexpectedly and for absolutely no fault of his own. For

Mother, Marie's motivations just didn't exist. There was simply no reason to kill a person. Mother was sleeping away Angus's absence, and that was Marie's fault. Even if it hadn't been deliberate.

Marie was surprised at her newly discovered affection for Mother. She'd always thought she resented her mother, thought she'd been unable to respect her. Now she remembered past holidays when Mother had been awake, alert, smiling and revelling in her children's Christmas happiness. Marie remembered Angus too, the stiff old Anglo who'd always brought them presents, and surprised herself by missing him. And the dinners Mother would cook, with Grandmother's help. Funny that Aline, this meek little woman, not much older than Marie herself, was now her grandmother. And unhappy about it.

Not that Grandmother had been particularly happy with Grandfather; there'd been enough Christmas battles and stormy exits from both of them. But at least Grandmother had had the strength to stand her ground against him.

She pitied Aline. She missed Angus. And she felt guilt for Mother's condition. Yet she was happy to be home.

What was this mysterious pull she felt called Christmas?

For Grandfather the transition from sleeping to wakefulness was an ill-defined thing. Years of waking after sundown with blinds pulled against the light had blurred the process. Today—this evening—for the first time in weeks, for the first time since the bloody incident with that damned crow, he gently drifted awake with a sense of calm comfort. Without paying attention to his own thoughts, he realized his wound must now be reaching a state of complete healing. He reached for his teeth and remembered that one day they too had ceased to hurt and finally felt natural enough in his mouth for him to feel nothing at all when they were in. He yawned and stretched; Aline had changed the bedclothes this morning and the mattress bore his imprint from years of close contact. How comfortable it was. In the darkness he fumbled on the side table for his patch before turning on the light. Healed or no, he didn't want to tempt fate, and the sudden light had already more than once stabbed him. He almost reached for the bell, which would bring Aline, but then thought better of it. He remembered it was the last day of December. He'd already been too long abed. Why not get up on the cusp of the New Year? Why not put an entirely new face on everything?

Aline had been good to him these past weeks. She'd nursed and fetched for him no matter how demanding or surly he'd been. He pondered how much he'd taken advantage of her in so many ways, only recently with the poor excuse of his health, and felt ashamed. It was not her fault the crow had tried to kill him. Even if she did harbour it, pamper it against his will.

And he'd never been a lazy man, never been afraid of hard work in his life. It was time to stop lying down. He rose and drew the blind up, letting in a little light from the rear of the houses across the lane. The lights and the luminescent snow reminded him again that it was the holiday. The telephone poles were strung together with snow-covered cables and topped with shining yellow lamps. The Gothic arches at the rear of the church directly across shadowed the faintly glittering stained-glass panes, and out of their corners and angles came dark greens and reds.

To hell with it. He felt good. It was time for a little cheer. There'd been enough misery this past year; he'd go down to his family and they'd celebrate that it was finally over.

As Hubert was stumbling drunkenly by Mount Royal Cemetery in the dark, Grandfather finally came down from his room. For the first time any of them could remember, he was smiling. Aline saw on his face the look that had attracted her so long ago. He didn't say a word. He surveyed the living room in silence, then crossed it to Father, who was sitting beside Mother, still stretched out like a corpse and sleeping. "Don't worry," he said to Father. "I've woken up. She will too." And he put his arm around Father's shoulder.

Aline was drawn to him suddenly and instinctively. She started across the room and then, as if remembering, halted just before throwing herself into his arms. He smiled and drew her close.

For a moment there was silence, as if none of them wanted to burst this peaceful bubble. Then

Jean-Baptiste said, "Grandfather, you've got your patch on the wrong eye."

There came a sudden knocking at the back door.

Ice had long since formed in Hubert's beard and moustache. When he yawned, it broke up and fell off his face. He looked up to see where he was: past both cemeteries now and coming along Côte-des-Neiges. It would be so nice to be home already. If only he hadn't argued so ferociously with the old man. It would be so nice to lie down right here and sleep. If it were summer he would. But now it would be foolish.

His head was pounding; he was all blocked up in the cold as if his sinuses and the base of his skull—and damn it, the top too—were shrinking. He should never have had so much to drink. But his father'd always had good taste in wine, and Hubert couldn't resist. He was never able to afford the vintages his father drank routinely. Bourgeois affectation.

Enough maudite neige tonight, all right. He started down the hill towards Atwater. Criss, if he had a sled now it would be easier. Down the hill all the way home. And to rub it in, he had to pass by anglo Westmount. He began to run downhill; he'd get past the Anglos as quickly as he could.

He slipped on the ice and shot out into the street with his leg behind him. Calice, that hurt. Stretched his muscle the wrong way. But he got right up again and started running. It was warmer that way. And if he fell, well, maybe he'd just fall all the way home. At least he couldn't fall up the hill.

He cheered up when he realized he was enduring this hardship out of his convictions. It was because of his political beliefs, which his father didn't share. And why didn't he? Hubert wondered. He was just as Québécois as anyone, he endured the humiliations of the anglicization of his homeland just as Hubert did, just as everyone in his felquiste cell did. Just as all francophones in Quebec (and the rest of Canada!) did, and had ever since the first humiliation of Montcalm's defeat by Wolfe. Wolfe indeed.

It had been a mistake to go home for Christmas. It was a mistake to think anyone could enjoy a normal life while anglicization proceeded behind their backs, while they were asleep. Every day and every minute the Québécois were threatened with assimilation into the great unwashed English mob of North America. Already too many of them had intermarried, and bred children who could no longer speak French—right here in Montreal, there were French kids with French names who couldn't speak a word of it. Families broken up by this linguistic gulf. There were grandparents unable to talk to their own descendants.

But the shame of it was the lack of realization, he thought. Like his father, no one seemed to understand that a passion to preserve the language was not simply a fanatical assertion of tribal will. For him a language was not simply a way of communicating, like the telephone or the postal system. A language is a way of thinking. It's a way of being, a way of life. If you take that away, you've destroyed an entire culture. You can't have French people who do not speak French. If they speak English, they are Anglos.

"Vive le Québec libre!" thought Hubert. There was no one else about; he left the icy sidewalk for the clearer road, and ran leaping down the hill. He began to shout. For once, it was good to yell out what he'd always only written down, what had been kept hidden for fear of the police. It was a new year; it would be a historic year. Now they were invincible.

"Vive le Québec libre! Le Québec au Québécois! Maîtres chez nous!"

The premier plays as important a part in this story as he does in Quebec politics; but here, although it's a briefer one, it's no less tragic.

The invincible Péquiste premier of Quebec, a man dedicated to forging a new nation for the Québécois, was liked and disliked and scorned and respected by anglophones and francophones alike. He was intelligent, resourceful and experienced. He'd been a war correspondent (for an American—English—paper); he had a lovely young wife; he smoked like a chimney even in the presence of the Queen of England herself; he knew how to take a joke; he'd been to school with the prime minister of Canada. In short, not just a cunning politician, but a man of the people as well. Marie and Hubert were among his many strong supporters. They considered him the absolute leader of the political side of their struggle, just as they were the military side; like Ireland's IRA and Sinn Fein.

The premier and his wife were discussing which English private school they should send their children to. Lower Canada College had its good points, not the least of which was its location, right here in Montreal. But Upper Canada College, while it was in fact in Toronto and therefore more expensive due to the cost of boarding, had the advantage that it would totally immerse their children in the English language and make them more proficient. It would also introduce them to a different set of someday influential classmates. There was no need to worry about entry into the right circles locally; how could there be for the children of the premier himself? But it never hurts to broaden one's sphere of friends, and if, some golden day in the future, Quebec should really achieve independence, personal friendships with the powerful people of Canada could not hurt their chances either politically or financially. Which was the point of sending them to English schools in the first place. It was insane not to be fluent in the majority language of North America.

This discussion had begun at the home of some friends where they had spent a quiet New Year's Eve, away for a brief moment from the minefield of public discourse. These friends had children at Royal Mount, just a few blocks from their Westmount home, and were extolling its virtues; the wife held a seat on its governing board. Now, hours and many drinks and more cigarettes later, after midnight mistletoe and suitable noise and hilarity, after another bottle of champagne, the discussion was continuing as they drove home.

Both were tired, both were cold. At this time of night, despite the distance, home was not so far away. There were few cars on the road and even fewer people. As do all Montrealers, the premier shot along the empty streets at highway speeds. He fumbled in his coat for his cigarettes and opened the pack easily with one hand. He jabbed at the dashboard lighter as the car began the long downward arc from Westmount Boulevard onto Doctor Penfield, where they would cross Atwater Street into Montreal.

As the car gracefully made the turn, the premier heard the pop of the lighter and reached for it instinctively. He took his eyes off the road. His wife screamed; he dropped the lighter, shot his head back up and saw, too late, Hubert.

"Vive le Québec libre!" shouted Hubert, waving his arms. The speeding car was behind him. "Quebec au Québécois!" He bounded across the intersection, heading down Atwater.

The premier spun the wheel and stomped on the brakes. The car slid on the ice-covered street, now completely out of control.

The premier yelled, "Merde!" But it did no good.

With a sickening thud, and without even seeing it coming, Hubert met his destiny.

They got out of the car; the premier staggered a little while hunting for a cigarette in his coat. "Merde," he said.

"Merde," said his wife.

Behind them, lying on the Westmount side of Atwater Street, was a body. The premier and his wife stood nervously in the empty street trying to decide what to do. Finding himself too nervous, the premier got back into the car to smoke. His wife, clutching her fur coat, shuffled from foot to foot in her high heels, feet freezing in the sub-zero temperatures.

"Tabernac," said the cop.

"Calice," said his rookie partner.

The older cop sat the premier's wife back in her car, beside her silent, smoking husband.

"Okay, don't worry. It's a routine thing, just an accident, right?"

The Péquiste premier turned his watery eyes on the cop, rubbed his face with his cigarette still in his hand. The hand shook like Mrs. Harrison's.

The premier's wife began to cry. "Calice . . . de ciboire . . . d'hostie."

"We'll fix it, don't worry," said the cop. He closed the door.

The rookie was coming over with a Breathalyzer.

"Criss. T'es-tu fou?" He grabbed it from the younger man's hand. "You wanna be the guy who breathalyzes the premier?"

"What do you mean? It's the law."

"The law. I mean, everybody's gonna think you're Lee Harvey Oswald."

"Oswald?"

"Yeah. And there'll be plenty hankering to be Jack Ruby. Tabernac, you got a head like a puck, you kids today."

"But we have to breathalyze somebody for the report."

"For all the report there's going to be you might as well breathalyze him," said the older cop, pointing to the corpse.

The rookie looked puzzled. "I don't think he can breathe."

"We'll give him a hand. Did you call an ambulance?"

"No. Sorry, I should have done that first. Calice." He started running back to the patrol car.

"Aw, Criss de Criss." The older man chased him, stopped him from making the call. "You got some things to learn for sure. No ambulance for this guy. Quick, now, we got a chance to clean up this mess if we act fast."

"What are you talking about? There's a dead guy out there."

"Yeah, and there's the maudit fucking premier sitting at the wheel of the car that hit him. You know what that means? That means unless we do something, you and me, right now, the whole goddamn Christ-fucked histoire du Quebec gets fucked up its own ass."

"Are you serious?"

"You kids are something. You think anything's changed since Duplessis died? Look, you and me gonna take our lunch break and use it wisely, and the premier is gonna go home and sleep it off, and tomorrow we're all gonna get up and start a new year just like we would have except for that bastard of a frozen turd out there. Then, in six or nine months, surprise, you and me get promoted. Okay? And if that's not okay, you know what? The maudit idiot of a Quebec premier goes to jail, instead of a referendum we get another useless election, those tits the Liberals take over, your wife will leave you because you reported the accident and the maudits felquistes will send you a little box that blows up when you untie the string. How's that? Okay?"

"Okay," said the rookie. "You don't have to yell at me. It's not my fault."

"Maudit wagon de Christ. I got to yell at somebody. I can't go yell at the premier." He slammed the car door but was calm by the time he returned to the premier and his wife. He leaned in the car window. They looked like stricken animals.

"Monsieur le premier, madame. Thanks for your co-operation, and we're sorry to have detained you. We hope you'll understand that under the circumstances . . . well, anyway, we won't need you any more. Please drive carefully, and have a bonne année. Okay?"

The premier and his wife looked at one another, then back to the cop.

He sighed. "Good night. Go home. Forget it."

Realization dawned on the premier. For the first time since he'd struck Hubert, something was happening that he understood. He stared at the old cop.

Not much older than the premier himself; same generation. The cop's eyes were warm, friendly, knowing. Briefly, the premier wondered whether he could be trusted. Not his loyalty, but his competence.

The old cop smiled. "Don't worry. When the snow melts, there'll be nothing left behind."

The premier nodded. He put the car in gear, lit another cigarette, removed his glove to shake the cop's hand. "Je me souviens," he said.

"What are we going to do with him?" asked the younger cop.

"We get rid of him."

"Dump him in the river?"

"No. He'd get stuck under the ice. He might drift downstream, but he'd wash up somewhere, someday. I got a better idea. An old acquaintance."

Aline and Marie had found something to talk about. Tourtière. They were filling individual little pies with meat and using cookie-cutter shapes to cut out bits of crust to lay on top. Both women remembered past Christmases, when their elders had done this for them; both were smiling and telling how wonderful their grandmother's tourtières had been.

And then the police came knocking at the kitchen door.

Through the frosted panes of glass Marie could see the cops, and Hubert, looking pretty bad. Her knees went weak. How had they found him? Why had he led them to her? Of course they'd beaten him; that would be obvious even without seeing his bloody, swollen face. Her heart pounded. She clutched at the kitchen counter to keep from falling. It was over. Jail. Even worse, Mother would find out Marie had made and planted the bomb that killed Angus.

Aline opened the door and drew back with a start when she realized the police were holding up a dead man.

"Where's the old man?" asked the older cop.

Aline was speechless. What had these people to do with Grandfather? Who was this dead tramp they were bringing into her kitchen?

Uncle entered the kitchen, saw the cops. "Calice de ciboire d'hostie," he said, and ran out.

"What's the matter with you people?" yelled the older cop. "Where's that maudit resurrection man? We got a New Year's present here for him."

Grace began screeching and fluttering in her cage.

Suddenly, Marie realized that Hubert was dead. She giggled. They weren't here to arrest her, they were trying to get rid of the body. He hadn't given her away. She felt almost giddy; being dragged from the depths of her despair was like standing up too fast.

In the great tradition of underground movements throughout history, Hubert had taken his licks and kept his mouth shut. He'd died to protect the rest of the cell. To protect her. She was still reeling under the blow of his death, but was now wrenched from the unsuspected and violent hatred that had burst into being with the thought that he'd betrayed her, to a shamefaced admiration for her noble, fallen comrade. And an overwhelming feeling of release. The kitchen had never been so warm.

She fainted.

FIVE

MYSTERIES OF MONTREAL

Grandfather and Dr. Hyde disliked one another intensely but had done business together for decades. Grandfather retained the distrust of all professions that had been beaten into him in childhood, through the priests, doctors, social workers and others who'd made it perfectly clear which end of the social scale he inhabited, and how much he owed to their kindness. He particularly disliked doctors, especially those to whom he was bound by economic necessity, and like anyone else he projected his self-loathing onto another when his own profit contradicted his sense of morality. He didn't blame himself for desecrating graves; he blamed his customers for the use they made of the goods he sold them.

His acquaintance with what exactly was done with the wares he peddled formed his opinion of all doctors. "Vultures. Butchers. They'll steal your kidneys while your back's turned." Or sometimes, if he was in a more expansive mood: "They plant 'em and I dig 'em up again."

So when the police came knocking at the back door with a body to dispose of, he knew exactly where to take it.

What a great fortune this particular corpse was for him. It boded well for the New Year. He'd never had one in mid-winter before, so it was a financial boon. At the same time, Dr. Hyde would be as pleased to see it as Grandfather in this dry season, and as the law of supply and demand operates in all businesses, he'd pay a premium for it. But best of all, and incredibly, for once Grandfather got to play the benefactor, and smugly relished doing a favour for his enemies—the cops.

This was one good corpse.

For Dr. Hyde, as for many doctors, a youthful idealism—a desire to help those in need—had drawn him to medicine. Such an ambition could equally have led him to the Church, except for the uselessness of such an institution in the face of the death of God. It wasn't so much that a dead God could not exist as that, even granting He did, a dead God was a God with no soul. It was an inescapable fact that since sometime in the nineteenth century, hospitals had been growing in number and size just as churches had conversely been shrinking. The century of Nietzsche, Darwin and Marx had proclaimed the ascendance of man through reason, and shunted aside mysticism and ritual, replacing them with technology and experimentation. The faith necessary for the foundation of the Church had been replaced by the demonstrable proof of science. Thus, the path to be tread by Samaritan ambition and megalomania was clearly marked.

Dr. Hyde's early history was a simple cliché. He was a brilliant student and a tireless worker. He was liked and respected by his seniors, his juniors, his contemporaries—in short, he was a pillar of the community and a man clearly headed for Great Things. Honours and promotions came his way as naturally as patients. His reputation burgeoned into fame, his clients came to consist of the famous, and problems were brought to him even if they were outside his field.

He expanded his field. He'd begun with neurology, the study of the nervous system. But cases began showing up that were clearly the province of psychiatry. So he turned from dissecting, weighing, poking, mapping and patching to listening, soothing, prescribing, interpreting and imprinting. He was famous in both hard and soft sciences. He was an innovator in both and a radical experimenter in combining the two; he led his patients through therapy, and he had them hosed. He listened to their dreams, and he dosed them with barbiturates. He probed their pasts with hypnotism, and he probed their heads with electrodes.

Some got better, and for that he was lauded. Most got worse, but that was clearly not his fault.

He had studied medicine, chemistry, biology, psychology; he had mastered surgery, mesmerism, anatomy. And he knew, in his heart of hearts, that all this had done no good. He was as ignorant as he had been in the beginning, poor fool. He could not escape the feeling that despite all his maps and models, all the reproducible effects were meaningless because none of them led to the seat of the soul. He could take apart a human brain or body, he could track the physical effects of emotions and thoughts on paper or film, but that wasn't enough. The real knowledge of what constituted the fundamental spark was still hidden in darkness, and Dr. Hyde was very much afraid of that darkness. Because if he couldn't find that brief illumination, that fleeting moment of Being inside any of his patients, he was afraid that he would never find it in himself. He was afraid it did not exist.

Dr. Hyde continued his experiments for years after his genuine interest had waned, only because his fear drove him to outrun his despair. He could easily dissect any number of creatures, and end up with a table full of dead meat. But if he started with a table full of parts, and managed to induce the same impulses and reactions natural to a living creature, would he end up with a living creature? If it lived, would it have a soul? It was the only way to put the question to rest. Was the soul a real component of a conscious being, or merely an after-effect of a certain material process?

At Ravenscrag, high on the side of Mount Royal, his private laboratories adjoined his mental hospital. Here he kept the results of his experiments, both when he had minor successes and when the failures were spectacular enough. He had a jar in which the hand of a hanged murderer still crawled up the side; he had a pair of lungs that had breathed by themselves for three days; he had a small brain that he suspected was still busy thinking.

These trophies were the result of his life's devotion to the Great Work; and it seemed as if it would all die with him. For if he had no real success, if the break-through did not come, it would be impossible to make his findings public. This was a side of his practice that could only be revealed if he managed to establish some conclusive proof.

And so for years his jars and solutions, his devices and desires, had kept Grandfather in business. And for years Grandfather had kept the doctor's research-es alive with his spade and his satchel.

Dr. Hyde strained to conceal his pleasure in acquir-ing a corpse of such positive freshness, for to give away his eagerness would only drive up Grandfather's already high off-season price. Yet Grandfather and Uncle too were themselves so pleased and relieved to do some unexpected business that all three postured and restrained themselves, and all three were so con-centrated on their own self-control—a discipline none had much practice with—that all were oblivious to the others' odd comportment.

Affecting disdain while examining the body, Dr. Hyde asked, "Have you taken to ambulance chasing now, Desouche?"

"Eh?" said Grandfather.

"He's unembalmed. He's not been buried."

For a second, Grandfather worried. But then, "Pickled or not, we take our wares where we can in lean times, Doctor. The both of us."

Dr. Hyde hmmed. "He's quite bruised. The blood's still draining from these wounds. Here . . .," he pointed, "and here," turning the head. "Ribs cracked. This leg's broken in several places."

"He's still dead," said Uncle.

"Yes," said Hyde, "perhaps dangerously so. Perhaps he'll be missed."

Grandfather took the inference. "Don't worry, Doctor. If my friends in the police are looking for him, they'll look under other rocks." And he grinned, for he'd never been able to say anything remotely similar, and with such confidence.

Hyde studied Grandfather's face. Friends in the police? Grandfather? That was an entirely new factor, and not one Hyde could welcome. But if it meant there was no danger in this transaction . . . This was no mummy. This one hadn't been unearthed after the indignities of formaldehyde and cosmetics. He couldn't have been dead more than a few hours—and he was practically fresh-frozen. This was worth losing sleep over; this was the one he'd been waiting for.

The black sky was passing towards grey, the only sign of dawn Montreal gets in winter. Dr. Hyde dismissed thoughts of returning to bed. It was time to work, for some things needed immediate attention and he could sleep later.

He stripped and cleaned the corpse to get a better idea of its condition. Broken legs, a crushed rib cage:

these he could replace, but he could do nothing for the heart, which had been shredded by the cracked points of the corpse's own ribs. The lungs had collapsed but merely needed reinflating. A few stitches required on the face. The main trouble was that much of the skull appeared to have been crushed at the back of the head and the delicate tissue beneath it pulped. Not so easy to replace.

He'd tried it once, in the late fifties, with apes: switched their heads. The operation had taken eighteen hours. The donor had died instantly, of course. The recipient had been kept alive artificially through the operation, and then died when the plug was pulled. There had not been even the remotest indication that more research, more experimentation, more anything, would have promised success. It was a complete and total failure. He'd been too demoralized ever to try it again.

In which case, the only thing to do here was remove what couldn't be saved and patch up the rest. Dr. Hyde spent some time carefully removing small, sharp fragments of skull from the jellied pinkish-grey mass behind Hubert's eyes before he put down his tweezers, picked up a scalpel and, with a sigh, simply cut out the bruised portions as if he were removing blemishes from damaged fruit.

Fortunately, this meant there were now large enough pieces of skull to cover what remained. He put Hubert's head back together the way Aline made a quilt. Fit a piece in here, stitch on one side, find a patch big enough, now one shaped more or less correctly to fill the gap, and there you go. At the end the head was closed up neatly, almost as if it had never been opened.

But it was a lot smaller.

✦

Why had Marie fainted?

She was no weakling in any sense. It's true, the kitchen had been even hotter than the rest of the house, what with the oven going for the baking. And she'd had as much cheap, sweet sparkling wine as anyone that night—more than some. And the sight of the police had scared her; the sight of Hubert dead had shocked her.

But Marie was young and in perfect health, and a hardened realist. As soon as she regained consciousness, with the mortician holding smelling salts to her nose, she knew the world was now fundamentally different. It wasn't simply that Hubert was dead, or realizing how that affected her work, the work of their cell. It wasn't that Mother was asleep or Grandfather in some strange happy mood, or Jean-Baptiste mysteriously delighted with a gift that was supposed to be an insult and a provocation, or that she'd found herself enjoying time with Aline.

No, it was something else. It wasn't just a matter of circumstance, and it wasn't just these feelings of guilt and familial loyalty welling up to overcome her dedication to the Great Work. There was something substantially and almost physically different. If not with the world itself, then with her. What the hell was this magically transformative power of Christmas?

Over the following week she found herself often dizzy, sometimes ravenously hungry and sometimes inexplicably nauseous.

She was, of course, pregnant.

Aline was now fully cognizant of Grandfather's trade. She felt as if a shroud had been drawn over her. She felt as if she herself were dead. For a single brief moment on New Year's Eve, she'd thought the old Grandfather, the charming, gift-bearing suitor who'd seduced her into marriage, had returned. Through her mind had flashed the thought that somehow his accident had changed things. That Grace had not just taken an eye but forever altered his perspective, and that he would henceforth see things in a brighter, clearer light. That he would love her and be worthy of love himself.

Instead, the horrible truth had been revealed. Resurrection man, the cop had said. She fought the idea that it could be possible, that such a person might still exist in the modern world; but Grandfather had come when he was called, and had taken charge of the corpse almost with glee. He hadn't been afraid of it or repulsed by it as she had been.

He was used to corpses.

He'd bundled it up like merchandise, and went off to peddle it.

The whole unholy business gave her the shudders. And now she realized the rest of the family had known what she hadn't. Had they been keeping it from her, or was it simply such a part of reality for them that they assumed she knew? What did it matter? It coloured her view of them all; but worse, it coloured her view of herself. She was his wife. She had shared her bed with him.

Her eyes were red with tears and her nose sore from the blowing. She wrapped herself up in her winter clothes and braved the January cold, and rode the bus to St Joseph's. She tried to pray to Frère André's shrivelled black heart, but she couldn't find the words. She simply knelt before it, hung her head and sobbed.

Jean-Baptiste continued working away at his play over the winter. He came out of his room only for meals, the washroom and when someone forced him.

Mother continued her slumber. Dr. Hyde had shown up at the door one day with a real hospital bed for her, with rails to keep her from falling out. He still had no idea why she slept, but he knew the army surplus cot they'd put her in wasn't going to help.

Father and Marie shared the task of caring for her, and thus spent more time together now than almost ever before. The clear realization that they had in common a concern for Mother was a kind of gift to them both. For Father it meant that Marie wasn't entirely alienated from the family—from him—as she had seemed in recent years. Perhaps she might be coming back into the fold. He'd always worried more over his daughter than over his son because it's common for fathers to do so and because Jean-Baptiste was usually home. For Marie his concern was a clear sign that Father still loved Mother; and if that was possible, after all the hard years, after all the mutual dissatisfaction, it meant two things: that love itself was real, and that a lifetime commitment could actually be met and sustained.

Uncle walked his dog whether it was warm or freezing, clear or snowing, and otherwise kept to his room and his cigarettes.

Aline spent most of her time in the kitchen, the closest thing she had to a room of her own. It simply didn't occur to her to displace Marie's things. She bedded down among them as if she were a temporary visitor and Marie would be returning from the attic shortly. Aline moved slowly about her tasks—trying to eliminate the stains from the porcelain sink, putting new shelf paper into the cupboards, cleaning Grace's cage—in between times of just sitting at the table, gazing out the window and across the lane at the blank stone wall of the church. Grace hopped about from the transom above the door to the top of the refrigerator, making the odd sound or flying round Aline's head as if trying to get her attention.

Grandfather realized that he was indeed beginning to see out of his new eye. He still took it out every night and cleaned it, and left it soaking in antiseptic, where it settled at the bottom of the glass, looking upwards. He discovered that although both his eyes functioned, they seemed to be out of synchronization or parallax or something. If he left the new one in and didn't cover his own real eye, his vision was occluded. They seemed to conflict.

So he still had recourse to his patch, but would shift it now and then from one eye to the other.

He was completely fed up with Aline, and as far as he was concerned, it wouldn't matter whether she moved back into his room or not. But then, moving the patch to cover his own eye, he suddenly remembered the way her face lit up so briefly on New Year's Eve, and all she had done for him; and that in fact she was really an attractive and young woman. His desire rose and he regretted their arguments and the circumstances that kept them apart.

Next morning, leaving the eye in its glass, patch over the empty socket, he thought to himself, Yet why should I deprive myself of my conjugal rights? I'm older than her, but I'm not dead. If I want a woman, I should have a woman. And if my wife won't co-operate, somebody else will.

And off he went.

There came a day when Marie faced the fact that she couldn't keep her pregnancy secret forever. She'd been mulling over what it meant for her. It was a branch in the road. It was the single most important decision she'd yet had to make, and whatever she chose, it would affect the rest of her life. Whatever she chose, she might live to regret.

She could either become a mother, or not.

Motherhood has often been a delicate question in Quebec. The early policy of the revenge of the cradle—preserving French numerical superiority by making large families a social and religious duty—was loudly espoused by the clergy at a time when they were still the most influential body in the province, especially outside the cities. Later, in the full flush of nationalist sentiment, to have children was to build the state; and when that state was still merely a province that had yet to carry a referendum on independence, every new French vote was a patriotic gift.

On the other hand, to have children and no husband was, if not merely the tragic misfortune of widowhood, clearly a sin. Fortunately for Marie this was at last beginning to change. Most circles in Montreal, English or French, would not have ostracized her. But even the most liberal would have made comments about the hardships she'd face because of someone else's prudery, and shake their heads in pity. Few would be openly happy for her, would see her child as a cause for celebration and another example of the joy of existence, the miracle of life. Having a child would still be a daring social move. And of course, because life was simply a slap in the face, Catholic Quebec had not yet seen fit to legalize abortion.

Marie also had the very real fear that if she committed herself to motherhood, she'd be abandoning her work. It might not make it impossible, but it surely would make it more difficult still. And it wouldn't be easy on the child.

In short, to have the child would be difficult; to decide to discontinue her pregnancy would be difficult; to secure an abortion would be difficult. With Hubert gone, she wrestled alone with this problem until she was exhausted and could wrestle no more.

Finally, she went to Father and asked for help.

Father was outraged, disappointed, scared, saddened; he was briefly afraid that the child might be Jean-Baptiste's—that's when the word *abortion* flashed through his mind. But after a moment's consideration, he was flattered and delighted that Marie had come to him.

Father lifted Mother off the bed, holding her in his arms like a groom with his bride. Marie pulled off the sheets, bundled them and unfolded clean ones. Why was Father silent? She almost wanted to yell, "Say something!"

When she'd done with the bedclothes, Father laid Mother back down in her bed. Marie arranged her hair, began to stroke it. Mother slowly turned, first her head, then her shoulders; then she hunched the rest of her body onto her right side. Father watched his daughter caressing her mother, and silently moved closer.

For the first time since she'd been a child, he embraced her. They both cried.

"And the father?" he asked.

"He's dead," she said.

That startled him. Should he pursue it? But if she confessed pregnancy, why would she lie about that?

This was not the time for a petty argument to divide them. The father was dead.

"And do you want the baby?"

"I don't know."

"You don't need anyone to go over the arguments with you. You're not stupid. And what I think doesn't matter. You must decide. When you've decided, let me know. But you're a Desouche. So we'll help you. No matter what."

"Don't tell anyone," she said.

"It's nobody's business," he said.

Marie made the decision; Father made the telephone call; Dr. Hyde performed the service.

It was a grey afternoon in February. The streets were black with old snow and moisture; the mountain's trees were bald and grey. They walked together up Pine Avenue to Dr. Hyde's office, their breath coming in great, laboured puffs up the hill. It was thirty degrees below zero, but they were both damp under their coats. Below them lay the flat field of the water reservoir and then the downtown core; above them, Ravenscrag and the cross.

Father waited in the anteroom. Marie lay in a hospital gown with her feet elevated. Eventually Dr. Hyde came in; he washed his hands and put on a robe but he didn't wear a mask. As he had with Mother months ago, he explored and probed and occasionally leaned back and stared in silence, as if considering. The room was bright with fluorescent light. Marie stared at the white tiled ceiling but saw nothing. She hadn't yet felt any pain and wondered whether it could be over already. Or had he even begun? Why was he simply staring?

He leaned in close between her legs and pushed her thighs apart, and touched her. She shut her eyes tight and suddenly remembered.

Father Pheley. The last time she'd been in a church.

Something entered her and she struggled to control her panic. She'd got herself into real trouble this time. It seemed to go on forever, and she was beyond thinking. This was not what she had wanted for herself, none of this had ever been in her plans. Somehow she'd been incautious and now her only salvation was in someone else's hands. Literally.

There. Now it was beginning to hurt.

"Just be calm."

She clutched her hands together, covered her face with them, began to gulp air.

"A minute more. Just a minute more . . ."

She yelped with pain, and suddenly felt the warm trickle of her own blood.

"There." He sighed and leaned back. "It's done. You can go home, Marie. You can rely on my discretion."

She stood and wiped tears from her eyes. He gave her tissue and she wiped herself. Sobbing, she put her pants on.

"Can I rely on yours?" He wiped his forehead and put his robe back on.

She left the cathedral in tears, as many penitents do. Her sins were many and grievous and she didn't understand them. Nor did she understand her penance. But she would never again go to confession, and since she cried hysterically whenever Mother asked her to, eventually Mother stopped asking.

The money meant nothing to him, but Dr. Hyde asked Father for it anyway. Father sighed and handed over the cash. He helped Marie with her coat and steadied her with his arm as they left.

Marie had lost both Hubert and his child but she was still burdened by his things, just as Mother had been with Angus's. She stood in his dark basement apartment with the ceiling pressing down on her. Just weeks ago the squalor had been invisible to her, immaterial and so unnoticed. But now, because something had to be done with his few belongings, she was forced to confront them. She tried to think what she might do with a hard, soiled cloth couch, a lumpy single bed and its sleeping-bag spread, a cracked plastic radio and his scattered laundry.

This was where they'd made their secret plans together. That bed was where they'd shaken the world, and each other. In the dresser drawers she found his notebooks and pens. In the closet she found stacked boxes of photocopied pamphlets and manifestos. Open letters to the press, the people and the prime minister; calls to arms, denunciations and revisionist histories of Quebec. They were signed with the rhetorical names of their committees, their cells, their organization. But in fact they represented the collected works of Hubert Lacasse.

Marie left behind the broken furniture but by default she was now the leader of her cell—it was the least she owed to her former comrade and lover, for dying in silence like a hero, like a martyr—and so she couldn't leave his papers, the record of his work and life.

But she couldn't allow them to be found in her possession, either, and when she returned to the attic at home where she'd been sleeping, she found the perfect place to hide them. She emptied her brother's boxes of chapbook poetry and filled them again with Hubert's pamphlets. She covered the top layers of manifestos with some of the original stapled booklets, closed the boxes and sat staring at the surplus on the floor.

What were these decaying sheaves of paper but a wasted youth? Cartons full of them had sat alone in the attic for years, since Jean-Baptiste had first begun printing them as an adolescent. Marie knew that some had never left their boxes. Jean-Baptiste had printed, collated and stapled his pamphlets in a rush of enthusiasm generated by the self-love his latest outpourings had caused. But then, panting in the afterglow, he'd come to realize their inadequacies, their emotionalism, their pretensions. Deflated, he'd simply shut the lids and let the paper moulder under the eaves like clothes he'd outgrown.

Jean-Baptiste would never notice how Marie had substituted someone else's writings for his because he never opened these boxes any more. And Marie rid herself of his excess poems by lining her coat pockets with them and smuggling them out of the house unnoticed. She smiled and thought of the irony: that it was she who was taking them out of the house. He'd never dared cross the threshold with them, and here she was, introducing them to the world.

And what did she do with them? She dropped them one by one into trash cans as she walked by, or balled them up and tossed them into the sewer. Or she'd heave a handful into the path of an oncoming snow blower. So they settled in place beside candy wrappers and old newspapers or bobbed on the half-frozen surface of thick, black water, or they fell like the packed snow and ice into trucks bound for the Victoria Bridge, where the whole frozen load was dumped into the river and floated gradually out to sea.

It pained Marie to have the ideas and sentiments of a true Patriote hidden under the irrelevant pretensions of her airy and distant brother. But then, rather than doing Hubert's works any harm, maybe his would do her brother's some good.

And they did.

Angus was getting the hang of things. If it wasn't getting any easier, at least it was becoming a little more familiar. He knew he was out of place. He felt the presence of his own things in the house, but he couldn't find himself. He went to look elsewhere, on the mountain, with his wife. Where else should he be? He battled the winds careening around the slopes, lost his way more than once and then found himself before the headstone. Now it had his name on it too, not just his wife's. But he knew he wasn't there.

And neither was she, he suddenly realized. His wife's grave was empty.

He allowed the breeze to carry him away and lost concentration. He drifted back to the house, where his things were, where his family was.

There was Jean-Baptiste, cross-legged on the bed, scribbling away in his notebook. Angus waited, patiently he thought, but it seemed like forever. Everything seemed like forever, now. Finally Jean-Baptiste stopped writing and looked up. Right at him, Angus felt, and willed himself to shout.

But it was no use without a tongue, without vocal cords, without lungs. Jean-Baptiste didn't hear anything, couldn't see anything. His stare was blank, his eyes empty and unfocused, and it made Angus uncomfortable, as though his grandson were looking right through him, as if he couldn't see him at all.

He gave up.

Work had begun again for Grandfather and Uncle. It had been hard to pry Uncle out of his hibernation, but Grandfather was eager to get back to business. He felt a new strength with the snow clearing and the sun returning. He began to buy the newspaper again, to follow the obituaries. He kept his eye open for stories of tragic early deaths; youngsters were better, more profitable.

But Dr. Hyde greeted them with reluctance, something he'd never done before. Surely these specimens were just as good as ever? And weren't the medical students' exams coming up soon? Demand was always high in the spring, what could be wrong? Hyde paid them less and less, became more and more surly, and offered no explanation to their queries and complaints. A man couldn't risk what they were risking if it wasn't profitable. If there was something wrong with their deliveries, he should tell them. This way nobody was happy.

But how could Dr. Hyde have told them the truth? That it had been many years since he'd had to rely on their scavengings for his medical students—since the laws about unclaimed bodies, prisoners dying in custody and public donations of remains had been introduced in the forties. That he'd been paying for far more bodies than he'd ever had a use for, just to keep the supply coming, just to gather an organ here or a limb there that might be suitable for his experiments. Or, if providence smiled on him, for his ultimate project.

But now there was one single organ he still required, and he'd realized they'd never be able to provide him with a suitable one, no matter how many corpses they delivered, no matter how long they toiled in the darkness on his behalf.

At last they came to argue. Dr. Hyde's form was outlined in the door where he stood by the light shining out into the yard. They could barely see his face, but by his stance and his voice they knew he was troubled, and whatever it was came out as anger towards them.

"I've no more use for the dead," said Dr. Hyde. "Don't bring any more corpses, or I'll have you arrested."

Uncle grunted angrily. Grandfather said, "All right, Doctor. But the police would want to know why we'd come to sell them. Your reputation couldn't save you from scandal at least. We'd all be arrested."

Words flew back and forth in the heat of the argument, but they all knew none of them would talk to the authorities. In the end, after the anger was spent, Dr. Hyde sounded not just exhausted but almost despairing:

"There's only one thing I need."

What he needed was a miracle.

Aline was miserable. The winter had been long, the spring merely allowed the dog shit in the backyard to thaw, and she struggled with the idea of leaving not just Grandfather's room but the Desouche house. When she'd married, her father had moved into a smaller apartment, and now she was afraid to burden him again with her presence. He'd no money, either, except his meagre pension, and she knew that sometimes he'd been reduced to sharing the cat's dinner. She'd no reason to stay where she was except for Grace, and she couldn't impose herself and the bird on Papa and his cat.

But Grace began to get more lively as the days got longer, and louder too. Aline still fed her bread crumbs out of her hand, and spoke to her as her only friend. Grace responded with her cawing and screeching, and at times Aline felt it was quite musical. If only her voice were a little less strident, not so loud. She began responding to Grace's calls by imitating them but pitching them just a little lower, a little softer. It became a game for them, and a little amusement in Aline's bleak life. The back-and-forth cawing and chirping went on longer, just a little longer, as if Grace had caught on that Aline was talking to her. Occasionally Grace would begin the game unprompted. Aline was charmed, and joined her voice to the bird's.

Grace was teaching her to sing.

Jean-Baptiste was dizzy. He'd been inside the world of his own head for so long, had concentrated on every line of dialogue in his play so closely, had dreamt its action over and over and over again so many times, that as he looked up from his small desk at the room around him, he felt almost as if it had magically appeared out of nothing at all, and the real world of his imagination had dropped out of existence. How strange it was: the unmade bed, the papers and magazines stuffed between the pages of scattered books, the dirty plates and cups he'd never returned to the kitchen, the laundry piled in the corners.

He gathered the cups and plates and went down to the kitchen. It was dawn, and he and Grace had it to themselves. He washed the dishes, gave the crow some bread; he splashed water on his face, stretched, and looked out the kitchen door and up into the sky. It was the same sky, but now he was different.

He'd finished a play. He was a playwright.

It was a complete surprise; he'd never had the least interest in the theatre and had rarely even been, except for school trips as a child. He didn't even like Shakespeare. But now he was a playwright, he had a complete script sitting on his desk upstairs, and he knew it was good.

But what to do with it?

St. Joseph's, a spiritual sanctuary like any other, had no locks on its chapel doors. It would be unthinkable to prevent a supplicant in need of solace from obtaining it. It would prove too shallow an opinion of the Lord's children to fear any might be tempted by God's material riches. It would be a miracle if anyone could, after climbing all those steps, have strength enough left to carry anything off.

Panting with the exertion before the great double doors, Grandfather and Uncle sat on the threshold to get their breath back and lit cigarettes while they were waiting. Across Queen Mary Road, at the foot of the hill they were on, lay the grey stone Jesuit college where Frère André had stared at the spot where they were now sitting and dreamt of the church they were soon to enter. The church where he was entombed and wherein lay, appropriately enough, his very heart.

Inside, before the heart itself, they found themselves alone with Frère André. Others were praying in the chapel, under the dome of the great altar, at Frère André's tomb itself and even in the original small wooden chapel behind the oratory. But here in the museum of the thaumaturge of Montreal, they were alone except for the presence, in the three display cases, of mannequins representing the priest in his original settings. There in the leftmost case was his entire bedroom, the very floors, furnishings, windows and ceiling from across the street; while the rightmost case held the tiny hospital room in which he had died—including the very bed and his very sheets, hospital white and hospital crisp.

And in the central case, facing the display of his heart, was the office he'd occupied, with the counter from behind which he'd greeted and admitted all visitors, all the days of his life.

On originally seeing this replica, Grandfather had given a start, for there stood Frère André himself, as if welcoming him into the church, life-sized and black-robed, and staring across at his own preserved heart.

Now, again, Grandfather frowned nervously and identified the grim thought tickling the back of his mind, where his conscience had lain buried and undisturbed for so many years—that Frère André was watching.

Iron bars; red-tinted plate glass; art deco reliquary. Inside? A human heart abandoned by its owner more than half a century earlier, yet known to have shed blood only a few short years ago. Placed there with reverence for safekeeping. It looks, Grandfather thought, like a potato. A big, unwashed baking potato.

While Uncle kept guard, alternately watching each of the two corridors leading into this museum, Grandfather took his tools from his coat and began to work. He wet a small rubber suction cup with his tongue—a foul-tasting Host—and grimaced, and stuck it to the plate glass. He ground a circle around it with the wheel of a large glass cutter, and stopped nervously—there'd been a loud noise, an odd kind of shriek—but no one seemed to have heard, and Uncle nodded him back to work.

He took out a rubber mallet and wondered if he hadn't just felt a warm breath upon his neck. But turning, he saw no one behind him except the mannequin of Frère André in his case—behind his own plate of glass, where even if he were breathing, surely his exhalations wouldn't penetrate the glass. Grandfather put his hand to the back of his neck. Was that condensation he'd spied on the inner surface of the glass, just below the mannequin's nostrils?

Of course not.

He held the cup in one hand, and smacked the glass a blow with the mallet. A hollow ringing; the plate trembled in its frame, settled, and let go the circle beneath the cup. Grandfather gently pried it away and set it on the floor.

Stupid. He'd not made the hole big enough to snatch the reliquary through. His own heart raced through a few beats.

"Hurry up!" hissed Uncle.

Grandfather put his whole arm into the hole, pressed his body and face against the glass. He began slashing the window of the reliquary in quick strokes, thinking to cut it out of its frame like a painting, and grab the bare heart itself.

It wasn't easy, single-handed. The glass was cold against his cheek; he couldn't directly see what he was doing and was forced to glance sideways at his handiwork. Of course, he couldn't see out of his left eye at all; it was covered by the patch. Damn that crow.

"What's keeping you?" came Uncle's voice, nervous and angry.

Grandfather lifted the patch from his left eye. It didn't really help much, considering he was trying to look through his own head with it.

Suddenly, Grandfather seized up. His heart had been stabbed by a needle, his left arm dealt an electric shock and his left eye—the glass eye—bit into his brain at the rear of his eye socket.

Frère André had sat down.

What the hell am I doing here? Grandfather thought suddenly. He found himself trembling. His knees were wavering dangerously, and he was supporting himself by leaning his armpit into the glass. He felt perspiration collect on his forehead and begin a slow trickling.

Warm. It was as warm here as it was at home.

Uncle came to get him. "Aren't you done yet?—Christ!" He rushed to catch Grandfather, who was slipping to the floor.

He tried to help himself by catching the lip of the hole as his arm slid out of it, but suddenly his body was very heavy and he hadn't the strength. He tried to reach the ground with his left hand before he fell to it, but somehow his left arm just hung there, like meat.

Grandfather began to cry. He didn't understand why. And it wasn't tears—if he'd felt any pain, he might expect a few tears—but he was sobbing as Uncle caught him and held him up, and he was as astonished and angry at himself as Uncle seemed to be, and realized, as Uncle swore at him and slapped him across the face, that he approved entirely. He would have done the same himself if he could, he thought in that moment. "That's right. Slap me again. Bastard."

And suddenly they were not alone.

What the priest and the janitor accompanying him saw was an elderly man in the throes of a heart attack being roughed up by an unsavoury character.

Both Uncle and Grandfather were speechless. Caught.

The priest took over Grandfather and sent the janitor flying to call an ambulance. As he was being dragged away, Grandfather regained his voice, and began shouting back to Uncle, "The heart! The heart!"

The priest attempted to calm him. "We've sent for an ambulance, you'll be all right, my son."

Uncle picked up the mallet and smashed the plate glass, and took the reliquary from its pedestal. He threw it to the stone floor and it sprang apart. Frère André's heart rolled onto the cold floor, under the gaze of the mannequin.

Uncle gathered it up, thrust it into his coat pocket and left.

Shocked, the priest crossed himself and murmured in Latin; he briefly thought he should chase the thief, but stayed with Grandfather instead. When the ambulance and the police arrived, he explained to the older cop and his rookie partner that Grandfather had been roughed up by some thug who'd stolen the sacred relic. The older cop looked quizzically at Grandfather, but wrote up his report according to what he was told.

So Grandfather ended up in the hospital again. A heart attack, they told him.

"No," he said. "Not me."

The attending physician explained to him just exactly what the classic symptoms and signs were, and how they matched exactly Grandfather's experience and condition.

"Hogwash."

The resident produced Grandfather's X-rays and charts and showed him where the damage was and how his cardiovascular system had been affected.

"Quackery. Smoke and mirrors. You know nothing about bodies. I know about bodies. Don't bother me with your mumbo-jumbo."

As he explained to Dr. Hyde, when his old business partner and family physician arrived to take over the case, "I let them bring me over in the ambulance just for show. It was a good diversion. Uncle's got the goods, speaking of hearts. And have you brought me any cigarettes?"

"We can't allow smoking in intensive care," said Hyde, and pointed to the frail woman under the oxygen tent.

Grandfather grunted and demanded, "When can I leave?"

"Well," said Dr. Hyde, "you did have an incident. I think you should stay a little while longer."

"I didn't have no heart attack. I'm as strong as a horse."

"Did your left arm go numb?"

"Yes, a little."

"Any pain in the chest?"

". . . yes. Heartburn."

"And you fell to the floor."

"It was just the shock of realizing that bastard was watching me all along."

The doctor started. "Which bastard would that be? You were seen?"

"Frère André."

"Oh. Anyway, I can't let you out."

Grandfather's eyes narrowed. "Listen, Hyde, I've got things to do." Which was a lie, really, but who wants to be stuck in a hospital ward?

"I, too, have things to do. I'm also held back by circumstances beyond my control."

"I see. My son will be here with the item soon enough. Tomorrow."

"Excellent. After looking over your results and examining you myself, I'm inclined to think that perhaps you haven't suffered a heart attack."

"That's what I said."

"But even though your case is probably not serious, in view of your age and your recent operation, I'd like you to stay for observation until, say, your son comes to collect you. I believe you may have had an exclusionary pulmonary deflation."

"What the hell is that?"

"A case of the vapours. You can go home tomorrow."

To Uncle's great disgust, Frère André's heart bled into his pants pocket, and many people stared in shock at him on his way home.

The heart had been bleeding since the reliquary was broken and it rolled out onto the floor. Perhaps it was the shock of the impact, or perhaps it was the contact with the air. Whatever it was, the heart continued to produce the thick, sticky liquid.

The heart wasn't really pumping blood. It was, more precisely, secreting the fluid, as an ice cube gives up water in the heat. Except that the heart was not growing any smaller with the effort. And it wasn't exactly beating, but it did seem to be somehow animate. It was more like a kind of undulation or a rippling, an uneven and irregular pulsing.

In any case, it was a problem for Uncle. He couldn't wait to get rid of it. In the meantime, he would've liked to simply lay it in the sink and let its sickly blood drip down the drain. But he couldn't let the others see it. So he placed it in an old zinc pail in his room, where it attracted flies whose buzzing annoyed him. He swatted them away from his face just as Grandfather had done when pestered by Grace, and finally went down to the kitchen and took the family fly swatter from under the sink.

When he returned to his room, he found his dog lapping at the pail. He poured the blood into the toilet. He was awoken twice overnight by the sound of the dog's tongue, and he swatted it away from the pail with a groggy curse. Through his dreary gaze it seemed to him that the dog had grown lighter-coloured and was now a mere pale shade of its former self: a ghost.

In the morning his black Labrador was a golden retriever, and its muzzle and tawny coat were flecked with burgundy droplets. It was bright-eyed and energetic, and Uncle's usual thundering curses and blows could do nothing to quell its puppyish behaviour.

Later, when he was carrying the pail and its contents—still excreting its viscous fluid, still quivering at the bottom of the bucket like some hapless, limbless frog—up the hill to Dr. Hyde, his dog refused to be left behind. It was following not him, he realized, but the pail. When it filled with blood he'd empty it into the gutter and walk on ahead, leaving his dog drinking at the curb. By the time he'd reached the corner of Pine and University, the main entrance of the Royal Vic, he noticed his dog was now albino, and its only remaining colour was the identical red of its eyes and of the blood on its muzzle. He emptied the pail once more. Passing motorists stared at this ghastly sight of a white dog, a bucket of blood and an ill-kempt man.

He continued up the hill of Pine Avenue towards the Allen Memorial, Dr. Hyde's institution. As he turned up the driveway he emptied the pail one last time and looked back for his ghostly dog, but it had disappeared.

SIX

THE INFLUENCE OF A PLAY

In the spring Marie organized a propaganda campaign. It would help keep her cell together, give them a sense of still accomplishing something now that Hubert was gone. Under cover of darkness, they crept along in ones and twos with pockets full of his folded tracts, and slipped them into mailboxes at random. They chose a different neighbourhood each time, in a different part of town, and a different night of the week, in an attempt to avoid falling into a pattern—a pattern was nothing more than a web to be caught in. This unpredictability also allowed Marie to choose the right moment for pamphleteering, when it might best bolster their flagging morale.

For the most part their feuilletons were ignored along with the rest of the junk mail people received. Except that it made some immigrants and anglophones nervous, and they complained to the newspapers and police.

And of course Hubert's politics were inadvertently mixed with Jean-Baptiste's poetry, and some puzzled people thought again how odd poets are, handing out verse door to door. Obscure and terrible verses which, for Christ's sake, didn't even rhyme.

But one man was struck by Jean-Baptiste's unusually direct dramatic words, and by the bravery of a poet who'd distribute his works door to door in the same neighbourhood and at the same time as the felquistes were making the rounds with their propaganda.

Now this man was a teacher of drama at a local college, and artistic director of his own theatrical company.

The Desouches' door was always open so as to let out the heat, but it didn't seem to be working, and had the disadvantage of allowing all visitors a presumed right of access. Professor Woland blew in like a hot breath through a damp scarf, stuffy and stifling. He paraded through the house as if whomever he might encounter would instantly recognize him, and his celebrity would by divine right make the house his own. He jaunted into the front parlour and encountered Mother in her repose. He stopped; he was disappointed there was no conscious soul he could overwhelm with his greeting. He frowned and brought his fist to his chin, stepped back into the hallway and called his greeting before him as he proceeded to the interior.

"Hello, hello. It's Woland. Professor Woland."

But the living room was empty. He heard the clank of dishes and turned towards the kitchen.

Aline was surprised by the sound of an unfamiliar voice, so obviously inside her house. She dropped a plate into the sink and went to see, drying her hands on a dishcloth as she went.

"Ah, miss," began Woland, as they almost collided in the doorway. But he couldn't continue, because Aline shrieked in shock.

Grace responded, cawing and screeching and fluttering about the ceiling; Aline jumped back.

Now Woland was shocked, by the noise of the two and their quick, frantic, purposeless movements.

"I'm so sorry, miss, I didn't mean to scare you." Woland was not happy. This wasn't turning out the great whirlwind of an entrance he was hoping for.

"Mais qui êtes-vous? Qu'est-ce que vous voulez?" Aline was angry. She'd been frightened by this stranger, and he had the nerve to walk about her home like it belonged to him. And he couldn't even speak to her in French.

Woland began feeling defensive. "Uhm, I'm looking for Jean-Baptiste."

This calmed Aline a little; perhaps he was some friend of her grandson's. Still, he was quite rude. She had a chance now to look at him for the first time. He was a tall man, and thin. He wore a light grey jacket, tight, with matching pants; black shiny shoes; black leather gloves; a blue tie rather like a cravat; and a small, high black hat. He had a pencil moustache and, somewhere, she suspected, a monocle on a ribbon. This was a friend of Jean-Baptiste's?

The commotion attracted Father, who stood now in the hall behind Woland. "What is it? Who are you?"

Woland turned to him gratefully. "Ah, sir, I'm looking for Jean-Baptiste. I understand he lives here?"

Father considered this question, which seemed to throw doubts on Professor Woland's legitimacy. If he was a friend, surely he'd know whether Jean-Baptiste lived here or not. Still . . . "Are you a friend of his?"

"Not exactly," began Woland.

"Then who the hell are you?" Father exploded. "Haven't you heard of doorbells?"

"Well, the door was open." Woland was beginning to feel the heat, and loosened his cravat.

"For Christ's sake. Your mouth's open, shall I put my fist in it?"

Woland was baffled by this fury. Somehow, he'd lost the authority he'd been planning to claim here. He'd never gotten the chance to assert it. All his day-dreams of sweeping the household, whomever it might contain, off its feet and into his plans vanished. The crow was still flying around, dangerously close, thought Woland.

"If I might just see Jean-Baptiste," Professor Woland rallied. A bad start, yes, but no reason not to sally forth. A few proper steps and he could put this unfortunate beginning behind him, get to the business at hand and still probably win the day.

"Oh. Whom shall I say is calling?" asked Father, with a false deference.

Woland pulled himself up. He was sure his next words were going to change everything. After this, he'd be back in his dreams. "My name is Woland. Of the Black Snow Theatre Company."

Father grunted. He walked slowly back down the hall to the foot of the stairs and, while Woland watched expectantly, shouted up:

"Jean-Baptiste! Some fairy from a theatre to see you."

"It's the oddest thing," said Jean-Baptiste. "I just finished writing this play last week. How did you know?"

"A play? Excellent! Just what I was hoping. Let me have a look at it."

"Well, I have to have it typed."

"Let me see." Woland grasped the book from Jean-Baptiste's hands and began flipping through its pages. At last he turned back to the front and began to read. He stood holding the book and his walking stick in the same hand, absently pacing in the room, nodding and "Hmm"-ing as Jean-Baptiste, who sat on his bed, could only wonder, stupefied, how indeed this man came to be calling for his play. Out of the blue.

"Of course it's just the first draft," said Jean-Baptiste.

"Yes, yes. I'm so glad you realize it," said Woland. "You wouldn't believe how many writers refuse to change anything. But no, no, I wouldn't worry if I were you. This is very good. Needs work, it's not yet a play, it's just words here on paper, but already I sense the potential."

"Good."

"Let me take this away and read it, and we'll meet again next week. You'll come down to my office, we'll have a nice coffee."

"I still have to type it," said Jean-Baptiste tentatively.

"Oh, your handwriting's perfectly legible." Woland put the notebook into his inside jacket pocket.

"Excuse me," said Jean-Baptiste, "but that's the only copy."

"Is it? I'll be careful, then. I'll make you a copy myself, at the office. Come by on Tuesday and I'll have a photocopy for you, and we can chat longer then. I'll read this on the weekend, but already I can tell we're going to work together."

"If it's all the same to you, I'd like the original book back." Jean-Baptiste held out his hand.

Woland shook it. "Oh, of course, how stupid of me. Tuesday, then, say eleven-thirty? Perhaps we'll have lunch." And Woland practically ran out of the room, flew down the stairs and disappeared into the street.

Woland threw the photocopy on the desk. Jean-Baptiste's heart sank as he saw that many lines of dialogue had been crossed out with wide strokes of a black marker. He knew this was going to happen.

Woland handed back Jean-Baptiste's notebook. He opened it and flipped a few pages. What he saw shocked him.

"What the hell is this?" he nearly screamed. Frantically he flipped through the notebook page by page. And on virtually every one of the pages, one or more lines had been obliterated with a thick black marker.

"Those are some corrections I've made."

"You've crossed them out!"

Woland shrugged. He'd seen this kind of reaction from writers before. As if they thought they knew something he didn't. "Sometimes a deletion is a correction."

"But you've erased my words. My words!"

"Calm yourself. Words are our common property. You don't own the language."

Jean-Baptiste threw down the notebook. "*This* language I do. Words I write down are mine. You've no right to delete them."

"I thought you understood there'd be work to do."

"You don't just erase the first draft! Changes, yes, but for God's sake, make the damned photocopy before you erase the words."

"But my dear boy, then we'd have two different scripts. How would we work together on the revisions?"

"Revisions?"

"Yes, of course. You must rewrite much of it according to my direction. And I can pay you nothing."

"What? Why should I agree? What do I get from such an arrangement?"

"Simply that I will produce your play. Your name will appear on it and you will have this credit. It will begin your career."

"And why rewrite? And which parts? Why not use my own words?"

"First of all, you have too many characters. We'll have to lose many of them. Actors cost money, you know. And you'll have to cut out these words entirely. You cannot say these words on the stage."

"I hear them on television."

"Perhaps. But the theatre is high art, and in high art we don't have every character begin or end every exclamation with a blasphemous expression."

"How about *merde*?"

"*Merde* is fine. We'll just switch all these *tabernac*s and *calice*s for *merde*. Shit has been acceptable onstage for over a hundred years."

And that's the way it went, for weeks. Woland demanded cuts and changes that baffled Jean-Baptiste, which convinced him Woland was a complete idiot who understood nothing. For his part, Woland made free with the play as if it were his own and continually insisted he was older, wiser and more experienced in the theatre than the young playwright. But Jean-Baptiste had to admit that at least there was nothing personal in these attacks and changes: he was often surprised when, at rehearsals, after a particularly fine scene had been played out, Woland would rise and berate the actors.

"No, no, no! Don't you understand what you're saying? Stop jumping on your lines, let the audience absorb them! Don't look downstage as you come in, you idiot!"

Nevertheless, the time came when he had to argue.

"You've completely made a hash of it. You've taken out all the transitional scenes."

"They were unnecessary, Jean-Baptiste."

"It doesn't make any sense without them. They were some of the best scenes."

"It doesn't matter. The audience will understand better what your play is about if we cut through the explanations and let the characters get on with it."

"But now it's too short, for one thing."

Woland heaved a sigh. And then, as if by magic, he said the one thing that could possibly have shut Jean-Baptiste up. "It's not about how long it is, is it? Is that why we're here? Look, son, you're a big admirer of Artaud, aren't you? Well, what did he say? No more masterpieces, right? Stop hanging on to your favourite scenes as if they're the best scenes. They're not even what the play's about. What we need is a play that will startle people, one that jabs in the gut. Right? Theatre of cruelty? I know it's hard for a writer, but liberate yourself from the text and see what's going on onstage. Okay?"

There was nothing for Jean-Baptiste to do but surrender; even though he couldn't bring himself to feel right about it.

On opening night Marie volunteered to stay home and care for Mother so that Father might see the premiere of his son's play with the rest of the family.

"I almost wish you wouldn't come," Jean-Baptiste said to them. "I think maybe it stinks."

Father was excited, happy and proud. "If it stank, they wouldn't put it on, would they?"

"Sure they would," offered Uncle.

So Jean-Baptiste sat in the front row, with Uncle and Grandfather on one side, and Father and Aline on the other. He was trembling as the audience took their seats: people actually showed up. Then he realized, of course, all the actors have family too. By the time the lights went down, he was soaking wet.

As the curtain rose a light appeared in the upper left corner of the stage, glowing yellowly. It grew brighter until the audience recognized it as a cross shining down from a mountain. The set was in forced perspective and looked as much like something from *The Cabinet of Dr. Caligari* as anything the audience perceived as a local geographical feature. From stage right two characters appeared, dressed in rags, bent over from the effort of pulling behind them a large chest, which might even have been a coffin. One carried a sack, the other a spade.

Grandfather's heart squeezed itself; Uncle hissed in the darkness. Father shifted uncomfortably, and Aline burst into sobbing tears. The rest of the audience assumed she was supplying atmosphere.

A sinking feeling developed in Jean-Baptiste's stomach.

Onstage, the two characters were silent. The chest was obviously genuinely too heavy for them to lift. It scraped across the stage and up the painted set; the actors were struggling, breathing heavily.

The closer they got to the top, the steeper the slope became, and the narrower the path they could take. It was, after all, not really a mountain but only a low sloping platform. The painted perspective began to look ridiculous: the chest didn't really get any smaller or further away. Finally, the huge box dwarfed the tiny shining cross. With a last desperate effort, the two actors pushed the chest over the crest of the hill. The audience heard the bulbs smashing as the light disappeared.

In the darkness, finally, an actor spoke:

"What was in it, anyway?"

"Nothing. It was empty."

"Why was it so heavy, then?"

"I don't know."

When the lights came up again, Father was no longer quite so proud. It had nothing to do with whether the play was any good or not. As far as that went, Father'd hardly noticed. But how could Jean-Baptiste have mocked his family so?

How could he have paraded them in front of the public? How dare he?

Father turned to Jean-Baptiste beside him. "What the hell is this?"

In act two, civil war had broken out. A barricade had been thrown up to protect what might be a hospital, a government building or even a prison. The actors were using real guns loaded with blanks, and the audience was going deaf. Styrofoam bricks were flying back and forth when the hero appeared, crawling, holding up a white cloth, waving it about as he approached the line of defence. The defenders ignored it, shooting wildly at him, pelting him with whatever came to hand. Since the props didn't harm him, he made it to the barricade and climbed over. Atop, he was met by a defender who held him back.

"You're not crossing this line, brother," he declared in a thick French accent.

"But I must get through. My mother's dying!"

"Don't worry. No one dies in English here."

At the end of act three the splinter group of murdering terrorists, who had been robbing graves to support the revolution, were now trapped by the police. When they began to fight among themselves, Woland himself, dressed as the devil and laughing maniacally, rode in a flying canoe across the stage and rained turds down on them as the curtain dropped.

The Desouches sat staring wordlessly at the stage as the actors took their bows and the audience politely applauded. They rose and shuffled out without comment. They wouldn't look at Jean-Baptiste, and made their way out of the theatre without caring whether he joined them or not. He followed behind worriedly, like a chastised dog afraid of being abandoned.

⚜

Although Woland had taken out ads in the papers, invited all the anglo critics, phoned and faxed all the media, and tried to drum up as much publicity as possible, as usual only a handful of people showed up for the premiere. The play got mixed but unenthusiastic reviews, and it seemed as if they'd all go home at the end of the week and forget all about it. For Jean-Baptiste it was a disappointment, but he wasn't happy with the final script anyway and felt the production had been uninspired. He consoled himself with feeling that at least he'd started. At least one production was done. He'd been written up in the papers even if only lukewarmly, and from now on he could refer to this experience as granting him some kind of entree into the world of the arts. An item on the resumé, if nothing else.

He did get invited, on the strength of it, to read some poetry at a monthly gathering in a bar on St-Laurent; and that was all the gravy he could really expect, he told himself. The play had led to something else. This second item, no matter how insignificant, also counted. He saw before him an endless succession of small steps leading off into a murky and ill-defined distance. But at least there was a path.

And then, on a slow week, noticing that the author's name was in fact French, the drama critic of the French-language daily *L'Obligation* came to see the Thursday evening show. His review was printed in the Friday edition and that evening the crowd was doubled. Woland was pleased; if this meant they could expect even a half-house on Saturday,

BLACK BIRD

193

anything at all on the Sunday shows would come near the mark of at least covering expenses. He was jubilant before the performance that night, springing around backstage and waving his walking stick in the air.

The cast was tired, had been disillusioned all week before near empty houses. They were fed up with the moody, irritable Woland himself, and they were weary of a play which through its failure with the public had let them down.

But something happened that night. The audience was charged; many had come not because the latest review pronounced it good, but because it hinted at something scandalous. Throughout the first act there was a smattering of laughter, and the cast was energized: they were being liked. Act two began to sing on its own, and the entrances and exits were crisp and sharp. The audience leaned forward with a new appreciation. There was a tension onstage, something happening between those people up there, and what were they going to do?

For the first time, the lines were delivered in the passion with which they had been written. The actors began to hear the words coming from their own mouths. Suddenly an offhand sarcastic remark took on a new significance, and when the protagonist turned away from the other actors to look out over the audience, the gesture was now full of import, the play was carried off in a new direction.

When the curtain rang down on act two, the audience realized with a start they were sitting in a theatre, and they had been enthralled. Their hands came together in true appreciation, and behind the curtain, the flushed actors could hear a woman in the first row say to her companion, "My God, what do you think's going to happen?"

The audience waited nervously for the denouement; the actors breathlessly changed costumes and shifted some furniture about onstage. Woland was jubilant. "This is the night. This is it."

The curtain rose on a hushed expectation. The protagonist entered, but then ran off left. No one cleared their throat; no one shifted in their seat. The actors began a slow dance towards the climax of the play, and though the words were coming from their throats by rote, they shared the physical tension of the audience and told themselves, under the lines they were delivering, Breathe slowly, relax your muscles. And even they began to wonder where exactly the play was going. Was this a tragedy they were performing? Yes, there was a heightened emotion present. But was it mere melodrama, would it all be burst by some unexpected comedy lurking somewhere in the wings? An actor heard his cue and moved about the stage in a predefined sequence, speaking his lines all the while, and wondered: have I just said that?

Suddenly, a wailing broke out. The noises offstage rose to a thunderous crescendo. The protagonist lowered her gaze from the heavens. Her face took on a look of dread as a horrible certainty gripped her, like a blow from an uncertain and frightening world. A turd fell to the stage. Another, beside her. As the lights faded, more fell, in increasing numbers as the final curtain rang down.

Half the audience rose spontaneously and began the applause.

But then, as the curtain rose again for the cast to take their bows, began a lowing as if of cattle. By the time the star of the show stepped to the centre of the stage, it was clearly booing.

It grew. Nervously the cast took their bows, looking with puzzlement into the stalls. What had happened?

The chorus of booing increased. A few brave souls were still applauding, trying to win the day for their approval, but it was no use. The disaffected had won the field. Many were leaning forward into their disparagement, cupping their hands around their mouths like funnels for the noise: BOOOO!

They began to throw their programs back up to the stage; some were torn and merely thrown in the air. An argument broke out in the lobby, but the critics were stronger, louder, more vehement than the supporters.

Distraught, the cast sat backstage and wondered: What went wrong? But Woland was still happy. In fact, he was ecstatic, for now, once word of this got around, they'd surely sell out the remaining performances.

And they did. They sold out the theatre for Saturday, Sunday matinee and evening. And each time, nothing but booing and catcalling, with garbage of all sorts thrown to the stage. Which of course only disrupted the actors, who naturally turned in terrible performances. There was still laughter, but it was no longer innocent: it was the punishing laughter of derision.

"Don't look so glum, Jean-Baptiste," said Woland. "Your name is made!"

Who began the booing? Marie.

Marie had been impressed with the reaction her brother's play had generated in their family. When they returned that first evening none of them would really tell her much of what they'd seen. Father seemed struggling to contain his anger, his face red and pursed when he thought of the play, and could only bring himself to erupt with, "He's betrayed us."

Aline was still puffy-eyed and began weeping anew as she climbed the stairs. "It's not that he said these things," she said. "It's that they're true." And she blew her nose.

Grandfather shrugged and said, "The little bastard used us. I hope he makes some money." And he strode down the hall to the kitchen, lighting a cigarette.

Mother was the single remaining member of his family with whom Jean-Baptiste was on speaking terms—and she slept.

What, Marie thought, could be in this play?

She laughed at the destruction of the cross in act one; she assented to the reality of the coming physical struggle in act two; she was offended by the existential epiphany, the realization that the struggle for ideals was as corrupt, hollow and egotistical as any revolution— Russian, French, American; but she was enraged, furious, livid, by the denouement: the FLQ betrayed their own ancestors and sold their souls to the devil.

Marie booed.

She informed her colleagues. Incredulous upon seeing that what she'd told them was true, it was they who'd instigated the booing that first night.

And the placard-carrying protests the second.

On that Sunday morning, his birthday, Jean-Baptiste sat waiting in silence with his mother. As one by one the family moved about the house without making any overture to him, he gave up anticipating any presents. He was no happier than the audiences had been about his play, but he went to the theatre anyway, since he was not welcome at home. Sent to Coventry.

Still, "This is your day, my boy," announced Woland. "Your name day. It's your birthday as well, isn't it? Well, I have a present for you: I'm extending the run. Today's performance will not be the last."

"But the crowd boos every night. They throw things at the actors."

"Awh, the actors can take it."

"I don't think I can."

"The theatre has been full for days. Packed. We're sold out both shows today, and the phone keeps ringing. Tomorrow we'll be dark, but we'll do at least another full week. Maybe longer."

Jean-Baptiste was angry. "But they're only coming to boo."

"Let them. If they're paying for the tickets, let them boo. Remember, Molière was booed. Jarry,

Cocteau, Sartre. You're in good company. We'd be crazy to close the show. What a splendid day."

St-Jean-Baptiste Day was always a time of high nationalist sentiment. During the bright afternoon's cheery parade, members of Marie's cell worked the crowds thronging the parade route on rue St-Denis, handing out denunciations of her brother's play—and pointing out how conveniently located the dilapidated theatre was, mere blocks away on St-Laurent.

And so with enough heat, enough beer and enough bravado generated by a flag-waving agent provocateur, a small delegation of louts spontaneously dispatched itself from the main route, detoured to the Sunday matinee and stormed the theatre in the middle of act two.

They broke windows out front and burst through the door shouting and spilling beer. A puzzled audience looked from the stage, where a bastion was being stormed by a single crawling anglophone with a white flag, to these boisterous intruders and wondered if this were all part of the performance.

But when the gatecrashers dealt some unlucky audience members a few quick and painful blows, fights began to break out, and the actors all fled in terror. Woland called the police and the sirens sent the Patriotes running. But by this time a few were laid out with injuries sustained in the attack, and others were drunk enough to be easy even for Montreal police to run down.

Only Marie escaped.

The ugliness and humiliation of having her friends arrested on their own national holiday, while celebrating their ideals and dreams, was simply too great an irritation for Marie to endure. To have been chastised and put down by their own police force, their own brothers! It was unspeakable. They were being suppressed openly now, for the crime of clamouring for their own freedoms, for their own rights.

It was a bitter pill for Marie to swallow, that her brother was so firmly lined up on the other side—les autres—even though he denied it. It was infuriating that it was her real brothers—her brothers-in-arms—who'd been arrested.

She was furious; she doubled over in a cramp; she bled into the toilet. Our blood is being flushed away, into the toilet, she thought. Something must be done.

"It's clearly a fantasy," said Jean-Baptiste. "Can't anyone see that?"

"Ah, you've touched a nerve, my boy," said Woland. "Stick with me and I'll make you famous."

"God, you're making me infamous. Half of what my family objects to wasn't even in my play when I wrote it. If this is fame, you can have it."

"How about wealth?" asked Woland.

Hubert lay in a private operating theatre surrounded by machines to which he was connected by tubing and wiring. His chest rose and fell. Now he had a new set of lungs which breathed by themselves. His left hand grasped the rail of the hospital bed like a baby's.

Just how does the heart connect to the brain? wondered Dr. Cameron Hyde. Is it a real, physical connection? Does this connection get stronger or weaker with age? Is this connection itself the answer to the search, the seat of the soul?

Could there be a soul at all? Does it need to occupy a space? If you lose, say, a finger, do you lose a part of your soul?

He carried the shuddering lump of meat in gloved hands to the operating table. Hubert's chest was held open by a device like an animal trap in reverse: a rib spreader. Hubert was breathing but he knew it not. And he was thinking, after a fashion, but with so much of his original brain gone, his synapses pulsed at the ends of broken chains like water pouring from the exposed pipes of a ruined building after an earthquake: pointlessly, wastefully.

Never again would he be able to close an argument, to wrap up a discussion, to come full circle and conclude a thesis, even to himself. But if the life of the mind was no longer to be his, he would have something perhaps more important. Soon he would smile at children, be generous to the elderly and frail, be patient with the lonely and comforting to the distressed.

Hubert was getting a new heart.

Angus felt scattered. It wasn't right to be bodiless: he couldn't *do* anything.

BLACK BIRD

201

He suspected Grace knew he was there. She kept looking at him, clacking her beak and flying right at him. And out the other side, it seemed. Somehow it felt as if she were trying to get his attention, but when he responded she'd just ignore him, like the others. He tried to follow her down the hall but she sailed away as if she were trying to outrun him. If only he had wings, like hers; it must be nice to fly. He should have flown when he had the chance, he should have taken a vacation in some other country just for the excuse. He'd never get a chance now. The closest he'd ever got to flying was a vague memory, almost a dream, of a split second in which, as his head sailed into the sky, his torso tumbled into the street and his arms and legs ran off in four directions. He shook it off. He wanted to run that one in reverse, collect up those scattered parts of himself and take control once more, be able to act, wake his daughter, do anything at all.

The debacle at the theatre raised the controversy over the play from a sidelight on the entertainment pages to a major news story. "New Meaning to Jean-Baptiste Day," went the headline. As a result, Jean-Baptiste's poetry reading in a small café was mobbed. Nationalists came out in force to continue the denunciations, and Anglos flocked in to support their shrinking culture.

Although he was nervous and decidedly did not like the kind of attention he was getting, still Jean-Baptiste had the foresight to bring along some of his backlog of poetry chapbooks, in the unlikely event that he might sell a few. Originally he was to be only one of several people reading, but as the crowd refused to be silent for the other poets, they all skulked from the stage one by one and stood fuming by as Jean-Baptiste, formerly a totally unknown element in their coterie, commanded all the attention. At the bar they nursed their wounded egos and whispered to each other their scathing criticisms of this juvenile's infantile poetry.

And they were right: Jean-Baptiste was a terrible poet. Nevertheless, an audience knows what it likes— or what it hates—and why, and rarely does a poet's opinion count with the public. So Jean-Baptiste was alternately applauded by Anglos who'd never been to poetry readings before in their lives, and booed by francophones who couldn't totally grasp the sentiments of a romantic adolescent's extravagant English. But both were content with the opportunity of reacting in a particular manner for the sake of their political leanings, and consuming as much alcohol as possible in the meantime.

Woland was there, of course, championing his discovery and leading the applause with great shouts of "Bravo! Bravo!" Beside him was the journal editor who'd invited Jean-Baptiste, looking nervously about the bar, wishing this had turned out just another slow Wednesday night like all the previous readings. Especially since the local TV stations were videotaping the event, and now the entire city would think this was the calibre of the talent he approved of.

For Mrs. Pangloss a trip to Boulevard St-Laurent was a trip to another world, even though it was mere blocks from the Desouche house. It represented to her all the things she disliked about the world: foreigners, Jews, students, artists—those who were able most easily to best her in an argument. St-Laurent was the crossroads of Montreal, where East and West met, where immigrants from so many countries formed the safety zone between English and French. The street was a veritable babel of tongues, a profusion of unreadable signage and inscrutable merchants, peddlers, beggars. To be going to this Sodom on the St. Lawrence after dark was her own personal trip to purgatory. Mrs. Pangloss got off the bus at Park Avenue and stood looking eastward along Prince Arthur, to the darkness beyond the churches on opposite corners of Jeanne-Mance. Streetlights glittered in the distance.

It had been any number of years since Mrs. Pangloss had been in a bar, though she'd been a sprightly lass, even if she said so herself, in those years before marriage and ungrateful children had so ruthlessly left her a bloated and overperfumed housewife. And certainly the bars she'd frequented even then were not of this type at all: dank and rundown and painted in dark, filth-obscuring colours. In a word, *Bohemian*. That's what she thought as she looked about the crowded, smoky sub-basement on the Main. *Bohemian*, meaning artistic, romantic, even intellectual,

204

but somehow with that unspoken undertone of danger, of illicit activity, of free speech and free love—and, worse, freethinking. She was not unaware of the rebellious turn of the younger generations these past twenty years: the beatniks, the hippies, the drug-addicted yuppies. She was a parent, after all. Her own children too had resisted the wishes of their elders, had ignored all sensible advice. Had actually gotten married, taken credit cards, travelled to Europe.

And although Jean-Baptiste seemed to be following this new trend of shamefully repudiating his parents, her curiosity combined with her sense of duty towards his mother—that is, her duty to perform as a stand-in for her friend in her time of sickness—led her to this dubious den she'd otherwise never have glanced at.

She wondered whether poetry readings always drew such crowds. That certainly wasn't the impression she'd been given from television or the movies. The exposed brick walls, the cigarettes, the tight sweaters and long straight hair of the young women: these were things she expected, and it gave her comfort to find them here. But where were the berets and the guitars? Where was the poster of Che Guevara, and where the circle with the upside-down Y? Why was there so much beer and so little of that bitter espresso, and didn't anyone at all play those funny little drums in pairs?

And the crowd certainly didn't behave in the manner she expected. None of them seemed to be listening at all to Jean-Baptiste's poetry. She wondered if he knew he was being largely ignored. Was he soldiering on bravely in the face of the excited table talk going on around him? How could he not realize he might as well be talking to himself? And as for the audience, why weren't they listening in respectful silence, waiting for the proper moment to begin snapping their fingers appreciatively? She couldn't hear him at all.

No matter. She'd come to show her support, and if she wanted to see what his poems were about, she'd just pick up one of those little pamphlets they were selling after the reading. It was a shame, however, that so many of these drunken French louts kept shouting about maudit anglais and calling for Jean-Baptiste to read in French. Who did they think they were? If people chose to speak English, that was their business, wasn't it? It was still a free country, wasn't it? And where was the waiter with her crème de menthe?

Mrs. Pangloss had decidedly mixed feelings about the French. For one thing, there were two different kinds of French: there were those in France, and then there were the local pepsis. She would gigglingly refer to either group as "French pea-soups," and she certainly decried the foolishness of the youth of both camps: atheists, communists, troublemakers on campuses both at home and in France.

On the other hand, they were at least Catholics. And if the local pepsis were ignorant, loud-mouthed clods who didn't understand how much the English in Canada had done for them, at least they weren't the snobs their European cousins were. And give them credit: they understood living without, just as the Irish did (Mrs. Pangloss was proudly Irish and cultivated her temper to prove it), and if she had to point a finger (though mind you, it wasn't her habit to do something like that; she believed in letting people be and not casting any stones—glass houses and first sins and all that) she'd have gladly admitted that at least in Montreal, it wasn't these French peasants who were the snobs and hypocrites, it was rather those heathen Protestants of Westmount.

But lately this separation thing had been getting out of hand. It's one thing for a few kooks on the outside to make fools of themselves in public, marching with signs and disrupting people's lives. But now, with an actual separatist elected as premier, look what it was coming to. More and more of these people were taking over the newspapers and the radio stations, more and more of them were demanding a referendum, were daring to speak their minds in public. Even here, where poor little Jean-Baptiste was just trying to read his poetry. Why should they pick on him? Wasn't he allowed to be a poet?

Although, from what little Mrs. Pangloss could hear over the rising din, it didn't seem like anything was rhyming. Take it from her, if you wanted poetry, Robbie Burns was your man. Not like this modern stuff, either all about sex and body parts, or about God knows what, without rhyme or reason or any shape at all, and all too often all too personal, as if you were listening to confession instead of poetry. Not that it's bad for anyone to make a confession, but you see what happens without religion: public confession. It only proved the need for priests, after all.

After three crème de menthes and too much smoke blown at her from neighbouring tables, Mrs. Pangloss was decidedly in a bad mood. She still couldn't hear any poetry, and now it surely seemed like the incessant chattering amongst the French at all these tables was a deliberate tactic to keep Jean-Baptiste from being heard. Now that was almost sacrilegious: didn't he have the right to cleanse his soul, even if he was probably an atheist? Even if he didn't realize that's what he was doing? Who could claim the right to keep anyone from their God? Wasn't it a sin even to try?

Wherefore she would show them.

Mrs. Pangloss rose from her table and forced her way across the room. No one took any notice of her. The air was laden with cigarette smoke and the smell of cheap beer. Those at the front, near the stage, were doing their best to lead the hall in a filibuster of French to drown out the pariah onstage. The television crews were taping panning shots across the room, Woland was nervously contemplating once more calling in the police, and Jean-Baptiste, bewildered, was simply reading to himself.

Mrs. Pangloss reached the rear of the room, where Woland stood beside the table with Jean-Baptiste's boxes of poetry. She reached in to take one.

"Madame," said Woland. "That will be three dollars."

"Oh, no," said Mrs. Pangloss. "I'm a friend. He won't charge me."

Woland began to argue, but she ignored him. He shrugged. It wasn't his business, after all. She pulled a chair over and used it as a step to mount the table.

"Madame!"

She steadied herself on the wobbly surface. Was it the table, or her three drinks? No matter, she'd be all right in a second. A few faces were looking towards her in curiosity. She cleared her throat. She opened the pamphlet, and began to read.

Since she believed she was reading poetry, she started in an attempt to capture a kind of rhythm. She soon realized there was none; Jean-Baptiste was just like all the other contemporary poets. No respect for the traditions of his art, no sense of what's pleasing to the ear. She abandoned her attempt to force the words into an aural pattern, and thought it safer just to read them out as best she could.

Around her now, people were actually listening. Their chattering stopped, and a circle of attention opened up. She noticed she could hear herself speaking. She looked around and saw surprised faces staring at her. She continued.

By the time the audience had quieted enough for her to notice that the only other voice she could hear was Jean-Baptiste's at the opposite end of the room, Mrs. Pangloss finally realized she was reading in French. It seemed odd to her: she'd assumed Jean-Baptiste wrote in English. She was still too drunk to listen to her own voice—perhaps for the only time in her life—and would have been quite shocked at herself if she had.

Even the audience listening to her was shocked. Here was a drunken, aging anglo woman, publicly declaring, in a highly accented but perfect joual, a revolutionary separatist manifesto. Even Jean-Baptiste finally gave up reading and stood watching her in silence. The camera crews quickly swung into action and flooded her with light. She looked up dazed, but when someone in the audience cheered her on, she returned to the text. When she reached the part where she was declaring that we in the felquiste movement will never cease our struggle, by any means necessary, a few people were drunk enough to cheer. Some were smart enough to get up and leave while they had the chance. And finally, remembering the violence at the theatre, Woland called the police.

Jean-Baptiste was wading through the crowd. He didn't understand what the hell Mrs. Pangloss thought she was doing, or even why she was there, but he knew instinctively that neither did she, and that she was in a dangerous position. He intended to rescue her from her perch and put her in a taxi home. But when he reached up to help her down, someone at a nearby table denounced him as "that anglo bastard," and several people jumped him at once.

To his credit, Woland leapt into the fray to help Jean-Baptiste.

By the time the police arrived, they were in fact needed to rescue Jean-Baptiste and Woland, who were being soundly beaten despite the screams of Mrs. Pangloss.

In sorting out the punch-up it came to light that the boxes of pamphlets had been brought into the club by Jean-Baptiste himself. On further inspection they were found to contain a large number of various illegal publications, of the type that had lately been distributed in mail slots around town. The remaining nationalist sympathizers were puzzled by this turn of events, but the police clearly saw their duty and arrested Jean-Baptiste as a member of the terrorist separatist cabal, and threw him into a cell at the Parthenais detention centre.

When Jean-Baptiste finally drifted off to sleep that night on his hard, narrow bunk, his cellmate pulled a rope out of his own bowels and hung himself from the bars on their window.

SEVEN

THE STORY OF THE EYE

Aline set pancakes on the table. Grandfather stared at his plate dubiously, adjusted the patch over his right eye and cocked his head for a better look.

"Thank you," he said.

"Who's going to visit Jean-Baptiste?" she asked.

Father said, "Fuck him. Little bastard."

She looked questioningly at Marie, who only shrugged in response and forked another dripping bite into her mouth. She didn't bother to ask Uncle.

"Someone has to go," she said.

Grace cawed from the porch.

Jean-Baptiste's first visitor was Professor Woland. Although in his own way Woland believed himself to be acting charitably, his was not a visit that Jean-Baptiste could appreciate. It was Woland who'd helped put him here, after all, with his grandstanding in the press and goading of the Péquistes and their fellow-travellers.

"Ah, Ti-Jean," he began.

"Don't call me that."

"Forgive my avuncular enthusiasm. I realize it must be unpleasant for you in here."

"Not at all. It's quite agreeable to wake up with a corpse swinging in the window. Cuts the light. You can sleep longer. Except for the yelling."

"All right, I'm sorry."

"And the screaming. Oh, and occasionally the sobbing."

"Okay, okay. But look at it this way: you're a political pariah, a riot broke out at your play and you were arrested at your first poetry reading. Clearly, you're a star. Why, this hasn't happened to a writer in generations!"

"I can see why they gave it up."

"You're a rebel. You're avant-garde. You're engagé!"

"I'm not interested, thank you."

"You disappoint me. Well, then, perhaps you'd be interested in your cheque?"

"My cheque?"

"Yes. We managed to sell enough tickets to pay back our expenses, and so you're entitled to royalties. Of course, expenses were high . . ."

"Of course."

"Therefore your cheque is small."

"I expected no less of you."

"Honestly, if you insist on being so unpleasant, I shan't stay."

"Just leave the cheque."

Woland handed it over and turned to leave. Just as he reached the end of the corridor, he heard Jean-Baptiste say, "You could have made it large enough to cover my bail."

When the iron door at the end of the passageway banged shut and the bolt shot into place, Jean-Baptiste listened to the steely echo die out and then turned his attention back to the cheque in his hands. He was right: it was too small to buy his release. But it was still more money than he'd ever had at once. Was it possible Father or Grandfather could help him out, top up this cheque and set him free?

He sat back down on his hard bunk, looked around at the concrete walls, the cracked floor, the open and stained toilet in the corner. He stood on the bunk and tried to look out the tiny window, but even on tiptoes he couldn't see over the ledge.

After a few days he'd calmed somewhat. He knew his way around a little more—whom to avoid, where not to walk, what not to say. He remained in his cell as much as possible. He asked for books, for paper.

And he kept looking at that cheque. If he could sit out his sentence, he would still have it when he got out.

Unexpectedly, Jean-Baptiste received a visit from Grandfather. In the first place he'd no reason to think Grandfather might have any sympathy for him, after the play; and in the second, he'd never had any reason to expect anything at all from him. Yet Grandfather was the first of his family to come visiting.

"Your mother would have come," he said, "but she's still asleep."

Jean-Baptiste nodded. "But Father won't come."

"He's a little disappointed in you."

"I'm not a felquiste."

"I believe you. But someone in the family is."

"I know."

Grandfather said, "I've never been arrested, you know."

"Funny, isn't it?"

"Yes, funny. Lately a lot of things have been funny."

"How do you mean?"

Grandfather struggled for a moment to put his thoughts in order. He hadn't realized that he had any to arrange, and so the surprise that he was about to explain something, as much to himself as to Jean-Baptiste, was like cold water on his face. Jean-Baptiste was startled by the look that came over him; he tilted his head up slightly, as if he were reading words off the ceiling, and the muscles around his eyes twitched as if he were asleep. He held his hands together in his lap with his fingers outstretched and leaned his back against the cold cement wall. It occurred to Jean-Baptiste that Grandfather looked more at home in this cell than he; in fact, in his cheap, ragged clothes and wrinkled skin, he looked like an early martyr accepting his fate. It was no longer possible to tell which eye was glass. At last he began to speak.

"You're still at the beginning of your life, and this is only your first lesson. At the beginning of my life I learned hard lessons about the reality of things and the appearance of things. In the orphanage I was shown, by people who said they were concerned with my well-being and my welfare, that the charity of others is a prison. A kind of slavery.

"I learned that the robes of a priest are the costumes of the world's greatest sinners. I was taught that in my bunk in the dark, before I was taught to read the Bible. The priests taught me to read the Bible so that I might learn to turn the other cheek; they wanted me to learn that to forgive those who trespass against you is holy, but it was they who were the trespassers. They wanted me to learn that my spiritual health was more important than my material well-being and that God and heaven existed and were waiting for me. But instead they taught me their keen interest in my body, and by their betrayal of their own beliefs demonstrated the empty and cold nature of the world.

"When I was old enough to work and fend for myself I learned that those who spoke of a fair day's pay for a fair day's work were making their own livelihood off my back, and that whatever they paid me, they collected double on. When I was occasionally able to make a profit off others, I learned that the goods I acquired suddenly needed protection for their own sake, that it wasn't enough to have acquired them, I must maintain them at an even greater cost. I learned that even owning things was a form of slavery and a prison.

"When I became old enough to vote I was told that I held the power of self-determination in my hand and that democracy would set me free. After I'd cast my vote, I saw that all lawyers were liars, that freely

217

elected governments were not loath to send in the army and that democracy itself was just a slave of capitalism.

"When I was old enough to marry I was told that love is what makes us human, different from the animals, that love was the supreme expression of the union of two souls. But after I was first wed I discovered the trap a marriage could be, the endless lifelong series of obligations and compromises that keep us from being ourselves for ourselves. I was told that children were our way to immortality, but I learned that their disappointments and resentments were a sure road to the death of my soul.

"Above all I learned that what the world calls happiness and wishes upon us is oppressive and self-serving, that the world cares not for individuals but only for the propagation of the masses, and never questions itself in this regard, and punishes all who question it. This is one thing you've learned today.

"So I settled into a life of small expectations, no ambition and a deep satisfaction in small, simple and immediate pleasures—which have always seemed to me the only ones worth having, as they're the only ones we can be sure of, which have no hidden motive behind them. Intentionally I would make myself happy any way I could, any way that cost not too much effort or money, any way that didn't involve a sacrifice.

"This didn't mean that I couldn't make others happy at the same time, or that I never wanted to make others happy. It's just that that was never my habit. Making someone else content was for me like a change in the weather or a new kind of food. It was just the variety, the spice, that made my own routine my preferred way of doing things.

"So there were times when I brought my wife gifts or flowers, or took her to dinner, because her happiness for that moment was a pleasure to me, if only because it was a relief from her usual misery. Or there were times, like now, when I bothered to talk to my children or grandchildren, to tell them stories or listen to their chatter, or offer such advice as I could.

"But in the main I wasn't interested in other people's troubles. I wasn't interested in planning or saving for any future project. I wasn't interested in moving to a better house or neighbourhood, or getting a divorce, or providing anything for my wife and children. I felt that everyone ought to provide for himself whatever he wanted as best he could. And since I wasn't interested in possessing anything for any length of time, I was content if there were only enough to eat and a place to sleep. I was happy with a cheap cigar or cheap liquor, or even cheap women, now and again, whenever the mood would strike me.

"The idea of expecting any of these pleasures, large or small, to be a regular part of my life, or a circumstance that I'd come to consider as normal, was repellent to me. I believed that a life of that sort could only be a weight on my shoulders. That was my idea of what others called the rat race, or the bourgeoisie: people trapped under the oppressiveness of their own lives, unable to escape from the burden of their material well-being. Or frightened in their hearts of some kind of a Judgment Day or moral censure if they should happen to work towards their own happiness at the expense of their responsibilities. I couldn't see an ordinary life lived in an ordinary way as anything but one kind of social slavery or another. And the only friends I had were those who shared these opinions in some way, who were usually thought of as unsavoury. The unemployed, alcoholics, whores, thieves, pushers . . . doctors.

"So my life went on and was full of things everyone experiences—money, poverty, sickness, health, divorce, marriage, death, birth. But also happiness, pleasure, surprise.

"And then this thing happened to me, that I lost my left eye.

"You'll think me just drunk again, or addled with the painkillers, or senile. But since I've had this glass eye in I've begun to see things differently. Of course it sounds ridiculous that I should see anything through a glass eye, and I don't know if I do or not. But I tell you that now things look different to me.

"And I don't simply mean that my attitude has changed. I mean I've seen things that I've never seen before. I've seen things that aren't easily explained by a merely material universe. And I don't mean that I'm seeing ghosts or spirits; though I've thought that occasionally, I've decided I was wrong. The world itself and everything in it is suddenly revealing to me what I can only call its moral dimension.

"When I was a child, the Church successfully beat any spiritual sense out of me with its hostility and hypocrisy, with its devils dressed as angels. Nevertheless I've been living my life all along with an assumption of the spiritual value of things. I set that value at zero, for everything. Everything, that is, except my own momentary pleasure, which I gave a value slightly above zero, but only because it relieved my suffering.

"But now I think that my suffering itself was a call, a sign that there must be some kind of value external to myself. And now I see that whatever that value is depends on how I see it. Because when I lost my left eye, I lost the ability to see things the way I wanted. I could no longer control what I saw.

"Some days everything would be normal, as it ever had been. Other days I would wake up with a renewed sense of ease, of youth and contentment. I was positively disposed to the world, and was willing to give a little to make others happy, or I wanted to make others happy for their own sake for the first time. I began to see physical things differently. I began to see the connections between things. I don't mean their causes and effects, but I could make out direct physical relations between objects, as if I could detect the forces of gravity that kept them in relation to one another. And I began to see things that I'd always thought impossible. I saw dead people get up and move unaided; I saw mannequins come to life, like Pinocchio. I saw myself inside my children. I see myself in you now.

"And because of that I'm trying to explain this to you. If I'm in you in any way, I don't want you to wait until the end of your life to understand what I see now."

Grandfather paused. He shifted slightly and cleared his throat, but kept his eyes away from Jean-Baptiste. He seemed almost embarrassed, as if he were forcing himself onward.

"It's become a comfort to me in my old age. I can move my patch over the eye I was born with and then with the new eye I can see everything in its best light, when I no longer want to see anything poor or evil. And then again, on bad days when on waking I open the wrong eye, I can close down the sentimental, optimistic organ and revel in the malicious and the tawdry. So if I go down to the cathouse on de Bullion street, with the proper eye I can see in the hookers what I saw in my dear wife, and I'm again consumed with love, love for the whole female gender. Or when the beast in me is rising and I want to debase myself with my inherited male cruelty, I can see them for the cheap whores they are, over-painted, tired, by turns lascivious and inhuman.

"Which eye is which? I ask myself that every morning before I dare open either.

"But then one day, for the first time, I looked at myself in the mirror while I was wearing the patch, and the part of me that hates the other looked upon the part of me that pities itself. Or perhaps it was the other way around; it's impossible to say. For the first time I was conscious of both my optimism and my desperation as if they were separate beings regarding one another. I felt both the weight of meaninglessness and the lightness of play, which had always competed in me to dominate my emotions, but which I was only able to experience in their pure states with the help of the patch. Except that this time, at that moment I stared at myself in the mirror, I was not only fully who I am but each separate part of me regarding myself. As if I were regarding my own twin sons, or an earlier me, with both nostalgia and scorn.

"I see that things which seem opposed are not. I see that things which seem in union are not. I feel like the image of a man with the devil on one shoulder and an angel on the other, urging me one way or the other. I feel like the devil's been missing for most of my life, and I've been carrying this little angel around with me. I know anyone who knows me must think it's absurd for me to say that, that I meant to say *devil* instead of *angel*. But I've said what I think is the truth. Even if it makes little sense.

"What I've learned is that these opposites have no meaning. Thinking of them as the reverse of one another has no meaning. Believing I've come to some spiritual awakening has no meaning. I don't believe I've discovered any kind of a truth, because that kind of a truth would be too simple and a lie. But I no longer believe it's even possible to lie about anything.

"What I'm saying isn't absurd, or paradoxical, even if I don't quite understand it myself. For the first time in my life I've been giving long thought to puzzling questions, and I can only say that I'm trying to live with my experience even when I know it must be faulty. Yet I continue to experience it as reality.

"And I don't expect that my saying this can do anyone any good. But it's made me feel better to tell someone."

When his grandfather left him to his cell, Jean-Baptiste thought about this strange confession. How it revealed a man living unsuspected beneath the grave-robbing reprobate, how the simplest of lives was no shield from the mysteries of Being, and how time itself reshapes our experience so that, at the end of our lives, their beginnings appear entirely different than when we lived through them. He took a pen and scrounged together some napkins, and in the time-honoured tradition of writers in prisons, began to write.

Prison was a place Marie had avoided as best she could. She'd known enough felquistes who'd spent time inside, even some who still were. It was common wisdom among them not to visit friends in jail. Signing the guest book was registering yourself with the police as a fellow-traveller. But this time it was different. She could hardly refuse to visit her brother. It was an awkward family obligation for everyone, since they were all angry over the play. But Marie couldn't help feeling guilty for his plight. So when they pushed her, she went.

It was always difficult between them. They knew each other so little, all they knew were their differences. Marie, nervous and claustrophobic in prison, fell back on sarcasm, the only opening she could find. "I hear you were arrested for reading poetry."

Jean-Baptiste wasn't happy to see her in the first place, and her opening words were irritating. "I was arrested because you planted illiterate propaganda in my boxes. It's your fault I'm here."

She tried to steer the conversation into banter. "It's true I wasn't there, but I'm sure if I'd been subjected to your verse, I would have called the cops too."

"I can't believe you. *You're* actually mad at *me*, aren't you? What the hell for?"

Marie was lost. Everything she said made him furious. She didn't know how to answer. "You're stealing the show. You're making us look like fools."

"Excuse me, but *I'm* the one in jail, here. None of this has worked out for me at all."

Marie sighed angrily. She had nothing left but a bitter defensiveness. "Sorry to disrupt your bourgeois ambitions."

"Ambitions nothing. That play wasn't what I wanted onstage. I got precious little of my own work up there. But I'm blamed for everything. The family hates me, but they don't understand how little control I had over the play."

"It's a little too late to start pleading innocence, Jean-Baptiste."

"For Christ's sake, no one even heard any of the poetry I was reading. Now I'm stuck in here, people think I actually wrote that trash of a play, and my family hates me."

"Stop feeling so sorry for yourself."

"Why are you mad at *me*? What do you want from me?"

Marie found herself yelling. "You never helped me. You never did anything for me or my friends. You won't help your own people. You refused to write for us, to join us, to help us or support us in any way."

"I never helped you? My family thinks I was fucking my sister the night Angus died, but I never helped you? Fuck you."

Marie was stung. She turned from him as her eyes welled up.

"Why the hell should I help?" Jean-Baptiste rushed on. "I don't agree with you. I'm not interested in politics. Politics is full of hypocrites. It's either Thieves for Democracy or Fascists for a Fundamentalist Dictatorship. I hate to think which you are."

They were silent a moment, looking away from each other.

"I expected more from you." Marie wiped her eyes. "You're smart, but you're wasting yourself on scribblings that do no one any good." She stood to leave.

"Well, I'm sure I won't be doing much more scribbling." Jean-Baptiste waved a hand in the air, like Woland. "My reputation will precede me now. I'll never live this down."

"I brought you some chocolate." She put a candy bar on the table.

He sighed. Quietly, he asked, "Have you got any paper?"

EIGHT

OCTOBRE

When Hubert disappeared Marie thought taking over as de facto leader was simply picking up another chore he'd left undone, like the dishes or the house-cleaning. But when she'd actually organized and implemented the pamphleteering campaign, she realized two things:

The others had accepted her leadership.

It felt good.

For once, her ideas had not been dismissed or trivialized. For once, she'd found herself directing the actions of others, and they'd seen the results in the newspapers. The whole town was abuzz with their actions.

From then on she was tacitly acknowledged the leader of her cell. She organized meetings just as she had in the past, scheduling them, making sure word got around, acting as general secretary and chair. Yet now, whenever a question came up, whenever a decision was to be made, it was left to her: her vote was supreme. And the actions and ideas discussed were all referred through her; she approved them, dismissed them, supported them or ridiculed them. And her approval was the cell's decision.

She'd always seen the struggle in Quebec as a struggle against the past, a struggle for the future. Everyone involved knew they might never personally see the changes they so desperately wanted, might never benefit from the kind of society—a French society—they envisaged for Quebec, the independent nation of the future. But they knew their children and their grandchildren would enjoy an autonomy that had never been possible for them, an identity as a fully recognized people in the world community.

But somehow, now that she was herself in some small part in charge of the necessary tasks to propel them towards that goal, Marie began to feel quite differently about the future, about what the results of her actions would be. She began to feel protective of her people and her cause; she began to accept the sacrifices they would all have to make—even as Angus had—for the benefit of the future generations. She realized some of these might be unspeakable, unthinkable, inhuman. But the future of Quebec and its people occupied a new place in her heart, not one simply of a youthful, rebellious nature but of an eternal, living affection that could never be shaken or broken, even if it could be disappointed. The children of the future, of the new Quebec, were Marie's children. They might be ungrateful, they might be disobedient, they might even be unforgiving.

But they would always be hers, and she would do anything for them.

⚜

Hubert haunted Marie like a guilty conscience. He would have been the father of her child, and they had killed him. They weren't even Anglos; these cops were fellow Québécois. But that hadn't stopped them from beating him to death. They were so blind to the problems that had made thugs of them that they couldn't see he was their saviour, not their enemy. And they had created the conditions that forced her to abort her child. How could she have given birth to another soul under these intolerable circumstances, which set siblings against each other, tore generations and families apart, weakened the well-being of the nation itself? How could she bring up a child as she herself had been brought up, under the yoke of economic and social oppression, without the means of determining her own destiny?

So many forces had been marshalled against them all their lives. The money didn't care for the underclass, the English didn't care for the French, and the politicians openly snubbed the electorate. And the successful French all followed the path of assimilation, of Uncle Tom. And the press, French and English, so controlled by the money at the top, which trickled down just enough to its middle-class servants to slake their bourgeois aspirations, couldn't fail to be against her friends. Not just in editorials constantly denouncing the felquistes as murderers and thugs, but even in the supposedly factual articles, so slanted against the FLQ for the sake of petty sensationalism and emotionalism, in the name of circulation figures. They cared nothing for their brethren without jobs, without education, without dignity . . . without real lives.

It was unbearable to think things would always remain the way they were. That families like hers would always suffer the miserable, grey winter that was life in Montreal. Forced into crime for a living, forced into belittling subservience for spiritual sustenance, forced into sleeping through life to avoid its pain. Grandfather, Aline, Mother. Even Jean-Baptiste she pitied; in this rare moment of reflection about her brother's world, she saw him, too, caught between reality and his dreams, saw how it was crushing him.

If they could kill and imprison her friends, if they could suppress her own ambitions and everyone else's, what chance did any hypothetical children ever have? If no one acted, if no one effected change, there would be no point in anyone ever having a family. What would happen to the family of the Québécois themselves? Her family?

She agonized for days. She wandered the city looking for a purpose, for a reason to continue, one way or another, any way at all. She spent time in Parc du Mont-Royal, walking the gravel road to the summit and the cross of iron; she gazed out over the city towards the river, the Pont Jacques-Cartier and the South Shore beyond. She wound her way through the tiny, quiet streets of Westmount; so isolated and rarely visited except by these residents. Million-dollar homes, huge shiny cars, but no sidewalks inviting riff-raff into the neighbourhood.

Something must be done to shake this up. There had to be a more fulfilling life for the Québécois than shovelling snow for the Anglos. There must be an act capable of awakening a sleeping people to their rights, their dignity, their destiny.

She was at a turning point in her work, her life, her relations with people, with politics, with her family—with herself. She had to accept the fact that there wasn't anything she could do to achieve her goals, that what she wanted was beyond her means. That her years of work and struggle had been wasted. Or she could accept that the work was bigger than she was, that the goals were larger than a single person could expect to meet, and give up everything else in her life to struggle for whatever progress might be possible—to let others see that things did matter, that things did change, if you were willing to take the long view.

It was a question of placing herself in a different context regarding the Great Work. It was a matter of recognizing that the Great Work was her master and she was the servant, not the reverse. She would write no more scripts in her head, have no more expectations that she was in charge or would get the results she anticipated. The Work existed separately from her, of its own accord and for its own reasons, and she was only an instrument of its desires.

If this made Marie recognize just how small she was, it made her see just how Great the Work was: it controlled people and events beyond their ability or even desire to stop it, just as money did, just as society did. Now she knew how hard her task would be. How foolish she'd been to think that a mere few years of campaigning would shift the balance between the great forces of Change and Inertia.

And that's what she was really fighting. Not just money and social conventions and apathy: Inertia. But now she saw the opposition as people just like herself—if only they knew it—people who had given their lives up to their own causes, people who'd been unknowingly mastered by their own ideals.

She was at that point where people shed their dreams, stop complaining and slip into the mainstream of life, into repetitive work and small comforts. Or where they consciously step fully outside, shed any sentimental or emotional attachments and get down to work: coldly, methodically and, very often, cruelly.

She could choose to continue the larger struggle, a struggle that would consume her and all her feelings and hopes, and would leave her no normal human life. Or she could instead give up the years already devoted to the work, and all the physical and emotional energy it had required, and retire into her family—her difficult, simple family, whom she both loved and hated.

Father was delighted to have Marie home.

"It's time we started working on putting this house in order," she declared. "Let's finish the framework between the kitchen and front parlour so Aline can get through without tripping over something or getting her sleeves caught on a nail. That's where we'll open the stairs to the adjoining basement as well, for your workshop. It'll be less work to combine them."

His own daughter back—and involved in the family. She'd never cared before, not like this: having an opinion, offering advice, even lifting tools to help—so much more help than his brother or father had ever been. Or his son. She was growing up. Not just that, but having her help in his project to launch a new career, to better the situation for all of them: it was a boon, a refreshing breeze that lifted his spirits and set his ambitions afire.

Years ago, when he'd been a younger man and Mother pregnant with their future hopes, he dreamt one day he'd work beside his son. Physical work like this, where you felt your muscles and sweat, where tools and materials passed hand to hand and where something actually got made. He held a beam as Marie yanked with a crowbar, and remembered that early longing. Now his son was in jail, a traitor to the family, and Marie, his daughter, was bringing him this unexpected satisfaction.

"Here, let me try it," he said.

"No, no," said Marie. "When it comes free you have to hold it. It's too heavy for me, but I can work this lever." And she put her back into it, instinctively holding her breath with the strain.

She's smart, too, he thought. She could make a difference around here. She could really change things if she put her mind to it.

Once that was done it was time to attack the basement in earnest.

"We'll throw out all this old trash of Angus's," said
Father.

"No," said Marie. "We'll work around it like everything else down here. It belongs to Mother now. She'd
never forgive us if she woke and it was gone. Any one
of these pieces might be a real treasure to her."

"You're right," said Father. He realized then that
he and Marie had always bonded through Mother.
She was their link, and caring for her was how they
expressed affection for each other.

"And there's plenty of room," said Marie. "In fact,
we'll raise partitions here and create a little room
where I can sleep."

"You're fine where you are. Why move into this
dank basement?"

"Jean-Baptiste will be back soon. They won't keep
him locked up forever. I need my own room. Right at
the end here, and we'll stack Angus's boxes right up
against it. It'll be quiet and snug. You can work in the
rest of the basement and never know I'm here."

"To hell with your brother. You stay where you are."

So that was that. If she wanted a room in the basement, she'd have to hide it.

Naturally the renovations took longer than expected.
The sheer amount of physical work was the main
deterrent. It loomed over Father's imagination like
an unyielding mountain, an implacable fate. But this
was perfect for Marie. It was easy for her to make her
own arrangements with false walls and hidden ducts

in the mass of lumber, plaster and dirt being moved about. With Angus's boxed possessions stacked up against her meagre four feet of false wall, no one even glanced over in that direction, let alone wondered why so much space was lost. And the sealed boxes of books, magazines and old clothes provided effective noise-proofing as well. Which would come in handy when her plan came to life.

Hyde sat in his office with only a desk lamp for company. He was going over his old case notes, reviewing every experiment he'd done for years, trying to remember every error, so as to avoid them all now. He knew he was close. So close, he'd spent some time just staring into the darkness collecting his thoughts, daydreaming the papers—no, the book—he'd write about his work, his experience, his life. It was important. Everyone would see that. He would explain it properly. But for that, he had to turn it over in his mind, prepare his arguments in a logical fashion. He'd wandered, luxuriating in the acclaim he imagined would be his. He scolded himself mentally. He must get back on track. He'd never been a daydreamer, never been a man of fantasy.

If it were possible to artificially create a being in the laboratory, Hyde thought, and that being possessed the traits recognized as the soul—conscious and deliberate actions based on desires and emotions, the ability to master mere animal instinct or reflex reaction, a sense of self that marks one's own individuality—then that would go at least partway towards demonstrating that these traits and the soul itself were nothing more than either a property of matter under certain conditions or inherent aspects of a complicated system. Perhaps even the governing component of a series of subsystems, all adding up to a conscious human being. On the other hand, if such a being were created and demonstrated none of these traits or qualities, then that might lend credence to the idea of the soul as either some kind of divine element that predates corporeal existence, and perhaps even outlasts that state, or a biological or genetic element that appears, matures and dies with each individual.

In other words, are we momentary or eternal beings? It's a purely scientific question, and the answer, either way, would revolutionize our existence.

That's what the whole ghastly business was about, the years spent taking people apart with scalpels, trying to get legs, arms and organs working and living, even if only one piece at a time. That's what the opening of skulls was for, piercing living, conscious brains with needle-thin electrodes and introducing random charges into an already working system. He still watched his own old films, black and white, himself in the bleached robe glaring out in high contrast under the operating lights, while the edges of the frame were dark, like a silent film from the twenties. One scene kept turning up in his dreams, a recurring nightmare: an ape waking, blinking weakly and then, clearly confused but instinctively and inconceivably horrified, trying desperately to scream—

but unable to do more than grimace, so wide it seemed its whole skull would fall out. Mercifully, it died almost immediately.

And the other memory, more comical, since he'd no qualms at the thought that the patient was—had to be—fully conscious during the operation. What happens when I touch you here, he'd asked. Burnt toast, Doctor. It smells like burnt toast. That one had made his name, early on, been broadcast to a world amazed at his daring, his skill, his sang-froid.

Hyde smiled. You ain't seen nothing yet, he thought.

Aline envied Mother. Whatever she was feeling, she felt it all in a dream, and even if it was some kind of pain or suffering, it wasn't real. Aline, on the other hand, had to face her situation and had no idea what to do. In fact, she was having trouble simply grasping what her real state was, having trouble keeping everything together in her mind to form a pattern or story or a clear picture. She knew only two things: that she'd never known the despair and anxiety that now consumed her daily life, and that her only relief was in Grace.

When she'd been a spinster living with her father, life had been small and difficult: money was a constant problem, they both missed her dead mother, and there was no hope of any improvement or change. Since she married Grandfather, she felt cut off entirely from her father, speaking to him only by phone. How could she see him without revealing the horrible secrets of her new, unhappy life? Impossible. And it would be unfair to burden him now, when he no longer had to stretch his pension to feed two and had become used to the lavish excess of a single bottle of Crown Royal every month. Bootlegger's, he called it, in English, repeating the story of how such a respectable anglo family had made their money during Prohibition. And he never ran out of cigarettes now. He travelled in a cloud happily, hacking only when he laughed a little too hard.

She missed her earlier life and pined to go back to the tiny apartment on rue Cartier at the bottom of the hill. But if she did that, if she broke down and confessed that her fairy-tale marriage had turned out to be Walpurgisnacht instead, it would be the end of his rye and his laugh. Even though she knew he wouldn't hesitate to take her back and would make no complaints. Pensions don't grow like inflation, and they'd both lived off his meagre stipend long enough. That had been one of her joys in an unexpected suitor, when Grandfather first came around so clearly intent on taking her from his house: that it would make things easier for him too.

Aline was puzzled why the Lord, who'd so clearly favoured her with a vision of the miracle at St. Joseph's, was now testing her so thoroughly. She'd only fled from one poorhouse to another when she moved in with the Desouches, and life since then seemed one endless, dark litany of disappointment. Grandfather'd turned bitter and vindictive, and had his horrible accident—which for some reason he occasionally seemed happy for. Mother'd been crushed by Angus's death; constant family rows drove Marie out of the house and back again; on New Year's, she discovered Grandfather's illegal and disgusting trade; Jean-Baptiste's play broke open a rift in the family, and then he was arrested. Finally, as if it were a sign to her personally that she'd been set adrift by the Good Lord who'd always protected her, the very symbol of their personal compact, Brother André's heart, had been stolen in broad daylight.

It was flabbergasting. Such brazen heresy. And it couldn't have been a simple theft; it was crazy to take something of no intrinsic monetary value. There was no shortage of more convertible church property lying about unguarded, that any common thief would more likely have chosen: the silver and gold, the jewelled objects. There was some other reason the heart had gone missing, there had to be. She'd been praying in front of that relic every Sunday since the miracle. Who else knew that? Only God Himself. What more direct renunciation could be imagined?

But why? Why had she lost favour in the Lord's eyes?

Marie swabbed Mother's face with a damp cloth, rinsed it, swabbed her arms. She turned Mother as necessary, lifting her arm, bending her leg, reaching as much of her body as she could. Marie performed these actions with a deep sense of guilt, for being the cause of her mother's condition. But also with a deep sense of sadness, because she identified Mother's way of handling her grief with the silence of the Québécois. In the same way that Mother was sleeping through a life otherwise unbearable, the great mass of her fellow Québécois slept through their political and economic suppression. If only they would awaken, how changed things could be. If Marie had transgressed by her actions, by causing Mother's pain, she would redeem herself by what was to come, by redeeming all her brethren, by awakening everyone to the horror of reality in Quebec, by showing how far they must go, by leading them away from a life made bearable only by intoxication and slumber.

The response to her brother's play stirred her. It proved she was not alone. It proved that her sentiments were shared, that hers was the voice of the people. Thousands were willing to follow, if only someone could lead. And hardened by her guilt, she knew her only happiness was in doing just that. In leading them out of their complacency and into the new future of Quebec. In awakening the province to its destiny as a nation she would redeem herself and her actions not only in the eyes of the world, but in her own eyes, and, if they knew it, in her family's eyes too. As she covered her with the cheap blanket, she knew that even Mother would realize that in fact Marie had been taking care of her all along. That a Quebec ruled by the Québécois was better for everyone, even the Anglos.

What the hell was Marie doing? Did she know herself? Angus tried to bring himself closer to her, and felt the anger in her, just as he always had. But now he detected something new too, beneath the frustration and the fear. As he collected himself and reached out to her, there it was, emanating from her like radiation: guilt.

Angus wondered what poor little Marie could be harbouring within her so painfully, and he wanted to help, to extricate the cancerous emotion that was now spreading through her every fibre. But he couldn't. It was like a barrier keeping him back; it repelled him as if it and he were opposite poles of a magnet.

Angus retreated, dispersed slowly and sadly. Why was everyone so hard to reach? Why in hell could he feel so close to these people, his family, and yet ever be unable to reach them?

As he drifted away he saw, as if out of the corner of his eye—Jesus, to have an eye!—Marie putting a small gun in her pocket and quickly leaving the house.

A gun?

The ride was like a dream. They'd gone over the plans again and again, even walked through the motions with kitchen chairs serving for the car, thought of every eventuality, tested their response to whatever might happen, immersed themselves in this task and its rehearsals until it seemed like the only real thing in the world. Now, riding in the back seat with a gun on her lap, Marie felt as if nothing at all were really

241

happening, as if she were dozing at the movies, transported along passively as impressions streaked by her eyes. She allowed herself this ten minutes of not thinking or worrying because she knew the others would look to her during the event itself. Just as they had in everything else up to this very point. But now, on the way, with nothing to do but sit in the car and watch the streets of Montreal float by, she let her thoughts wander.

A switch closed in her mind, and she gave herself over to the inexorable progress of the plan, executing every step towards the goal as if she were herself a series of dominoes falling against one another. She had a dim presentiment of watching the march of events as if from outside herself, and she could see ahead to their end as clearly as if she were following the course of a stream downhill. But she had lost all volition, and while she watched her mind toss back and forth the feeble emotions connected with a sense of right and wrong, of guilt and purpose, without assigning any of them a value higher than another, she suddenly discovered the helpless, directionless sense of floating above events like a cork on the water that others must feel—the others she'd always accused of apathy, of collusion, of stupidity—when they throw up their hands and ask despairingly, yes, but what can *I* do about it?

Somewhere she struggled within herself to reconnect, to force down those troubling, amorphous feelings of danger, of error, of failure, to grasp herself firmly and be once more in charge of her own destiny, responsible for her own actions. To claim them as hers, as right, as inevitable. As she'd always felt when she was most proud of herself.

But she discovered now that she was truly under the influence of the events that had led her here, to this car and this action; and though she knew she could still change her path, choose to step away from the otherwise inevitable, she knew she had at last given herself over to the plan itself, finally acknowledging that she had striven so hard and for so long towards such an unreachable goal that she had wholly submitted to the Great Work and acknowledged herself inferior.

If she was ever to regain any strength of her own, if she was ever to steer her own course again, she could do so only along the path already chosen. There remained only one direction in which to move. The shore she'd left behind had disappeared over the horizon—there was no harbour on any side—and all that was left was to press on and trust that somewhere ahead lay a new landing.

Marie got out of the car with the gun in her hand. The two others were nervous, hiding their weapons, fearful of being seen, waving their hands in a frenzy of signalling: The gun, the gun! Put it away!

She drew them together. "No. This will go like clockwork. Do as I tell you, don't hesitate, and we'll be gone in five minutes. Everyone up to the door." She shoved them along the path, and they went hurriedly.

Marie tightened her jaw, strode up behind them and knocked loudly on the door. She had a second to breathe deeply, and then it opened.

She barely measured the maid's face before all she saw was her own fist pointing the pistol at it. Her other arm snapped out, grabbed the startled woman's shoulder and pushed her back. She shunted the maid aside, barked an order to one of the others and stood in an open hallway, pointing the gun in a quick sweep.

Jesus, she thought. What do I do now?

They were watching her, waiting for instructions. The maid, in a chair by the door with a gun held at her temple, cried.

A toilet flushed upstairs. Marie held the pistol out before her like a shield and carried herself on legs locked like a dancer's. She felt taller. She was breathing deeply and evenly, and even though she was aware of every detail around her, as if she had all the time in the world to observe her surroundings, she was moving up the staircase faster than she wanted, effortlessly, with the momentum of a child down a slide.

She had no idea what she was doing, but felt no impulse to stop or slow down. One of her colleagues followed her. At the end of the hall, light spilled from a door, flickering with the movement of people inside the room. It drew her like a moth.

She pointed her arm around the corner and followed it in. A man and a woman turned from a mirror where they were dressing for dinner. The woman was startled and grabbed the man's arm as she exclaimed. The man jumped back and yelled an obscenity. Marie pointed her arm at him. He cowered.

He's afraid of me, Marie thought.

In an instant the couple were more collected, and indignant. They choked out angry questions.

"Shut up," Marie barked. "I'm in charge." I'm in charge, she thought; they don't know who I am, and they're going to do what I say.

The wife was sat on the bed; the husband's head was covered, his wrists bound. "Down the stairs." They marched him down, past the maid, and the four of them poured out of the house and across the lawn towards the waiting car, all without breaking stride or speaking.

They doubled him over, threw him across the floor in the rear of the car, and everyone scrambled to get in. The driver had the engine running before the doors were closed, and the car lurched and swerved all at once before straightening and charging down the street flat out.

Marie slouched down in the car as much as she could. Ahead, across the street, was her house. In the darkness she waited, watching passing traffic, until one by one the lights went out, as first one then another of the Desouches went to sleep.

Still she waited. A couple of lights came on again, and then an hour later Uncle and Grandfather left by the front door, turning the lights out and locking up behind them. She waited.

Finally she drove the car slowly and quietly to the end of the block, turned right onto Prince Arthur Street, turned again up the lane that separated the church from the row of gabled houses. She turned off the headlights, took her foot off the gas, and the car drifted slowly towards the rear of her home.

She stopped the car, killed the engine. She paused. She carefully got out of the car, opened the rear door and pulled the stumbling, bound man from the back seat. She'd left the basement door unlocked. As quietly as she could she got him into the house. Father and Mother, of course, would be asleep; Aline too; Uncle and Grandfather had left, and Jean-Baptiste was still in jail. She led him to the secret room.

⚜

It wasn't the sort of French that John Cross was used to hearing. It was full of scatological terms, religious references, oddly pronounced English words and others impossible to identify. It wasn't accented in the manner of French diplomats or of English private school instructors. It was not, and had never been, the language of diplomacy.

But its message got across to him and he acquiesced to the bag over his head and the pistol in his neck, and to being jerry-marched blindly across his lawn and thrown forcibly face down into the back of a small, musty-smelling car. Then there'd been a series of drives, changes of vehicle, waits in unknown apartments, listening to these lower-class hoodlums arguing, being pushed here and there—all without seeing a thing. He'd been struck when he spoke, he was not offered water or food, and when finally someone thought to take him to the bathroom, even then he'd not been allowed to remove the bag. How was he to see what he was doing? He wasn't: he was helped.

It was perhaps the most frightening moment of the entire ordeal. He stood with his hands tied behind while someone else unzipped him, pulled him out and said, "Piss." He couldn't recall ever having felt so vulnerable, so small. And, when the woman laughed, so emasculated. Not even in public school.

It seemed a terribly long time had passed, and he was afraid for his life. He was faint from hunger and thirst, and sometimes, sitting in a darkened room or a closet, he couldn't tell if he was awake or asleep until he jerked alert. But there was nothing to see and often nothing to hear. His attention was concentrated on his body. It ached. No position, standing, sitting or lying down, was comfortable. His muscles were tense and cramped, and he trembled all over when he tried to force them to relax.

He became angry at the British Foreign Office. Stupid bastards. If he'd been posted to Africa or the East, they would have given him a bodyguard or at least some training for this sort of thing. But then, who could have expected a British diplomat to be in danger in Canada? Which was why he'd chosen the posting, naturally. The idea of taking his family to a country that required the precautions of a bodyguard was out of the question.

After a final interminable ride with the car radio blaring and so many turns around corners that he'd never be able to place himself, and then some interminable wait where he'd thought they must simply be parked on a busy street, he'd been bundled down concrete steps. He assumed it was a basement. Boards groaned close overhead. He was sat down on a bunk or a cot. The springs creaked under his weight. A door closed; the chain of a bulb was pulled. His hands were untied and blood ran back into them. But he wasn't allowed to rub his wrists as he wanted. His left arm was grabbed and he felt a handcuff applied, and heard its mate rasp against steel.

Finally the paper bag over his head was removed. He saw her face. Her eyes were dark and shadowed, her cheeks flaccid and her mouth held shut by a kind of resigned determination. Suddenly he was more frightened, not less. He was in a tiny unfinished room, barely more than a closet, with no more space than was necessary to stand or to lie on a cot. The bare bulb glared and swung inches above her head. Was it she who'd laughed at him?

She struck his face. "Don't look at me."

He looked to his cuffed left hand. It was secured to the frame of the cot. The mattress was barely an inch thick over the rusted springs and the linen wasn't fresh.

When she removed his gag, he said, "For God's sake, let me go."

She scoffed. "None of us can be free as long as we're all in chains. Here's a sandwich. There's a pail under the cot. You might as well relax."

248

"Why are you doing this? Why me? Let me go, please!"

"I'm sorry. Though I despise you, it's not personal. And I won't let it become personal. No conversations."

"I am a representative of Her Majesty's Government—"

She slapped him.

"I am a diplomat, and I demand you release me right now."

"We hope to release you as soon as possible. Get some sleep. It's rather late."

When she was done, and climbing the stairs to the kitchen, she thought, I've done it. I've really done it. She quietly opened the door, stepped up into the kitchen, shut it again quietly behind her and flicked on the light.

Grace squawked and fluttered above the refrigerator. Marie jumped, and then laughed. She looked at the settling bird. "I've done it," she said, and laughed again. It felt good to tell someone, even the bird. And the bird wouldn't squeal.

Grace folded her wings back and clacked her beak, and turned her head, staring at Marie from a single eye. Clack. Clack.

It went on for days. He saw only her. She brought table scraps as if he were an animal, or sandwiches or fruit. He asked for tea, and to his surprise, he got it.

She emptied his bucket every day with evident dis-
taste. When he pleaded and cried for release she
struck him. When he demanded his rights as a British
citizen, she scoffed and struck him.

"I beg you to be reasonable."

"It's too late for reason."

"I'm a human being just as you are."

"It's not possible to reach me on humanitarian
grounds."

"Can't I have a radio? At least a newspaper? For
God's sake, what day is it? How long have I been
here? Does my family know I'm alive? The police
must be looking for me."

"I'm sure our police are looking for you. It's
unfortunate for you we aren't hiding in a doughnut
shop."

He slept; he ate; he cried. He lost all track of time,
of day or night. He ached for a cigarette. He missed
his wife, his children. He reviewed his life and cata-
logued his regrets. He tried to think his way out but
became unable to distinguish between his plans and
his dreams. He prayed.

He'd tried everything he could think of to get himself out of this fix, and none of it worked. He fingered
the chain around his neck and, as he prayed, thought
of trying to pray with his captors. If reason and logic
had failed, if emotionalism had failed, perhaps this
tactic would not. What had he to lose by it?

It was the only thing that could make a difference.
It was the only answer. And with his hands bound and
mouth gagged, the only thing he could do.

Jean-Baptiste was led into a small, windowless room. They sat him at an Arborite table on which lay a jumbled piece of cloth. The big, older cop, promoted to detective as he'd predicted himself that cold winter's night, leaned across the table, staring Jean-Baptiste in the eyes. At the same time he unfolded the cloth and revealed a revolver.

"Pick it up," he said.

Jean-Baptiste looked from the overhanging, mustachioed, pot-bellied detective to the gun lying on the table, its muzzle pointed towards him.

"Pick it up," said the cop again.

"No," said Jean-Baptiste.

The cop folded the cloth and put the gun in the desk drawer. "Okay, forget it." He lit a cigarette, wordlessly offered one to Jean-Baptiste. He stood and walked around the room, behind Jean-Baptiste and back again. "Heard the news?" he asked.

"No," said Jean-Baptiste.

"No? Don't listen to the radio? Newspaper? Television?"

"No," said Jean-Baptiste.

"Talk to the other inmates?"

"I keep to myself. I'll be out soon."

The cop laughed. And then he held his tongue with a smile on his face, long enough to make Jean-Baptiste wonder why. "Not soon enough for some," he said.

"What?"

"Somebody's trying to get you out."

"Someone paid my bail? That's ridiculous, I'm being released next week."

"No," said the cop. "No one's paid any money for you."

Jean-Baptiste waited as long as he could. "What are you talking about?"

"Who are your friends?"

"What friends?"

"Your buddies. Who do you hang out with? Drink beer with, smoke pot with?"

"You want me to snitch on pot smokers?"

"Maybe. If it makes you comfortable to put it that way."

"I haven't got a clue what you're saying."

The cop stood up and smacked his hand violently on the table. Jean-Baptiste flinched. "Who the hell are your friends? What are their names, where do they live?"

Jean-Baptiste said nothing.

The cop calmed down. "Okay. Let's be straight with each other. You're in here for spreading treasonous literature."

"That was a mistake. Those weren't my pamphlets. My own literature may be bad, but it's not criminal."

The cop sighed. "Right. Everyone's innocent. That's why we're all here in this lovely resort hotel, as a reward for our virtue."

"Whatever you say," said Jean-Baptiste.

"Okay. You're not a felquiste. You didn't write those manifestos. I believe you. Too bad the felquistes don't."

"What do you mean?"

"Let me tell you the latest news. There's been a kidnapping. A British diplomat. Not for money, not for ransom. He's been taken by the FLQ. They're threatening his life. And you know what they want to set him free?"

"I haven't got a clue."

"They want you out of jail."

"What? You're insane."

The detective passed him a photocopied sheet of paper. A crude drawing of a Patriote formed the background, wearing a long toque, a pipe dangling from his mouth and carrying a long rifle. All the FLQ communiqués bore this image. He read the text. It was both a manifesto and a list of demands, written in a half-educated, proto-Marxist style. It rambled a bit, revealing its author's uncontrollable anger, even calling the Canadian prime minister a fag. Most of its points were familiar to Jean-Baptiste from his sister's rantings, and from newspaper reports of previous communiqués. But what was important was a single item on the list of demands: the release of all political prisoners.

"Who wrote that?" asked the cop.

"I don't know. I don't know these people." But at last Jean-Baptiste realized he knew exactly who had written this one, and he understood very well why, and how it was just another wrong turn in a maze, a maze that might somewhere have a hidden exit, but was just as likely to have only wrong turns and unexpected collisions with mirrors.

"I don't believe you. Are you sure you've never seen this gun before?"

"No."

"It was found at the kidnapping scene." He unwrapped it once more, but was careful to handle only the cloth, not the gun itself. He held it out to Jean-Baptiste. "Take a closer look. Many guns look alike."

"I've never held a gun in my life and I won't start now," said Jean-Baptiste.

The cop put the gun away. "Okay. Just one more thing and you can go back to your cell where you belong. Get up."

Jean-Baptiste stared.

"Get up, stand away from the chair. Come on, quick!"

Jean-Baptiste stood in confusion. He was scared. He knew the cop wanted his fingerprints on the gun, wanted to connect him to the kidnapping. My God, what had Marie done now? Was she really involved? Was it really some warped attempt to get him out of jail? It seemed hardly likely, when she knew he would walk free in only a matter of days; besides, there were other friends of hers still in prison, some in this very jail. She probably never thought he would be questioned, since she certainly knew he wasn't in the FLQ. That is, if Marie even had anything to do with this kidnapping herself. But that manifesto . . .

The cop opened the desk drawer and took out a long, flat and slender length of polished wood, with a grip at one end long enough for two hands.

254

"All those manifestos and other treasonous crap are in French." He walked around behind Jean-Baptiste. When Jean-Baptiste turned to follow him, the cop stopped him. "No, no. Stand still. But all your 'literature' is in English. You like the English? You like English games? Eh? You ever play cricket?"

The cop began to strike him, first across the shoulder blades and then up and down his backside. Jean-Baptiste's knees buckled when he was hit on his calves, but he caught himself before he fell. He stood quivering under the blows and made sense of the pain by thinking how Grandfather had been right, that he was beginning to learn the way of the world and the hard lessons it offered. Right now he was learning how easy it was to be punished for someone else's actions, and how little Justice cared who suffered its retribution, as long as someone suffered indeed.

Marie was sleeping only fitfully. She was nervous. Never before had she risked so much, carried such a burden so consciously over so long a time without relief. The fewer people who knew the whereabouts of the hostage, the better. Even her friends didn't know.

She took pains to hide it from her family. She could never count on a time to fetch his meals or clean his waste. Father was keeping a regular schedule but Grandfather and Uncle were bound to be awake after dark. Even though Dr. Hyde wasn't buying their corpses any more, those graves were still full of rings, diamond tie clips and gold teeth. And Aline seemed to have as much trouble sleeping as Marie. Only Mother was really getting any rest.

It was starting to drag on. She cursed herself this time. Could she really have been so stupid as to think the authorities would capitulate according to her schedule? She should have seen it coming. Incompetent and shit-scared politicians furiously chattering among themselves instead of doing something—wasn't that just the reason people like herself were necessary, to cut through all the hypocritical bullshit of the parasitical poseurs? Meanwhile, the thuggish Keystone Kops could think of nothing more effective to do than run around arresting all the usual suspects. And even that was an insult in its way: hundreds of supposed fellow-travellers were cooling their heels at the Parthenais Detention Centre. Musicians and singers, nationalist newspaper columnists and university professors—writers, for fuck's sake. They'd corralled all the eggheads and hippies in town and thrown them all together in a giant conference centre, as if stifling the most eloquent portion of the population was the same as striking the most active or the most productive. They were all probably forming new committees in their jail cells right now, planning their sociological dissertations and avant-garde film scripts while listening to the first drafts of new pop songs and merrily enjoying this period of imposed self-importance at the taxpayers' expense. It maddened her, even more so when she was struck by the realization that Hubert would have loved it. The only saving grace was that it showed just how close Quebec was coming to open revolution: the authorities had jailed the intellectuals.

How in the world those fools confused academic status with bravery and conviction was beyond Marie. But at least it kept them from her door for the time being.

She poured the contents of the zinc pail into the toilet. It was the same pail Uncle had used to carry the heart up the mountain. This was what Cross and his kind produced, she thought. From birth to death, more and more of it every day. Piles of shit to stifle others with, to humiliate others with. And she was left to clean up after him.

Worse, when she'd returned the pail, he'd said, "Pray with me."

"Mange de la marde, maudit tête carrée. Calice." She threw the bucket to the floor.

Thereafter, every time she stole unobserved into the basement and opened the door on him, there he was on his knees with his head bowed, praying, with the gold crucifix that dangled from his neck held between his outstretched fingers. No more pleadings for freedom or newspapers or to write to his family. Just catechisms, and invitations to join him.

And then she'd have to go upstairs and listen to Aline reacting in shocked horror to the news reports about the growing alarm over the "crisis." Whether the Quebec government was doing all it could, what the Canadian and British governments thought, what these anarchic madmen demanded in their communiqués, and whether all this was going to have a positive or negative effect on any upcoming referendum.

And when Mother's friends came visiting, how obviously frightened they were, even in broad daylight in their own hometown. "Who knows what'll happen next?" asked the cigarette-puffing Mrs. Harrison, waving a column of ash precariously over the parlour carpet. "They're crazy."

And Mrs. Pangloss, with, "I'm telling you, God is punishing us. The world's going to hell because we've reached too far. Ever since the Americans went to the moon, look what's come to us: a separatist government, for Christ's sake, and now this. We're being punished."

Yes, thought Marie. We're being punished.

And then, incredibly, came a joint televised conference with the prime minister of Canada and the Péquiste premier: two long-time political enemies, two old university classmates, announcing the imposition of the War Measures Act.

Even as they spoke, Canadian troops were being deployed, in numbers not seen since the Second World War—Angus's war—on Canada's own soil. As she listened unbelievingly, Marie began to hear a thunder from the sky. Downtown Montreal was being invaded. Such drastic measures were deemed necessary in these extraordinary times, to protect the population and ensure the survival of Democracy itself. Neither Canada nor Quebec would be held hostage by terrorists. Let the forces of evil do as they would; but the Péquiste premier assured all Québécois, of every political opinion, that he would have no dealings with criminals.

Marie was aghast. Through the window she could see the lights of a convoy of military vehicles passing on Park Avenue, right in front of her house. In the sky she saw the slow dance of enormous helicopters descending over downtown squares, and still, atop the mountain, the cross glowing in the early evening twilight.

So there it was: the Canadian government showing its true colours. Democracy? At the end of a gun barrel. They voted in the Soviet Union too. And also had these massive military parades.

She had to get away from everyone. She dashed to the basement and stood in darkness, trying to reconcile her conflicting, charged emotions. She was afraid. Damn it, she was scared. They'd just sent the whole fucking army after her. She paced and stumbled over things. Slowly her eyes grew more accustomed but she hardly noticed. She wasn't thinking of her physical whereabouts. Why did everything turn out so contrary to her expectations? What was it that frustrated her ambitions even in her successes? She was caught now between her own prisoner and her family, an inescapable trap.

The whole of her life had been a trap, and it was her parents' fault. Why did they have to mix up their marriage like that, the way Canada tried to impose a union between French and English? She hated the

English. They never understood, not from the first. She hated being partly English. It meant she was tainted; it meant she must hate what she was herself. It was just like being part of her frustrating, hateful family. She didn't relish being poor, she didn't relish listening to her friends when they railed against Anglos, because they all knew that somewhere deep inside her was something that hurt when prodded. She didn't relish her family's way of life either: their insular, provincial opinions, their acceptance of the English, their source of income. She didn't want to belong to a family of body snatchers.

Yet she couldn't escape them. Through the arguments and the bitterness, through the deprivation and discouragement, they supported her. They were familiar to her. She knew their faces and their habits, she knew how they spoke and what pleased them, she knew how little they cared for her ideals, how futilely they pursued their own ends against her wishes and advice. She had a place amongst them, and that was as stifling as it was comforting.

And the only way to make more room for herself inside her family was to strike back when their image of her contradicted her own image of herself. She must scream, she must argue, she must threaten violence, as she always had. As she had since infancy. She was not like Jean-Baptiste; it wasn't possible for her to withdraw to some private reality where everything was mixed together fantastically and improbably, where things were never what they really were, where they changed into their opposites to suit his understanding. Things meant something else for her brother, meant something she'd never imagine, because he was so Anglo. It made him think in another way, a way that conflicted with hers. She was Québécoise, French, and more so than some without English or other blood, because for her it was a conscious choice.

Still, if it weren't for the English, she would be totally French. Quebec would be French. It would be New France, France with a new outlook, new opportunities, a new face. The best of all possible worlds. But history had been against it. Just at the moment when France itself had embraced the clearing away of the old in order to free itself for the future, Quebec had been grabbed by the English and stifled, held down and repressed. No wonder Quebec had been backward, poor, religious for so long. The Great Darkness.

The revolution had been a long time coming. It was time for a cleansing.

It was probably time to empty that bucket again. When she opened the door, there he was, praying. He disgusted her. The smell from his pail was strong and he hadn't had a bath in days, and his hair was stringy, greasy, unkempt. His clothes were limp and wrinkled from prolonged use. His face was dark with stubble. He didn't even look up at her, continued his whispered mumblings into his hands as if it were she, not God, who was absent. As if he was too good for her, too good to notice when she entered. That was so typical of the English, assuming their superiority and enforcing it for their own benefit while proclaiming their humanitarian intent.

How could this man, this English man, be allowed to exist, to live, when Hubert had been plucked out by death? And in his arrogance he calls upon the power of his God. The English have always had God on their side; they've always claimed divine right. It was always God who was against us in this province. Even the French Catholic priests, black-frocked vultures, pederasts, preaching the revenge of the cradle as if it were for our own good, as if it meant something liberating for us. When for so many it was a trap, a stifling inescapable slavery whose only alternative, the only choice she'd had—what else could she have done, even if she'd wanted the little bastard?—was a haunting, a loss, a bereavement unrecognized by anyone else, as illegitimate as the birth would have been. Not a baby, not a death. No hopes and fears, no loss, no gains, no future—one big No, the vote the English campaigned for: No.

What was really needed in Quebec, even needed all over the world, was a Yes, an affirmation, a welcoming, an embracing . . .

All of them. The doctors, the priests, Hubert himself. Even her father with his typical male expectations of what she was worth—every one of them had reached right inside her and killed something. Was death so easy to mete out? Like serving dinner or handing over a business card?

John Cross expected his religion to lift him up and set him free, this same religion that had so effectively and for so long suppressed and restrained the people of Quebec, and Marie personally. Worship was painful, a physical suffering just like Christ's, and she bore the scars from her youth, she still bled where she'd been marked in that profane baptism. But he seemed not to know this. He seemed to truly believe that his faith would protect him from any physical trial, as if when his saviour had died for his sins he'd also agreed to take on any corporal suffering that might occur.

In a rage she knew she'd have to show him, to break through his mindless, brainwashed innocence with an immediate and very material demonstration. It was a revelation: the chain around his neck. She took the cross from his fingers, enveloped it with her own small hand and twisted the gold links into his neck.

The ends of the crucifix stuck out between her fingers like the points of brass knuckles. His face turned red, he struggled, his eyes turned up. She beat him with her free hand, twisting the chain again. He gulped air as she loosened her grip but she only took more slack in her own hand, and began strangling him in earnest.

"Where's God now, Mr. Cross? Has he forsaken you at last?" The crucifix dug into her flesh as he struggled desperately. She was afraid he'd break free and so held her right hand over her left, using the strength of both fists to contain the cross. He was making harsh, dry barking noises and his face was so red and full it seemed it might burst. He convulsed, and the points of the cross bit into Marie's hand.

With barely enough breath, shooting out of him like a rude noise from a freed balloon, John Cross tried to say, "You alone are capable of building a free society."

He managed enough for Marie to recognize his words, words straight out of the FLQ manifesto. But it was too late now. She'd long ago passed the point where she could abandon this direction in her life. It was like the arrow of time, moving ever and ever forward. Even if she was capable of doubting her immediate actions, her current struggle, she was beyond being shocked back into any kind of repulsion at what she'd become or what she was doing. She was incapable of sympathy for this man or even for herself now, and was performing an act as coldly as drowning an unwanted kitten, or slaughtering a chicken for dinner.

"You alone are capable of building a free society."

It wasn't even ironic, as perhaps Cross had intended it, much less an appeal to any personal morality it might waken in her. It neither strengthened nor weakened her resolve, it neither amused nor chastised her. Somehow John Cross had drained the phrase of any meaning just as she was extinguishing his life. Words. All that remained of it were words.

And that was exactly the problem with words, and had always been the problem, and why she resented her brother so, and his love of them: they changed. In some magical way the same words that once had been a solace, an inspiration and a call to arms could now be an accusation, a derision, an insult. The very words on which rested all her certainty were suddenly the cause of all her doubt.

Slowly he turned purple, and just as he gave up the ghost and went limp, Marie felt her own flesh breaking. He slumped; he was dead. She relaxed her hands; as she did so, she felt a sharp bite and a warm trickle. She opened her left hand and let the crucifix fall out onto his chest.

Her palm was bleeding.

Just the one.

The certainty of Cross's corpse became for Marie the one fixed point in a universe of doubt. She was suddenly flooded throughout her body with a shuddering of her muscles, each one tightening and loosening again in an instant, and then her stomach shrank in on itself and rose up again under her rib cage.

But all his muscles had relaxed.

And whatever her doubts or certainties, she was now left with the problem of the corpse. As if she had finally inherited the family business.

Marie vomited uncontrollably.

Into his bucket.

NINE

Aline was humming a lively La Bolduc tune as she plunged the knife into Grandfather's right eye with her left hand. She had decided to name this year's jack-o'-lantern after her husband. She remembered how much her own mother'd enjoyed Halloween, sharing it with her daughter and teaching her its liberating spirit:

"And now, who's the biggest pumpkin-head in our lives, Aline? Who do we dislike this year?"

Aline would name some current neighbourhood bully or some rival classmate, and her papa would call from the living room with the name of a current politician or his boss, and her mother would cackle with glee and suggest her sister-in-law, or Aline's babysitter—whom she'd caught flirting with Papa—and then her mother showed Aline how much fun it was to stick a knife into a pumpkin named for an antagonist.

Aline's mother loved Halloween. It was the one day in her proper Catholic existence when she didn't feel bound by her social constrictions as a woman. It was practically the only time she laughed aloud, and she sang as she prepared for the trick-or-treating. 267

She smoked cigarettes. She had a drink, and then another. She even swore, by God.

And she played dress-up with her infant daughter. They chose the proper clothes together, they bathed together and brushed out each other's hair, they dressed. Then came the neighbourhood kids ringing the bell, and they were all dressed up too. It was fun for Aline to see the surprise waiting on their doorstep, and what her mother's reaction might be. For sometimes she smiled and welcomed the gangs of children, and sometimes she screeched and cackled at them like a witch.

At that, Aline always responded with her own squeaky giggling, as the surprised and frightened kids ran in all directions. Her mother slammed the door. "That was one of those Trembley brats. They're all bastards." Together the dressed-up ladies laughed and ate the candy themselves.

Her mother died young, in the fifties, but Aline still allowed herself to keep playing the Halloween games her mother'd taught her. It was a link between them, a time when the universe or God allowed the dead, good or evil, to circulate without hindrance among the living on earth, and Aline felt closer to her deceased mother. It was the only day she felt able to think the unthinkable: "If you're so good, God, why have you taken my mother away?"

She set her one-eyed jack-o'-lantern in the parlour window, lit a candle in its head and went upstairs to dress. She showered and dried her hair with a hand blower set at full to make it frizzy, and powdered it with talc to make it grey. In her bathrobe she pulled out all her black clothes of any kind, and threw them all on the bed. When she'd chosen a long black dress with long black sleeves and a long black shawl, she thought about whether or not to wear jewellery. And what kind? What goes with such a dark outfit? No, nothing at all, unless—yes, just a single, glittering, pure white diamond on a simple ring, like a talisman, the only jewellery a witch *should* wear!

And so naturally she thought of her mother's engagement ring. She remembered she'd left it in Grandfather's bedroom. She'd better rescue it before he pawned it.

She stepped into the hallway, thinking of the fun she'd have with the children tonight. She stood in front of his door, dreading to go in. He was still asleep. But it would be worth it to complete her outfit for the evening.

Aline stole in as quietly as possible, leaving the door open just a crack to let in light from the hallway. She stood just inside until her eyes adjusted, listening to Grandfather rumbling in his sleep. He'd left the window open and it was cold in the room, except by the radiator under the window, which was too hot to touch. She hated being back here. It was harder than she'd bargained for. Somehow it was still musty, like the whole house. No matter how hard she tried to clean it, it was cramped and closed and mouldy. The house defeated her.

Aline closed the window, tried to shake herself out of her sudden, despairing reverie, and looked over the dresser for her jewellery box. She opened it and searched among the pile of plastic and glass for the one true stone she had. She found it. Instinctively she put it on the same finger as her wedding ring. And then she thought, I should wear only the one ring; any other detracts from its importance. So she took them both off, put on her mother's diamond again and placed her wedding ring in the box.

On the dresser was a small framed photograph of Grandfather and Grandmother on their wedding day. They were young, dressed as well as poverty ever allows, standing on the steps of a small parish church. What could she have been like? *Grandmother*. No one would ever call Aline that. Her husband was too old, and she no longer wanted his children. How could this other woman, smiling in the photo just as Aline herself had on her own wedding day, have lived with such a horrible person for so long? Had his children? Was she aware of his job? She must have been. Yet she was a Catholic woman too: they were standing on the chapel steps with the priest above them in the doorway.

That must be it. She'd been caught in the same trap as Aline. Lured in and then unable to escape. Grandmother had lived her life as his wife not because she approved or even tolerated him, but because she was Catholic. And now Aline would too.

On Grandmother's hand, holding up her bouquet, was a small whitish spot severing one finger: her wedding ring. It wasn't possible to distinguish it from the one Aline had just removed.

Aline realized the horrible truth: her very wedding ring had been scavenged from the dead. Her heart sank. She wasn't bothered by its being used, second-hand; she wasn't stuck up like that. But knowing that her husband hadn't enough respect for either of them to allow his first wife to go to her rest with the ring that consecrated her marriage, or his second wife to live among his family with her own ring, her own dignity, was approaching the unbearable. To think that Grandfather had robbed even Grandmother's grave meant that he'd never thought of either marriage as anything more than a simple change in his civil status. It meant she had found herself among people who knew no respect for boundaries, be they personal, societal or legal. It struck her with dread that she was wearing Grandmother's old clothes as well. Never before had hand-me-downs or second-hand clothes from a church rummage sale weighed upon her mind; but she realized these dead woman's clothes were hers simply because her husband hadn't bothered to throw them out.

A dead woman's ring, a dead woman's clothes. They signified not acceptance into the clan as she'd first thought, but that she was accepted as a substitute and not a person. That her own, individual life was over; she had been declared dead. Without ever having been allowed to live and speak for herself.

And no one was bothering to do anything with Angus's things either; they were still boxed and piled against a wall in the basement, like bricks in the very wall. The Desouches did not honour the dead; they lived off them. They built their lives off the dead, scavenged everything wherever they could find it, feared letting anything go as if to save it up was like saving money, putting away for the future.

But was that a future worth having? To live in the clothes of the dead, eat off their plates, read their books, give their toys to the children?

Hyde was nervous. It was a new feeling for him; he hadn't had so much riding on success or failure since his medical school exams, and then he'd been prepared. All he'd had to do that time was show that he'd learned, prove that he knew. This time, he didn't know. No one knew. This time he was not demonstrating a command of all the facts. This time he was creating knowledge, literally, without precedent. He was on the edge of his profession, and he was edgy. Years had been eaten up in waiting for everything to come together.

And he was no longer young, not by any stretch. He could easily wait out the rest of his life without another opportunity. Yet he knew as well that some things needed more time. He knew some of his techniques were still too rough, that no matter how great the success he might display for himself tonight, it would be short-lived. His patient would probably not survive long, if at all. He adjusted the camera, inserted a film cartridge and set it rolling.

His patient would by no means be a complete,

normal subject. It might not walk, or see, or talk, or any of a thousand other normal things. A real mess. But if it lived, if it only lived unaided, for the briefest time . . . that's all he wanted, that's all Hyde needed. Proof. That's all anyone ever needs. A few seconds of film.

He was going to use electroshock. (He'd had mixed results with it in the past, remarkable success and shameful failure both, although those experiments had been performed on live subjects. But it did physically stimulate the tissue.) And adrenalin. A dose enough for a horse, in a syringe the size of a caulking gun. Chemicals and electricity: after all, what else was a man? It was time to find out.

He couldn't wait any longer. There was no way to tell which scavenged part might suddenly reach the end of its useful life and thereby doom the whole experiment. Loose ends or no, rough, untried techniques or no, there was no time to lose.

He charged his machines, lit his lights, donned his gloves and filled his syringe. He had no trouble inserting it through the wound in the sutured chest. He pumped the liquid directly into the heart. When the syringe was totally empty he quickly looked his patient in the eye. He saw nothing, but hadn't expected to. He turned to his machine, flipped the power switch, set the dial to a low charge and pressed the button.

It made a sound like a door buzzer.

But there was no answer.

He pressed it again, longer. He increased the charge. More. More. He set the machine on full and leaned on the button, gritting his teeth. No, no, he couldn't fail now, no . . .

The overhead light dimmed. In surprise Hyde took his hand from the button. The light came back. "Bah," he exclaimed, and pressed again with all his force, as if the more pressure he applied, the more power would flow.

The light blew. The machine stopped buzzing, so Hyde took his hand away. In the darkness he felt his way to the door. Light spilled in from the hallway. He looked back at the operating table, but the patient was inert. Hyde went down the hall to the utility room, where he replaced a blown fuse.

He felt a physical release of tension, as if he'd stopped after running, or as if he'd finally been released from a small enclosed place. "I have failed, at last. It has happened: my worst fear." Yet he felt no emotion. He was not hurt or angry. He'd always wondered what he would do, what he would feel, if he should fail in the Great Work.

Nothing, seemed to be the answer. His worst fear had been realized and the world still went about its business, regardless. He breathed deeply, stretched his back, shut the electrical panel and went back to the operating room.

Where the patient was breathing.

There was a lot of pain. And then he noticed he wasn't quite sure where he was waking up, as if he were hungover in a strange place. But there was an equal amount of pain in his chest, as if he'd eaten far, far more than he should. Except he was also ravenously hungry. He was too weak to rise, so he regurgitated where he was. Fluid rose in his mouth like a combination of searing bile and an oily marinade. It slid down the back of his throat and he gagged loudly, coughing his head up off the pillow. It stabbed the back of his skull, while his chest felt like it was tearing open.

He flailed his arms, snagging them in the tubes speared into his veins.

Dr. Hyde approached and held him down. He loomed overhead, laughing through white teeth. "Relax, relax." Hyde administered an injection and wiped away the waste while the thing that used to be Hubert, among others, slowly calmed.

"Now," said Hyde. "Who are you?"

Hubert blinked slowly and inhaled shallowly—a deep breath hurt too much. His eyes shifted back and forth to take in the surroundings, but they were indistinct in the darkness that lay outside the glare of the overhead light.

"Who are you?" repeated Dr. Hyde.

Hyde's eyes were glowing, his whole body taut, his arms locked straight on either side of the patient, and he gazed directly into his eyes as if looking for something lost down a hole. Hubert looked away.

"Answer me."

He felt a little clarity resolve out of the pain and confusion, and tried to speak. He made a whistling moan but hadn't much strength.

"I think fluid's draining into your lungs. Can you speak?"

". . . yes . . ."

Hyde gripped the patient's arms urgently. "Who are you?" he hissed.

"I don't know." He had an inkling that in some previous life he might have been able to answer the question. "Who are you?"

"I'm Dr. Hyde. I'm your doctor. I saved you."

"Saved me?"

Hyde giggled. "Yes. Saved you up, as a matter of fact. You're the ultimate transplant patient. Parts of you from all over. But I need to know—who are you?"

"Don't you know?"

Hyde snorted. "That's not the point. Do *you* know? That's the point. Tell me—do you know? Do you feel it?"

"Feel what?"

"Do you feel yourself? Do you feel your soul?"

"I don't know. What is a soul?"

Hyde turned away, angry. He stood with his back to Hubert. He faced him again.

"I'll explain. It's possible you have amnesia and your memory will return. But it may not. So here's the important point: if you know who you are, if you have a self, then you have a soul. But if you don't—if you're just an animated amalgam of interchangeable parts—then I've created a monster and you have no soul. If you, as an artificial man, have no soul, then the soul of a natural being transcends mere matter. It's not just parts."

"Parts. Brought me back?"

"Yes. You were dead. All of your parts were dead. Which part is dominant? The heart or the head? Who are you?"

"You did this to me?"

"Yes."

"Why?"

Hyde shouted. "To prove or disprove the existence of the soul." He calmed a little. He reached over and grabbed Hubert by the ears. His face was flushed, and though he shouted, he was restraining himself. "I need to know. I need to know if I have a soul."

Hubert stared into his eyes and saw the searching. A rage was building in his head. This man had done something horrible to him. But a sorrow was emanating from his chest. This poor man was still searching his eyes.

"I will help you find out," he said. He reached both hands up around Dr. Hyde's neck and strangled him.

Hyde was so startled he hadn't enough time to react. The patient, gazing eye to eye with him, was demonstrating the proper qualities. Conscious, deliberate action. Was it anger he saw in the monster's eyes, or pity? A desire to help Hyde, or to strike out in revenge? It didn't matter. What mattered was the success of the experiment. Even though, in this burst of final insight that Hyde saw as a brilliant light, instead of knocking on God's door, he was nailing God's coffin shut.

Hubert watched the surprise flash over the doctor's visage, and then the fear mounting with the redness of his face, until his eyes rolled up into his head and he collapsed.

Hyde was heavy atop him. He couldn't move. He slept.

Green helicopters burped out green troops, trucks rolled noisily and brashly through scattering city traffic, and within hours the army had secured all that it cared to secure. No politician was without his guard, no bus or railway station or bridge off the island was unwatched, and the only foreigners granted easy access in or out through Dorval airport were another army: the press. Flashbulbs and tape recorders from around the world descended on Montreal in numbers unseen since Expo 67, because something was happening the like of which had been unknown since 1837.

All the government buildings were policed, all embassies and consulates watched, every major street patrolled, and all the millionaires in Westmount had their own personal soldiers at attention just outside their front doors.

But no one was watching the wretched houses on Park Avenue or in St-Henri or the Point or the East End. In those lowly neighbourhoods, unworthy of attention or protection, life progressed as usual, with cheap beer and cigarettes and black-and-white televisions. The parents found what solace they could on their meagre wages and the children excitedly, delightedly, ganged up for trick-or-treating.

All the graves opened up and the spirits came drifting down from the mountain. It was Halloween and the streets rang with the laughter of goblins and witches and ghosts, demanding their annual due. People all over Montreal handed out bribes of sweets and small coins to ward away trickery, mischief and worse.

Except in Westmount, where soldiers armed and ready kept the rich anglophones safe from the children of the poor.

Gangs of ragged scarecrows, and zombies with axes buried in their heads or backs, still ran from door to door long after dark. Aliens with glowing eyes and flashing zap guns demanded their tribute, fairy princesses waved their glittering wands and leprechauns charmed; black-masked stripe-shirted robbers held open bags marked with dollar signs; skeletons rattled, pirates set their beards afire, and a Frankenstein lumbered unnoticed through the streets, bleeding at the seams in his flesh and trailing catheters.

The cold, rattling damp of autumn clung to him and he sought warmth and relief.

He was attracted by the noises of laughing, yelling children. He found them running up and down streets dodging cars and grouping at doors, where they were welcomed and given gifts. Flocks of them scattered and split seemingly at random, but when one rang a bell alone, she'd find herself swallowed into a gaggle of revellers before the door opened, and have to assert herself for her share.

Up and down the street, house lights blinked on and off like fireflies as doors opened to disburse candy to children, and jack-o'-lantern grins flickered in windows. Light and heat—and doors opening to let it out. Hubert fell in with Moonie McCairn and his friends and looked not so out of place with their costumes, and not so outrageously large or adult beside the hulking Moonie, though that was no concern of his. He was handed apples and ravenously enjoyed them; and then the door was shut, and he followed the children again.

Jean-Baptiste stood naked with his back to the mirror, turned his head and examined himself. The cop had done an excellent job. There were no marks at all. He was surprised, considering the pain he'd felt at the time. It had been a week before he could sit or sleep on his back. During the day he'd stood leaning his elbows or forearms on the horizontal bars of his cell, holding a book in his hands just outside the cage, gazing past the bars to read—bars that disappeared when he was swept into the story.

Once he was satisfied that his backside was unscarred, he noticed how pale his flesh was. No suntan this year. Not just his torso, but his arms and face. He'd missed the hottest part of the summer. Grandfather'd always said about Montreal, "Ten months of winter and two months of hell." He'd suffered from the heat in August as everyone had, but he'd been stuck inside.

Now he was looking forward to getting out, was gathering his things together for his release next morning, but he was not looking forward to going home. Father had never come to visit.

He thought about the cheque he still had from Woland; maybe he should take a vacation. What else was he going to do with the money, really? He could hand it over as a contribution to the house, as a peace offering. It might help Father with his plans or pay some outstanding bill, or buy some new clothes for whoever needed them. But though that might smooth out his homecoming, even though it was more money than he'd ever had, it wasn't enough to make a big difference for anyone at home. It might ease things for a week or so, even provide some small treats like an early Christmas, but it wouldn't be long before the money was gone and forgotten, swallowed into their lives like a mere drop in the proverbial bucket, and then things would be the same as they had always been. They'd skimp and save so as to limp from one week to the next, never daring to spend an extra dollar, always worried there'd be too little on the plates. No, a single injection of cash would do nothing to alleviate their worries.

He noticed he'd put on weight. Three meals a day, regular as clockwork, for two whole months. That he'd miss; he'd eaten better in prison than at home. Now *that* was a crime. He'd learned things inside, though. Like there were damned few inmates who hadn't shared his penurious upbringing. Not a lot of university graduates or corporate executives. He'd learned about state control of the poor, and how property was considered more important than people. He'd thought a lot about what Grandfather had told him.

Jean-Baptiste had spent two months at the mercy of the paltry shelves of the prison library. He was disappointed to find no Diderot or Borges, and even worse, no Henry Miller or Pauline Réage. Thus he'd plowed through the *Tales* of E.T.A. Hoffman and the *Contes cruels* of Villiers de l'Isle-Adam. For the first time he'd been forced to squirrel out the meaning of a story he hadn't immediately grasped. It gave him training in patience, the patience necessary to sit thinking for hours, worrying an idea or concept just beyond his reach. The patience he'd need if he was going to finish the novel he'd started writing. *Even the Nuns Are Grey* had originated in his imagination as something like *Balconville* or *The Tin Flute*, but somehow was turning out much darker than he'd anticipated. Funnier, too.

It was set during the Rebellion, and began: "In a town where even the nuns are grey, where coal is still burnt against the cruelties of January and the winter holidays are the important ones, I was born at the beginning of summer. The midwife led the women of the house in assisting my mother, while my father was in the basement attending to his secret occupation as an abortionist . . ."

But he was having trouble keeping things realistic. Occasionally a disruption would occur, and the character he'd made an elderly patriarch would suddenly turn into the pirate Hook or Bluebeard, or later show up in the story as a Cyclops:

"He dominated us all with his cruel laugh and physical unpredictability, as if having only one eye had kept his personality from rounding itself to the fullest . . ."

And yet only two pages later: "His constant silence, coupled with the accusatory look of the single immense eye in the middle of his aged forehead, loomed over us relentlessly as the summer sun . . ."

He'd thought he wanted to be Kundera or Calvino, but discovered himself some odd hybrid of Lautréamont and Clark Ashton Smith. In order to keep himself more reined in, he gave himself the task of writing up descriptions of his characters as if they were members of his own family, and produced portraits of them he could refer to in his story.

Of Aline he wrote: "Her hair is limp and dull against her pale neck. She is nervous, always moving, never at rest. She crosses herself and holds the crucifix that hangs on her neck. She speaks a common but prim French, so that a language I always think of as languorous and eloquent seems pinched and sharp. She's small."

Uncle and Father became neighbours, "ineffectual twins, neither with any apparent occupation, who nevertheless seemed to divide the day into equal shifts, for one was never seen during the day, the other never after dark. But they were easily distinguished, because one was a drunk and the other was missing some fingers."

His sister became the wife of a Patriote, and the drive behind her husband's dedication, herself handing him a cleaned and ready musket, or passing messages back and forth with other wives. He'd already written in a scene at the climax where Marie, now widowed, becomes a prime agitator in the riots that burn down Canada's first parliament buildings in Old Montreal.

He couldn't seem to find himself a place among them, either as the runt or the prodigal, until he fell on the idea of a young defrocked Jesuit making a little noise at the Literary Society on account of some licentious poems in the manner of Nerval or Baudelaire.

It was difficult keeping all these elements working together, because he had to figure them out as he went along, and his mind kept changing about what they meant or which character they were about, and he spent hours in silent contemplation until some other prisoner made a noise or commotion in some other part of the block, bringing him back to the real world of his stinking jail cell with a start.

He looked over his scattered paragraphs and could think of no way to arrange them all together in a sensible manner that wouldn't contradict what he'd read in the musty *History of Canada* the prison possessed. He went back to the library and looked more closely at the Canadian writers he found, and then threw away his original opening, replacing it instead with pages of description before even bringing a character into the scene, let alone having an actual event happen.

Once he'd done this, he recognized it as an odd recapitulation of the early English novel, where a title character begins by explaining his lineage back several generations. But being transposed to the colonies, characters who couldn't claim a pedigree were validated by family lands instead, by their real physical presence in a landscape of material objects and forces, not a milieu of social rank and grace, or lack of it.

It was easier when he could sit again. He had finally hit his stride; he'd become familiar enough with the daily routine of prison life that he simply fulfilled his given role when necessary and spent most of his time on his bunk, either staring blankly up at the sky through the bars or scribbling madly in his note-books. And now it was finally the end of October and he was being released.

Now what Marie needed was a gravedigger. Did she dare ask help from Grandfather or Uncle, both so experienced in that line? Could she go to Father with this problem as she had with her pregnancy? Did she have any option but to try shoving this skeleton into its closet? Of course not. One way or another, Cross must be disposed of without arousing the authorities. It wasn't just for herself: even an ordinary murder would have destroyed all their lives, the investigation revealing their secrets large and small— from their theft of electricity and gas from neighbours, and the ghoulish profession of Grandfather and Uncle, to the body of a foreign diplomat and her clear connection to the bombings and robberies of the FLQ.

Yet the worst of it would be the family's—Father's— knowledge of what she'd done—the terrorism that slowly mounted from political scare tactics to the murder of one of their own family, Angus, and finally into the creation of an international incident. In their own home, no less. She lowered her face into her dirty hands and sobbed. She couldn't bear the shame of Father finding out. She imagined the complex mix of disappointment, fear, anger and hopelessness the knowledge would cause him, and she felt all those things herself.

Under the bare bulb of the hiding place, with John Cross sprawled unnaturally on the floor, she sobbed over the corpse as parents do over the bodies of their own children.

She was alone. No one could help her in this. And this was a problem which could only be buried. With Grandfather's spade she began to dig into the earthen floor of the hidden room in the basement. It was long and hard work. She kept having to brush tears away from her cheeks, and so smeared earth and blood from her hands over her face. And she was unused to handling the spade, and blisters formed on her palms alongside the gashes—blisters where Grandfather and Uncle had grey, dead calluses on theirs.

❧

Angus was frustrated. Without a body, he was tossed about on the winds like a cloud of dust, and felt sometimes his motes gather close enough to resolve into wakefulness, and other times as if much of himself had been swept away and lost in the ether forever. Or was this just another dream of Mother's? Was he truly still anywhere at all? Or just in her unconscious and unrestrained head?

The heat was like a desert, and the mass of blinding dust was a storm that was partly himself and partly simple patterns of air moving across rippling dunes. He was a mirage of himself, lost in the infinite particles swirling in forces he couldn't resist.

Yet there she lay, asleep, and that bothered him so: Wake up, daughter! Wake up! You've got your life to lead, you've got your family.

You've still got your own body, damn it, and why don't you use it? Oh, God, for a body to rest in—yes, rest in: all this flying apart in circles and clouds makes me nauseous. And falling in piles of dust on other, scorched deserts of dust—no water, no rest, no will of my own any more—and you just lie there, with a perfectly good body, you can get up and turn the thermostat down—it's killing me, but I can't be killed, just desiccated and floating on currents of warmer and warmer air.

Oh, God, for a body to speak with, to wake my daughter with, to live and die with . . .

Meanwhile, in the parlour, Mother's friends took the opportunity of seeming concerned for their still-slumbering friend to abandon their own homes and save the expense of handing out candy. Since they had little to say on their own behalf, they spent some hours gnawing the trivia of neighbourhood gossip, and then lamenting worldly affairs.

As far as Mrs. Pangloss was concerned, the troubles all began on July 11, 1969. One giant leap indeed. That single event could account for all the noxious prodigies plaguing the world at large: the unpredictable raging of the weather, Angus's horrible demise, Grandfather's just deserts, Jean-Baptiste's success-cum-notoriety, Mother's persistent somnolence, Frère André's missing heart, and up to and including the kidnapping of the British trade minister by those horrible criminals (what—pray tell, what?—would the rest of the world and Mother England think now of their once faithful, proud Dominion?); not to mention Mr. Pangloss's creeping impotence.

Mrs. Harrison quietly cackled in sympathy, with a teacup held under her chin.

As a matter of fact, according to Mrs. Pangloss, all these disasters had clear forewarnings, if only proud, ignorant men had heeded the signs. It was the simplest process to trace back through history the calamities brought about by each aeronautic advance. Every one of these scientific achievements, Mrs. Pangloss averred, was a correlate of moral decline, tied in inverse proportion to the others. Had not jets occasioned a flurry of hijackings, and the opening of the hungry maw that was the Bermuda Triangle? Were not propeller planes and rockets the direct cause of the London Blitz and Germany's unfortunate craze for Hitler? Even the age of dirigibles had eaten itself, vis-à-vis the "unsinkable" *Titanic*, which left its mark even in Montreal's own Mount Royal and Côte-des-Neiges cemeteries, and ended with what is always referred to as the *Hindenburg* Disaster; oh, the humanity.

Certainly, and with pride, had *she* been a peasant farmer in France (though perish the thought: herself a dirty, garlic-eating frog!) she, too, would have pitch-forked a Montgolfier for a Satanist, or worse. There's no denying the wisdom of the folk, even if hygiene isn't a priority in the culture. She'd always said, you can't blame people for what they are; it was God's own business to reveal His wisdom as He saw fit, and if the Lord Himself was content that some of His creatures couldn't speak proper English or wash the fields out of their hair before sitting down to dinner, who was she to question the Lord? Though really, bombings and kidnappings were going a bit far; that's just taking advantage, and surely not what the Lord intended, no matter how twisted the thinking He put into someone's head. Let it be said again, as it was said in the beginning (and hope, at last, mere foolish mortals might listen): Man Was Not Meant To Fly, Icarus.

Imagine: herself arrested in an FLQ sweep, and her husband dragged from his work to bail her out. They ought all to be rounded up and shot, or deported. Bombings and kidnappings and God only knows what else . . .

And Mother still lying there like a corpse.

Mrs. McCairn clucked more than once and shook her head, either in complete sympathy, or just possibly without the will to argue, resignedly.

When the doorbell rang again, Mrs. Harrison jumped and sent ashes scattering over herself, and Aline hurried down the hall from the kitchen with Grace following her in the air and landing on her shoulder.

It was delightfully nostalgic for Aline. In her own neighbourhood, her mother wasn't the only adult to dress the part when handing out treats. It was a creepy delight for the children who stood on the threshold, surprised to find the staid, controlling, ordinary grown-ups decked out in black and masks and darkness. The reversal of roles threw the younger ones into a confusion of identity. After all, the children knew they were only playing at being ghosts and ghouls and grave robbers; but adults most definitely did not play at dress-up. Adults were the forces of stability themselves, the agents of comfort and security. So who *were* these people answering the knock on a neighbour's door, and just where were the neighbours? Could these life-sized, lifelike evil spirits be real? Could they have done away with the ordinary, familiar grown-ups who lived here? Were their neighbours bewitched or scared away, or worse— buried in the basement?

Aline, dressed in mourning, with her dark lace shawl still smelling of mothballs and a great, cawing, curious raven staring down from her shoulder, opened her mouth and let out her best impression of Mrs. Harrison: she cackled with glee.

"Viens t'en, mes petites. Come in, come in, my pretties. Hee hee hee hee, have some candies!" And she doled out chocolate kisses and toffees and sugar candies. And for the smallest, most adorable pastel fairy princess she reached into her bag and brought forth a large, shining red apple, and knelt down before the child. She was trembling before the giant, sinister witch and her familiar, wanting to bolt, but petrified right where she was.

Aline was having too much fun to notice the child's fear. "Now, my little precious," she said, "take this apple home with you, it will put a rosy blush on your cheeks—but beware! You dare not eat this before going to bed—for apples will give you a tummy ache and you won't . . . get . . . any . . . sleep!" And she thrust the apple into the little girl's bag.

Suddenly, to Aline's surprise, the fairy princess burst out crying, and all the now terrified goblins and monsters scattered from the porch, down the stairs and up the street as quickly as they could—some dropping or even abandoning their treasured sweets as they ran.

All except the Frankenstein, who stopped to gather spilt candy into his mouth, and Moonie, whose mother was sipping tea with the ladies in the parlour.

Now Aline was half pleased with herself for having given the children a chill to tell their parents and all their friends at school about, and half saddened that she might just have overdone it with the young girl.

Oh, well, that was probably enough for the night anyway, since it was getting so late. In her broken English she bid Moonie enter to find his mother, and expected the other child to be off home, but . . .

Child? With the hallway lit only by a few candles for added spooky effect, Aline couldn't be sure. A friend of Moonie's might be another simple soul, and somehow he looked familiar—but he did look too old, and he did look a mess. Was that some kind of costume? With a torn and bloodstained hospital gown, and ragged bandages on his head and elsewhere, and those lines in his skin like wounds and stitches? A homemade, poorly made outfit, surely. Cobbled together from what scraps a destitute family with an idiot son might salvage from their closets and rags. But even Moonie didn't eat candy from the dirt. And his clothes looked as though they were wet in the darkness. Aline sighed. She couldn't let this one wander off unsupervised, obviously. She'd have to bring him inside and at least try to clean him up, try to find him something to wear, and shoes too—how can anyone walk the streets without shoes? Aline quickly glanced away from those dirty feet with a feeling of revulsion—his feet were clearly of different sizes.

She pushed him ahead of her down the hallway, past the door to the basement stairs, and thought, Of course. Angus's things, all boxed and waiting downstairs. She'd find him a completely new set of clothes from head—good Lord, that really looks like a massive wound—to toe, if a pair or a couple of mixed pairs of shoes might be found, close enough to his various sizes, to fit. But anything might be better than the scraps of his costume. As he entered the lighted kitchen she saw the pallor of his face, and how one leg seemed olive-complected while the other was a pasty white, and his arms were rosy-fleshed on the left and suntanned on the right.

Grace squawked and flew around the ceiling madly and unexpectedly. Aline ducked her head as the bird flew by; never had Grace done such a thing before. She seemed agitated, and veered in a new direction too quickly, colliding with the ceiling light. The bulb snapped and the room went dark. Aline was startled and held still while she heard Grace settle atop the fridge. She moved to the cupboards carefully and brought out more candles. She remembered the momentary glimpse she'd gotten of the newcomer; she was unsure of what she'd seen.

He looked completely made of a patchwork of scraps, as if to match his costume, and he looked innocent and without experience of where he was and what was happening. In fact, he looked so horrible altogether that suddenly she feared his own family might have abandoned him some time ago and left him wandering the streets. She sat him down at the table and looked at the liquid drying on her hands. It looked like blood.

She rooted in the fridge to offer him milk or juice, and when she turned back to her guest at the table, Grace had perched atop his head and was picking with her beak into the wound.

"Oh my God," she exclaimed, and rushed over to beat the bird away.

But Hubert put his hand up and his palm out and said, "No."

"She's hurting you," said Aline, and made another move forward.

"No. Doesn't hurt. I like the bird."

Aline thought, of course it's not a real wound, it's just makeup. If this poor simple soul likes having Grace on his head, leave them both be. But it was disturbing to see her beak dip so deeply into the bandaged spot. It seemed as if Grace were trying to pick out a berry or a nut she'd glimpsed among the mess. She seemed to grip something and twist it this way and that as if she were working it loose.

"Burnt toast," Hubert said.

Aline realized she'd been staring at Grace. "What?"

He looked puzzled. "Burnt toast," he said.

"Are you hungry?"

He nodded. "Yes."

Aline sighed. Of course she could give him at least some toast. It would be better for him than all that candy he'd been gorging on. She put two slices in the toaster and pushed the lever all the way to the right, the darkest setting. Burnt it is.

Hubert's eyes lowered. He seemed to be looking at nothing at all, slumped in the chair like someone totally despairing of life. Aline felt like that sometimes. "Do you have parents?" she asked.

Without looking at her he said, "No."

"Any family at all?"

"No."

"Do you have a place to live?"

"No."

Aline suddenly realized how far she'd committed herself to this disturbing stranger. She really expected him to be simply lost, and that she'd just track down his home or his parents, or whatever institution he might be in care of, and hand him back. But now she was afraid she'd have to actually take him in, at least overnight. It was too late to call anyone now to do anything for him. No social agency or government office or even church would answer a knock or a phone call now.

The toast popped. Grace flew up to perch on the window frame. Hubert handled the toast like a child, unsure of his grip and awkwardly trying to fit it into his mouth. His eyes were still downcast, his shoulders hunched over as if he lacked the will or strength to sit up straight, and he masticated noisily and let crumbs fall from his mouth.

Aline burst into tears and lowered her head to the table, sobbing. It was just like having breakfast with her husband. He was unwashed, uninterested, ungrateful and uncommunicative.

Grace fluttered down to rest on her back. She cocked her head, leaned in behind Aline's ear and squawked. Aline heaved and sobbed again.

Hubert had finished eating and sat, blankly. Grace hopped across the table, up on his shoulder and eyed the hanging, bloody bandage. She picked. He grunted. Grace prodded.

"Sing," said Hubert.

Aline raised her flushed face. The wave of despair had ebbed but tears still streaked her face. "What?"

"Sing," he repeated. "Your voice."

What was she going to do? How could she take on another burden? The whole household had become her burden: Grandfather, Mother, everyone else. No one looked after themselves, no one lifted a finger to help her. She had no life of her own, no friends, no hope. All she had was Grace. And now this basket case, another helpless burden, had landed in her lap.

He raised his eyes and looked straight at her. Grace had to jump to his head to reach down into the sticky mess. "Your voice is your heart," he said. "The heart is the strongest part. Follow your heart."

Aline laughed nervously and wiped her face with her bare hands. "Get off him, Grace," she said. She got up, walked around the table and held Grace with both hands so she couldn't fly away. "I can't stand it, even if you don't mind. It's too creepy."

She brought him to the basement, which was harder than she imagined because he was quite incompetent with the stairs. He stood unsteadily, watching her opening and sorting through boxes until she offered him some clothes.

"I'll leave you with these, you can change yourself. We've no extra beds in the house, but you can sleep here on the floor. It's hard, but not any dirtier than you already are. Wrap yourself in these blankets, and in the morning we'll call the welfare people. Somebody else can give you a bath."

As everyone retired, turned off the television, locked the doors and went to bed, Grandfather awoke and stretched in his bed. It was musty and warm as always, but he took note of it almost for the first time. *Almost*, because as he was feeling the touch of the stale sheets and blankets as never before, he realized they'd always felt that way. And with the window closed, how stuffy and warm it was.

Through the wall he heard his wife crying in her bed. Nothing had changed. But he took no satisfaction in it; that was new. He put his eye in, blinked, felt the paste in his mouth. Why should he now begin to feel guilt, where before her tears had justified his angry pleasure?

Exhausted, Marie had slept on the cot beside the grave. Earlier she'd stirred, half woke on hearing scrapings and bumpings at the wall, and voices in the basement beyond. But it was quiet now. She lay in the darkness in the small room without windows, with the knowledge of what she'd done, and felt how airless and hidden and muffled it was in there, as if she herself were dead and in her coffin.

She might as well be dead. She'd failed at everything, had lost everything. Burying Cross had been her only choice, but it was really a stop-gap measure. She couldn't leave him here indefinitely; someone would find out someday. Even the false wall she'd built for this tiny hole she lay in was only ever supposed to be temporary. She must think of what she was going to do.

How do you get rid of a body? Who could help her with that question?

At the kitchen table, Grandfather lit his first cigarette of the night. He opened the previous day's newspaper and read. He'd never noticed before how quiet it was. He heard the house creaking; he heard the occasional car race past on its way down Park Avenue, or the bus. He opened the window and heard the tree gently rustling in the cool breeze. He heard weeping still, and looked up to the bedrooms overhead. No, it wasn't Aline. She was silent now. But he still heard it. He moved away from the window and heard it louder in the centre of the kitchen. He moved towards the hallway, and there—he heard it more clearly still, through the basement door. Someone was crying in the basement.

Finally, Marie turned on the light, wiped away her tears and stood up. She was hungry, she needed a bath and she had to pee. She took up Grandfather's spade to return it before anyone noticed it missing, and stepped into the basement. She reached for the hanging bulb, closed the door behind her, flicked the light on and stepped around the boxes of Angus's things. She looked up.

A man stood slouching, his head down. It wasn't

Uncle or Father or Grandfather or even Jean-Baptiste. He lifted his head. It was Hubert.

Marie screamed.

"Marie," he said.

Grandfather yanked open the door and charged down the stairs. At the bottom he found Marie standing terrified before a stranger. She was holding his spade, in self-defence, he thought. He drew closer and saw the horribly shambling mess that shifted its weight from one foot to the other.

"Give me the shovel," he said to Marie, but he had to reach over and take it from her hands. As he stepped up beside her he looked the stranger in the face.

"Jesus fucking Christ," he said. This was the man the cops had brought to his back door, the man—the corpse—he'd sold to Dr. Hyde.

Without hesitation Grandfather lifted the shovel and swung it like a baseball bat. He broke Hubert's nose. Hubert swayed backward and grunted. He lost his balance and toppled over.

Marie ran up the stairs. Hubert! Where had he come from? He was dead, he was dead! How could he be here? She heard noises in the basement. Grandfather was beating him with the spade—should she stop him? Should she help him? Good Lord, she couldn't let him try to bury Hubert—he might find Cross.

She dashed back down the steps and grabbed Grandfather's arms. He'd been bending over Hubert, whose head had cracked against the gas meter and lay awkwardly against the pipes and the grey stone of the foundation. "No, no, don't!" she pleaded, and held on to Grandfather's arm as he made a swing right at Hubert's face. She yanked his arm and he missed Hubert, but he hit the pipes and the soft lead of a fragile solder joint, and after the short clang came a sharp hissing and the pungent smell of gas.

"Christ, we've got to get out of here," said Grandfather. "Wake everyone. Get out of the house. Call the fire department."

"Are you crazy?" said Marie. "They'll find him."

Grandfather looked puzzled. Why would she care? "He's an intruder. We've got a gas leak, we could all be killed. Get out, let's get out!"

Marie stood still, looking from Grandfather to the unconscious Hubert. She was breathing heavily in short bursts, her mind racing so fast she couldn't think. Grandfather grabbed her arm and tugged her along after him. He was filled with a sense of urgency and worry; he couldn't really make sense of the situation, but somehow he felt, above everything, the need to get Marie out of danger. That was new too. Putting someone else first.

Hubert crawled up the wall until he stood unsteadily on two feet. He picked up the shovel and examined the thing that had broken his nose. He could feel the pain, but he wasn't bothered by it. He dropped the shovel. It struck against the stone of the foundation, and two tiny sparks shot out. They pleased him. He raised the shovel again, and dropped it.

The explosion threw him to the foot of the stairs. He'd lost an ear, and the other rang painfully.

But the flames were nice and warm.

Aline ignored their pleas. "Open the fucking door, Aline," shouted Father. "No one's kidding around here." But Aline lay still. Grace fluttered around the bedroom cawing, and Father and Uncle pounded harder and harder on the door.

In the hallway they were all shouting at one another:

"How'd he get in?"

"Who the hell is he?"

"Why didn't you take care with the shovel?"

"Why didn't you do a decent job with the soldering?"

"What're we going to tell the cops?"

"Aline, the house is on fire. You have to get out."

"Forget her. Let her die. I'm getting out."

"For God's sake, someone help me with Mother."

Who is this person lying with a head split open? And look, great seams along his chest, his arms, everywhere. But nothing, no person in there.

There was a disturbance in the house, but more than that was unclear. Was this person responsible? He collected himself and moved closer. He drifted down against the warmth that pushed back at him, and still, there was no one in there. Repulsive. What

301

an ugly, beaten monster. But when he got close enough, there was a thrumming, a pulsing that welcomed him. He offered no resistance. He settled in through the sutures and the gaps in the flesh, and he began to feel. His chest rose slowly, contentedly. Everything else hurt, hurt like hell, but his chest drew in air—air!—and he felt a kind of release of tension, as if some ordeal were over, and he was once again welcomed and loved.

He slept.

He woke to the sound of strident cawing. He might have been dreaming of vultures.

Hot. Why is it always so bloody hot? Red, orange flames, dark black smoke—what have I done? What did I do or not do? To be here, enduring this? I did what they told me to. I kept my nose clean, I didn't cause trouble—is this my reward? Bodiless, in hell?

But those are my things burning—and I'm lying on stairs—fuck, my head hurts—my back—my chest—

He gasped the air, and then realized he'd done it. He looked around. Everything hurt. A jet of flame sprang from the wall and everything was catching fire. He struggled to rise, but had trouble with his legs and arms—

—these are not my legs and arms—

He crawled up the stairs. Black smoke billowed out the doorway into the hall. He crawled out of it coughing, raised himself on the door, took huge gasps of cleaner air.

This was his daughter's house. He staggered down the hall and held himself up on the parlour door frame. There was screaming and thumping coming from upstairs. His daughter lay sleeping on a hospital bed. He slowly put one mismatched foot in front of the other and swayed unevenly, flailing his arms out to balance. Behind him he heard someone running down the stairs. He reached the bedside and steadied himself with both arms locked, and looked down at his sleeping daughter's profile. Behind the sagging lines of middle age he saw the bright eyes and curiosity of the girl she had been. He saw his long-dead wife's chin and smile, saw his own nose, saw her in her wedding gown, saw her in the hospital bed with a newborn in each arm.

Behind him he heard, "Jesus Christ."

"Wake up," he said to his daughter. Nothing. "Wake up. Wake up!" Nothing. He reached over to her ear, drew in his breath and yelled, "Wake up!"

Just as Father grabbed him by the neck, Mother's eyes fluttered. "Wake up," he croaked.

She opened her eyes.

And screamed.

Father yanked so hard the head came off in his hands. He yelled and dropped it. Mother scrambled from the bed, and the body fell where she had lain.

He was dead. Finally.

Aline was so depressed she convinced herself they were only playing some horrible Halloween gag on her. But Grace was agitated, shrieking and flying about, fluttering at the window. Aline got up to open it. Even though they'd abandoned their pounding and screaming at her door, it sounded like they were doing just the same elsewhere in the house.

When she had the window open, and Grace had darted out into the cold night air, she realized she could hear the sirens of fire trucks screaming towards her.

My God, had they been serious? She hurried to the bedroom door and flung it open. A wall of flame came rushing up the hallway towards the air pouring in from her window. She retreated. It really was a fire. How could things continue to get so much worse? Wasn't there ever an end to the suffering?

She had no choice now but to go out the window, just as Grace had. She stepped onto the roof of the kitchen and saw flames licking over the lip from the windows below. The roof was hot on her bare feet. There were no stairs or ladder to the ground, which seemed infinitely far below. Behind her the top floor of the house was engulfed. In minutes the roof would collapse beneath her.

Grace flapped in her face, cawing. She beat the bird away, but it came back, flying around her in ever-widening circles, calling. Aline was confused. "Grace, go away, we'll both die."

The bird herded her to the edge of the roof. Across the lane the church was dark and lifeless. Aline couldn't bring herself to jump: it was too far across to any other building or down to the ground. She'd always been timid. She turned and ran to the other edge. The church was behind her and she faced the flank of the mountain. The illuminated cross glowed out of the darkness. Grace flittered about her face again, and Aline staggered, almost went over.

She was frightened. Grace screeched, almost hovering in front of her, over the empty air. "Oh, Grace," she said.

The bird called out to her as she had during their singing lessons, with the notes and strains of the tune they'd worked out together. Aline turned and saw, on one side, a wall of flame advancing towards her from the rear of the building, and on the other, the coloured glass of the church windows flickering dimly in the shadows. There were angels circling in the air, leading the risen one up, in a scene of the Ascension.

She had always wanted to fly. She sang with Grace. She had to raise her voice to hear herself above the cracking timbers, and the wind and fire howling back and forth at each other. She felt the tar of the roof go soft under her feet, heard the groaning and snapping of beams giving way. Jump? She could no longer afford her fear.

She flew.

⚜

The firemen worked through the night to put out the blaze, but they were lucky to be able to contain it to just a few buildings on either side of the Desouche home. The sky gradually lightened, though as usual it was overcast, and so it couldn't be said that anyone saw the sun rise. But what emerged from the darkness was a smouldering pile of rubble where the house had stood, and on the sidewalk in front of it, some miserable figures wrapped in the cheap blankets they'd been sleeping in. The firemen collected their hoses and stole away. The police opened the street to the morning traffic.

Grandfather surveyed the smoking ruins through his glass eye and thought, along with what little we owned, I've killed another woman. Part of him was bitterly ashamed. But still, he felt now as if he'd been reborn. The past lay consumed, inert and powerless to hurt him. It was late in his life for a man to begin again, but now nothing else was possible.

He saw Marie staring blankly at the ruins, hugging herself against the damp, and shuddering. He threw his arms around her and held her close, and he himself felt comforted.

Marie was light-headed with exhaustion and dread. This was what her years of continued and increasing dedication and work had brought her to. The devastation was complete. She surveyed the open field of ash and char; the fire'd been fuelled so efficiently by the gas that nothing recognizable was left, not any of their possessions or that horrible zombie Hubert, or probably even Cross in his grave. At the edges of the exposed pit that was their home, timbers and pipes and scraps of the neighbours' dwellings and of the funeral parlour could be distinguished, and across the lane the grey stone wall of the church was blackened; but in the centre, where the blaze had begun, the largest surviving object was a small dark lump like a burnt potato. Unnoticed, it continued to ooze blood.

In the cold of the November morning, Ville-Marie de l'Incarnation Desouche stood, homeless.

Jean-Baptiste walked home from Bordeaux jail to save the bus fare. He'd never been so far out of his own neighbourhood before, never seen so many unrecognized streets and buildings. Yet they were all unmistakably Montreal. Countless French street names, street-front balconies and staircases, black ironwork and grey stone, and carved gingerbread doors, lintels, gables. Grey churches with green peaked roofs. Buses with brown and cream paint, red brick schools covering whole blocks, six storeys high, corner stores with their doors literally cutting the points of corners, always painted the same green as those church roofs. Enormous quantities of beer and cigarettes being carted up or down the block by ten- and twelve-year-olds fetching for their parents.

He walked streets with names like Henri-Julien, Cartier, Dollard. The city was alive with its ghosts, took special care to remember its dead, and surrounded itself above and below, on all sides, with the past, with corpses, with death itself. The invisible visitants of the Catholic spirit world haunted his every step, dogged him in all his travels: coming along St-Joseph he discovered St-Denis was blocked with construction, so he continued to St-Laurent.

From Ste-Agnès to St-Zotique, from Ste-Anne to Ste-Thérèse, the dead came back to life every moment of every day in Montreal, and poked and jabbed, laughed and derided the inhabitants ceaselessly, in every quarter of the city. There was no escape from their influence, from their judgment. Like the demons of a preliterate culture they swirled in the winds gusting down from the mountain, flipped hats from heads, inverted umbrellas, tossed leaves and garbage at faces. These imps of the past, ghosts of Montreal and gremlins of Catholicism, were a gang of adolescent troublemakers getting their revenge on the living for the direction they were taking, for paving their cemeteries, for toppling their statues and church spires, for the fact of not having died yet.

It all looked so shabby, like the home he was returning to.

Coming along Pine Avenue he noticed the darker smudge of smoke against the overcast sky and was conscious of foreboding. He turned down Park Avenue and saw one remaining red truck pumping water where his house used to be, and traffic edging its way around the obstruction. He saw neighbours and strangers hanging about. He stopped where he was. He saw Grandfather embracing Marie; he saw Uncle in his dressing gown, smoking and staring. He saw Father, and Mother—clearly awake, still in her nightdress—hugging each other, crying, laughing, so that he couldn't tell whether they were devastated or overjoyed.

From this distance, when he looked at his sister, he saw Father's features, just as he could see Uncle's face in Father; he remembered looking in the mirror and seeing his mother's eyes looking back at him, and how she'd always said he had Angus's eyes. He couldn't bring himself to move any closer. He'd been too long away to feel at ease with them now, under these circumstances. And he couldn't bear to confirm that they'd all lost everything, that all his books, his poetry and scribblings and boxes of magazines, were gone. In a puff of smoke.

All he had now were the notebooks he carried with him, and the uncashed cheque. He turned about in the street, looking up the hill of Park Avenue, looking back the way he'd come, looking westward across the street. He looked at the papers in his hand, covered with his own messy scribbling. Patriotes. Rebels. Abortionists. Poets. It suddenly seemed too real, not historical at all, not even as fantastic as he'd feared. But how could he write any of this? What had happened when he dared approach the truth in his play? What good had come of it, for anyone?

It suddenly seemed so unimportant.

Jean-Baptiste had had enough of writing what he knew. It only caused trouble. He vowed he would never again write down a single thing in a realistic mode, because whether it had ever actually happened to him or not, whether he actually believed in it or not, everyone would think it was the literal truth. As if simply because *they* had absolutely no power of imagination, no one else had any either, and therefore whatever he put down on paper was talking out of school. Kissing and telling.

Enough. From now on he'd write only about other times and other places, preferably places that never really existed, and mix up all the times together whenever it pleased him. And he'd describe only characters who were complete idiots, because everyone who read his work would think they were wise, and therefore that he'd made them up. And events that were clearly impossible, fantastic things out of fairy tales, because people would think they were somehow metaphors for a secret truth.

There was only one direction open now. He'd tear up his notes, his scattered drafts, and begin again. He moved down the street to join his family. A string of words occurred to him:

Montreal, an island . . .

ACKNOWLEDGMENTS

For various kinds of support over the years since beginning this book, I would like to thank the following people:

Bruce Basilières, Roy Berger, Tess Fragoulis, Barbara Gilbert, Denis et Raymonde Gilbert, Heather Marcovitch, Laurie Reid and John McFetridge, Lorne Stephens, Stephen Welch and Beany Peterson.

Many thanks to everyone at Knopf Canada, especially Noelle Zitzer, an excellent and tactful editor and the perfect foil for my extravagances. And thanks to Lena Sukhova, for reading the mail.

I gratefully acknowledge the support of the Canada Council for the Arts, the Ontario Arts Council and the Arts Council of Toronto. If we don't support our culture, we will lose it.

MICHEL BASILIÈRES grew up in Montreal with his French father and Anglophone mother. He now lives in Toronto, where he is writing his second novel.